I0545460

CLAIMS
OF THE
HEART

A SEQUEL TO FATED HEARTS

ALINA K. FIELD

Copyright © 2021 Mary J. Kozlowski
ISBN No. 978-1-944063-38-2

Havenlock Press
PO Box 1891
La Mirada, CA 90637-1891

April 12, 2022

This is a work of fiction. Names, characters, places, and incidents either are the product of the author's imagination or are used fictitiously, and any resemblance to actual persons, living or dead, business establishments, events, or locales is entirely coincidental.

Cover Design by Melody Barber

Since a perilous fall, Lucie Macbeth has been seeing more than a settled future as the heiress to a Scottish barony.

The visions plaguing her include a man—one far above her class and breeding, and English to boot. He's engaged to a duke's granddaughter as well, and thus wholly inappropriate.

Though she can't marry him, and she won't become any man's leman, when the Sight warns her of danger to him her conscience, and her heart tell her she can't walk away.

With grateful thanks to William Shakespeare, the master at adapting history, myth, and legend to meet the requirements of his audience.

Claims of the Heart is a sequel to *Fated Hearts*, a retelling of *Macbeth* and part of the Love After All Tragic Characters in Classic Literature project wherein:

"With complete artistic license, and an abundance of hubris, a group of Regency romance authors are retelling some of the great stories of literature, setting them in Georgian England, and giving these tragic heroes and heroines a happily-ever-after."

Hear my soul speak. Of the very instant that I saw you, did my heart fly at your service.

—THE TEMPEST, ACT 3

CHAPTER ONE

At the Theater

April 1816
Near Hunstanton, Norfolk

"Two letters arrived for you, my lord."

Tristan Hamilton Howton, Earl of Rudgwick, Major in His Majesty's Horse Guards and a decorated veteran of the Peninsular campaign and Waterloo, extended his arms for Darby to pry the wet coat from his shoulders and ease it over the lump of wood at the end of his right arm.

The valet's disapproving clucks both amused and annoyed him. Mother had tracked down his late father's valet and hired him away from the rich cit he'd been serving. Upon Rudgwick's return from Flanders, Darby had been waiting at Rudgwick Abbey, the ancestral pile in Cambridgeshire, happy to be back serving nobility, yet missing his favored Savile Row haunts.

In Darby's view, Rudgwick Abbey was paradise compared to their present abode, Thornview Farm. With four rooms below, four bedchambers above, and a few small attic rooms for the housekeeper, cook, and two maids, Darby had been sleeping on a cot in the dressing room. Rudgwick's friend, Lord Jeremy Bolton, who had inherited the estate late the previous year from an aunt, was in alt, declaring himself perfectly happy with the cozy cottage and the small income that came with it. And it wasn't entirely a bachelor establishment; Jeremy, too kind and dutiful to ever be a true rake, had offered shelter to another female relative, an elderly cousin and her even older companion.

Rudgwick stepped into clean trousers and held up his arms for Darby's assistance, annoyance niggling at him. He needed a man to tend to his boots, keep his clothing in order, and button his left cuff. Otherwise, he preferred dressing himself, even, or especially, during his time in the army.

"I fear I won't get the salt stains out of those—"

"Yes, yes," Rudgwick said. "A fair day for sailing it was, though, Darby. Are you not glad we're back from touring all the byways of Norfolk?" He'd left Darby behind while he and Jeremy rode hither and yon for the last few weeks, making do with help from inn servants. "Had we supplies on board today we would have made for Inverness."

Jeremy's new home had come with a yacht, a smallish one, in truth, too small for a comfortable journey to Scotland. An old school friend and former naval man, Jeffrey Musbury, had traveled up from his cottage on the River Ware to assess the craft, pronouncing it sound for short days of sailing, and inviting them to join him in summer on the two-master he'd been refurbishing.

Darby made a grumbling noise in his throat and fetched the letters. "A brandy, my lord?"

"Yes." He sighed. There'd be another nagging missive from his fiancée's grandfather, and a lamenting one from his steward.

Darby set a full glass before him. "Shall I break the seals for you, my lord?"

"Why not read them as well," he snapped.

Darby blinked in the way that Mother did before she straightened her shoulders and walked away from his churlishness. The valet was of an age with her, and, like high-born ladies, he'd learned patience and forbearance in the face of surly noblemen.

"Apologies, Darby." It wasn't Darby's or Mother's fault that a French mortar had blown off his hand at Waterloo. "That was uncalled for. Thank you. I shall manage."

Darby dipped his head and left, carrying off the wet and soiled garments.

Rudgwick took a healthy swig of the drink. They'd found cases of spirits in the manor's storeroom, good French brandy, and gin from the Lowlands. It seemed that the free trade reached even the west coast of Norfolk. As pillars of society, he and Jeremy would be expected to support the increased efforts against smuggling, but they had no qualms about availing themselves of Jeremy's late aunt's stores.

He closed his eyes and let the brandy ease the phantom throb in the hand that was no longer there. Then he shuffled the letters one-handed.

One fat missive and one thin. Both had been sent to London, where he was supposed to be in residence, and forwarded on. He broke the seal on the thin one and read.

Sir Thomas Abernathy, a baronet attached to the Home Office, inquired about his health, and asked about his availability to assist with a matter of interest to the Crown. A reply at his earliest convenience would be appreciated.

His curiosity was piqued, but he couldn't help wondering if Mother knew Sir Thomas and if she had put him up to it to orchestrate his return to town.

The second, heftier letter was addressed in a man's scrawl and sent post-paid from Edinburgh.

He hastened to break the seal and flipped to the signature, laughing out loud when he saw who had signed it.

Colonel Finnley Macbeth, Baron of Calder, had written to him. His wife, Greer Macbeth, corresponded with Mother, but the Colonel had never done more than send greetings via those letters.

That called for another dram of brandy.

And then he began to read. A lengthy passage reviewed the Colonel's recovery (he was mending apace), reported on his cousin, Lord Menteith (still in France), and discussed the plans for the two boys Macbeth had taken charge of, his late cousin Banquo's sons. But that was all a prelude for an important request.

> *Your lady mother informs me that you should be in London by now, and so if it would not be an inconvenience to you, I would be much obliged to ask a boon from you. There's a solicitor by the name of Stephenson in the City, who has knowledge of Banquo's business matters. He's failed to reply to several letters, and I can only assume he's ignoring them. I've asked Lucie to pay a call on the man. Lady Fiona has offered help from her man of business, and I've sent Hyde along to London with Lucie.*

Lucie. The name all but leapt from the page. Lucie was in London!

However, of late I've had misgivings and worries that, given Banquo's criminal nature, this Stephenson may be a shifty character. Lucie being Lucie, she's likely to find the danger an enticement and plunge ahead. Moreover, I know that a title can often open doors that would otherwise remain closed. If you could see your way to offer Lucie assistance, if your new bride has no objections, I would be most grateful.

He read through the letter again and then pulled the bell. As he returned to his seat the door opened.

"That was quick." He turned and saw that it was not a servant, but his host.

Jeremy was a younger and handsomer version of his brother, the Duke of Northam. A handsomer version of Rudgwick as well, with the same height, dark hair, and gray eyes, though they were completely unrelated.

"At your service, my lord," he joked. "The servants are busily preparing for dinner."

"Will you pack my trunk, then?" Rudgwick teased. "Ah, there is Darby, poking his head in behind you. Darby, we are leaving for London in the morning."

"We are?" Jeremy said.

"You may come as well if you wish. I've been summoned to go to the aid of the Crown." *And Lucie Macbeth.*

***

She opened her eyes and came out of the darkness into the red glow of the sun on the horizon and the sound of muffled voices and the chuffing breaths of a struggling horse.

Pegasus had fallen.

Oh, Hades. She must see to him.

Before she could stir, someone loomed over her, her vision too fuzzy to make out who it was. Fear rose in her, and then settled. 'Twas not Jamey Paisley, praise heaven. If he thought to touch her again, she'd... why she'd have a piece of—

"Shhh. Lie still, lass." The voice was one of Menteith Castle's grooms.

Pegasus. How badly was he injured? She pushed at the soft turf, the damp soaking her gloves. The rain had stopped before her ride, but days of downpours had left the soft places soggy and slick, and...

It had been her fault. Jamey's kiss had paled next to that of another man, and then he started to paw, and push, and demand a decision...

She had run and bade him not to follow. Only, she had looked back and seen him mounting.

She'd galloped hard, getting away, running, and running, and running, and then the ground had given way, sliding straight out from under them, and... She lifted her head and pain exploded in it.

"Lie still." A hand touched her shoulder, and she sank back into a dull throbbing.

Velvety grass cushioned her and gave off a sweet odor whilst a breeze tickled her brow, eased the shattering pain and shards of glittering light, and chilled her moist cheeks. She'd been crying and hadn't known it or—she levered a heavy hand and swiped at her face. Her kid glove came back red.

And then... a cloud moved over her. A gloved hand reached for her.

"Oh, my love." Grim lips, shaded by dark scruff formed the words, soundlessly. She heard them in her heart. She knew him there also.

Her hand touched his and she floated up, up, up, into strong arms that settled her onto a soft bed.

"Oh, my love." His lips formed the words again. She couldn't hear the words, but she knew them. She knew.

Stuff and nonsense. Lucie Macbeth, Maid of Calder, blinked the obsessive thoughts away and took in the dizzying view from Lady Estelle Walby's box at Covent Garden. The previous year, she'd attended a play at Drury Lane with her parents, Colonel and Mrs. Finnley Macbeth, Baron and Baroness of Calder. Grand it had been, but not so grand as this, nor so high up.

Truth to tell, she wasn't fond of such heights, which was probably why the vivid memories mixed with imagination were clattering about in her battered head.

This sight, Covent Garden theater, this was a real vision to store away for the long winter nights at home in Calder. All around her the boxes glittered with rich silks, sparkling jewels, and the glint of the glasses of the *ton's* well-to-do spying on other attendees. She must stay right here for the evening instead of wandering about in the past or some unbidden daydream.

"Come along then, ladies." Lady Walby's relation, Lord Grallon, pointed out their plushly appointed seats.

"I haven't attended a performance here since the fire." Lucie's elderly distant cousin, Lady

Fiona Carlin, took Lord Grallon's arm and Lucie followed behind them, seating herself at the end of the row next to Lady Fiona. "It's breathtaking. Shall we switch, Lucie, my dear, so you may see the stage better?"

"All the world's the stage here, isn't it, madam?" She'd attended a few glittering balls in Brussels the year before, but nowhere had she seen so many gaily attired ladies. Perhaps it was the matter of the war ending that made the *ton* more festive, as well as the fact that the theater, unlike society balls, was open to people of all ranks. Some of the most beautiful ladies peering out from private boxes would be members of the demimonde.

Lady Walby leaned across Lady Fiona. "You look very well tonight, my dear Lucie. You're sure to catch the eye of the gentlemen. That gown is brilliant."

Lucie murmured a thank you. The gown was, in truth, magnificent. Mother might never have allowed her to wear it. Father would have insisted on a more intrepid escort than the elderly baron, or a large fichu.

Given the bright red of her hair, she herself had been doubtful about this shade of vermilion. When she'd requested a red gown, Lady Fiona and the modiste hadn't dismissed the notion. They'd insisted upon this hue with its rich, almost golden shimmer, and at the first fitting, she'd seen the magic. The richly colored *peau de soia* fabric floated over an underdress of white silk, embroidered, and trimmed in gold, dipping low at the bodice. More gold trimmed the overdress and floated along the tasseled waist and hemline.

She wasn't given to vanity, not much anyway, but tonight she'd found a comely stranger staring back at her from her dressing table mirror. Lady Fiona's maid had twisted her hair up Grecian style, twining faux pearls through the creation that matched the ones at her neck, and teasing out face-framing curls. A light touch of powder had even hidden most of the freckles that were the curse of the ginger-haired.

Catching the eye of the gentlemen wasn't her goal tonight, though it might be a welcome diversion. 'Struth there *was* one gentleman plaguing her thoughts, and he wasn't free. Though she supposed if she encountered him during her sojourn in London, he'd be unable to annoy her as he'd done in Brussels. After all, their only connection was His Majesty's army, and here, they were moving about in different worlds.

In any case, to her knowledge, he wasn't in London. If he appeared tonight at Covent Garden, well, her heart was safely hidden within her vermilion gown, her future was secure in the Calder barony, and she had no need to be wooed. Tomorrow or the next day she would make another attempt to see to her father's business in London. Tonight, she merely wished for the entertaining spectacle of the actors, both on and off the stage.

"And how are the preparations for the grand birthday ball proceeding?" Lady Walby asked.

"Famously." Lady Fiona winked at her. "Isn't that so, Lucie?"

She laughed. "Very true, my lady." She'd turned one and twenty a fortnight before, and Lady Fiona had surprised her by announcing that she was hosting a ball in her honor. "Or so I assume. I can't claim any credit though since Lady Fiona has kept me in the dark about the preparations."

"Tell her, Estelle, that she must have a gown specially made for the occasion. She wants to wear this one again."

"Never turn down an offer of a new gown, my dear." Lady Walby raised her opera glasses. "Oh, do look. Is that not Bridgehampton across from us? And my godson, Lord Jeremy Bolton, with him."

The hair on the back of Lucie's neck quivered and, in no need of an opera glass, she followed the line of vision to the box directly opposite theirs. The Duke of Bridgehampton was a powerful peer, and quite a controlling man as well, if the stories could be believed.

"He's come out of mourning then," Lady Fiona said.

Bridgehampton's son and heir, Marquess Grey, had died several weeks earlier of an unsavory wasting disease brought on by his dissipated life, or so Lucy had surmised from the few details she'd gleaned from her father's servant, Hyde, who was well informed on that sort of gossip.

She'd never seen either man, the duke or his son the marquess, in the flesh, but surely the tall white-haired gentleman was Bridgehampton. The dark-haired young man standing next to him must be Lady Walby's godson.

Unable to turn away, Lucie watched as Bridgehampton remained alert and erect, surveying the vast array of boxes, one by one, until he came to theirs and his eyes landed on her. A jolt went through her. Surely the blasted man didn't know of her, didn't recognize her. Yet if looks might pierce a tender girl's heart, well...

She was no tender girl, though, not after the frights she'd experienced and the horrors she'd seen, and so she sharpened her gaze and thrust back at him, while all else melted away, the only sound being the slow *drub-drub-drub* of her heart beating.

A sharp squeeze of her hand stirred her.

"You are well." Lady Fiona's words were a quiet command, not a question.

Lucie turned and met sparkling topaz eyes so like her own. She often imagined her paternal grandmother might have looked like Lady Fiona. She often wondered if her late grandmother had been plagued with the Sight as well. Not that what she was experiencing, small lapses in time with intense *experiences* and *feelings*, could be called the Sight. After all, she'd suffered a terrible bashing. Her head had been badly concussed... and she'd lost Pegasus.

She hauled herself out of the threatening pit and fixed her attention on the dear lady next to her, forcing a smile. Whatever it was, this so-called gift—curse more like—was so new to her, she craved the guidance of those who had borne the burden longer.

Father might be able to help, but he was in Scotland. She hadn't seen him since this awakening, which started after she left Edinburgh with Lady Fiona.

Besides, she would hate to trouble him by calling to mind his past painful memories, not now that he'd survived the war and reunited with Mother. If Lady Fiona was gifted, as Mother suspected, she might help. It was a mere matter of screwing up the courage to ask. But she wouldn't tell what she was seeing. There was little to tell, memories of the frightful accident being mixed up with glimpses of a man she must never know *that* way, glimpses that were stirring and intimate and absolutely impossible to relate.

The older lady squeezed again and tipped her head toward the opposite box. Lucie glanced over and her heart skipped a beat, and then started racing.

CHAPTER TWO

A Vision

Across the theater from Lucie, a braw, dark-haired man, as tall and straight as the duke, stood in his grace's box, a young lady upon his arm.

Drawn like a giddy moth, she lifted her chin and met his gaze, bridging the yawning space, watching his mouth soften into the quizzical half-grin he displayed to such advantage.

Tristan Hamilton Howton, Major Lord Rudgwick, was, in fact, in London, in the flesh. He was here and looked ready and willing to annoy her. He looked hearty, healthy and well too; not at all impaired. As fully recovered from his injury as a man who'd lost a hand might be.

She let out a breath. She'd wondered how he'd fared after she and her parents left him in Brussels. Mother parsed the news she received in letters from Lady Rudgwick, and Lucie was too proud to ask after him.

She was glad to see him looking so well. Now she must simply keep the chasm between them as wide as the pit of this theater. Easy enough to do, given their different social circles.

He wasn't in uniform tonight, yet he'd still make hearts flutter, and the cocky smile said he knew it. Wide shoulders filled out the elegant dark coat, and strong thighs the legs of his trousers. He was, after all, a horseman, a cavalry officer with a stable of the finest horses.

With a quiet breath she attempted to quell her pounding heart, to blot out the seductive smile that she saw over and over in stirring visions of a future that could not be, that must not be.

She mustered a bored, *how-annoying* tone. "Rudgwick is here."

The young lady on his arm must surely be his fiancée. Even from this distance Lucie could see that the lass was a beauty, petite and dark-haired, her gown filled with the sort of generous curves men ogled. She was the type of girl the *ton* called a *diamond of the first water*. A good match for Rudgwick. They would have beautiful dark-haired bairns.

In the duke's box, the occupants shifted and Rudgwick looked away. Lady Walby's godson spoke, and then Rudgwick's young lady spoke, and then the duke said something that made the girl stiffen. The godson disappeared. Rudgwick seated his lady, spoke to her, and then, still standing, leaned over the railing and watched the swirling crowds in the pit. The duke sat.

A handsome lady of middling age entered and stood at the back of the box—Rudgwick's mother. Lady Rudgwick lifted her chin, looked directly at Lucie, and smiled, astonishing her so much that she couldn't help smiling back.

Rudgwick moved up next to his mother and Lucie held her breath, wondering if he would come to annoy her in person.

"Rudgwick has been with Lord Jeremy in Norfolk," Lady Walby said. "Jeremy recently inherited a property from someone on his mother's side, and Rudgwick went along to help him see to it. Rudgwick is looking quite well, is he not? I've heard they've made him a hand. But look, Jeremy has disappeared. He'll be on his way to pay his respects, wait and see, and I shall introduce you to him, Lucie. He now has a manor house and an income—small, but adequate—and I daresay it's time for him to think about marriage."

"We shall certainly invite him to your birthday ball," Lady Fiona said, with a sly glance at Lady Walby.

The poor fellow had no doubt already been invited. Lucie refrained from doing something so vulgar as rolling her eyes. Lord Jeremy would be looking for someone to supplement that small but adequate income, someone a step up from a poorly endowed Scottish girl like herself.

***

Rudgwick bent close to the ear of his mother, Lady Sarah Rudgwick. "Did you mean to torture me, Mother?" he teased. "Or was it the old man you were hoping to discompose?"

"Whatever do you mean?"

"*You must escort me to the theater tonight, Rudgwick,*" he murmured in a falsetto voice.

"This new production of *A School for Scandal* is said to be wonderful."

"Hmm."

She gazed up at him, her eyes shining as they so often did when she looked at him. "I may have heard that Lady Walby would be attending with friends. In any case, I feel a sense of great accomplishment this night. You are smiling."

So he was. He couldn't help himself. He'd arrived two days ago and was pondering the best way to approach Lucie and offer his assistance. The sight of her always kindled his spirits, and more. And tonight, she looked especially well. Damnably fetching. It was good that he'd seen this play before.

"What a pity the duke wouldn't stay at home," Mother whispered.

Bridgehampton's presence would keep Rudgwick from visiting their box. His grace was in just a high enough dudgeon to cause a scene. But Rudgwick had at least laid eyes on her, and she on him.

"Do you never fear his grace's wrath, Mother?" Mother had supported the engagement with Bridgehampton's granddaughter until Brussels. Since then, she'd demurred—quietly so as not to stir the old man's ire. He suspected her goal was the same as his own, to break off the engagement entirely.

He studied her sparkling eyes, wondering what she was planning. Probably nothing. She was most likely merely setting the stage for him to improvise the action.

"I see that Lady Harmonia's headache has providentially lifted," she added, ignoring his comment.

His fiancée, Lady Harmonia Haughton, had risen from her fainting couch the moment she heard the news that Jeremy would be part of their company. Her grandfather, the Duke of Bridgehampton, a crusty old grandee with impeccable intuition and a determination to have things his way, had risen as well from his brandy and pipe and resolved to accompany them.

Grandfather and granddaughter had already had a row, or as close to one as the aptly named Harmonia would come. She'd just expressed a desire to accompany Bolton and greet Lady Walby, a friend of her own late godmother.

Lucie might be of interest to Harmonia as well. Mother might have mentioned the Macbeth family, with whom they'd lodged in a leased villa in Brussels after the great battle.

Bridgehampton, of course, knew of Macbeth and his lady and daughter. And he did not approve.

The duke made it his business to know everything about Rudgwick's business. Thus, Rudgwick had discouraged Bridgehampton's offer to join him in Brussels, delayed his return from Flanders to England for as long as was possible, and upon that return, planted himself in the country.

Imagine if the duke knew of the kiss he and Lucie had shared during the duchess's ball? Imagine if Colonel Macbeth knew Rudgwick had been kissing his daughter? *Hah*. He might have died before the battle had started. No one knew of the kiss he'd stolen outside the Richmond residence after delivering a dispatch.

That kiss. His heart had pounded as loudly as the distant cannons signaling that the battle had started. He hadn't wanted to risk death before kissing the impudent, saucy, delectable Lucie Macbeth, and after, he'd tucked away the memory and headed off to the battlefield. And damnation, he wanted to kiss her again.

Miraculously, he hadn't died. Nor had his fiancée, Harmonia, thrown him over when she learned of his injury. Not that the duke would ever let her cut ties with him. The duke had a plan, and everyone must fall in line with it.

"The lady seated next to Lucie, is she Lady Fiona Carlin?" Mother asked.

"Yes." He'd met Lady Fiona the year before, in the hellish week of the London Corn Riots and Bonaparte's escape from Elba.

"Much recovered, it appears. I heard there was an injury or illness requiring a recuperation in Bath for a spell. I suppose Lucie served as Lady Fiona's companion there."

They shared smiles. He'd learned of the sojourn in Bath in the letter from Macbeth and had made the same assumptions. "Perhaps we should compare intelligence reports, Mother."

"I'm bound to know more. I've been in town the last few weeks while you've been rusticating in the country."

"I've talked to him about that." Bridgehampton's hearing wasn't the best, but he'd worked out Mother's last laughing declaration. Now, his booming voice set Harmonia to fidgeting. "Time to come and take up your responsibilities. You're fit enough."

Rudgwick bit back a retort. The last several weeks in Norfolk had been heaven. There'd been no society to speak of, no need to put on airs. They'd surveyed the house, buildings, and land, and visited tenants. They'd hunted, traveled the highways and byways including the old Roman Peddar's Way, and sailed.

Before that, he'd been holed up at Rudgwick Abbey, learning how to turn his remaining hand from weak to strong. He wouldn't have a servant spooning food into his mouth or writing his personal letters, and he'd manage his horses, dammit. He was fit enough to get back to all of his duties except the one that most concerned Bridgehampton. Meeting that duty would require him to ignore his own heart.

"Damned foolish battle. Why you didn't stay here and marry—"

"Duke. I serve the Crown, and the Crown needed me." More than the Duke of Bridgehampton had.

The Howtons and Haughtons were kin, separated by a few errant letters of the alphabet and positioned on different branches of the same family tree. The late Grey had been a poxy, corrupt fool, and nothing but trouble for his father, especially during the last years of war. It was whispered that the duke had scraped him out of one predicament after another, covered up his graft, perhaps even saved him from a charge of treason. And he'd failed at the one absolute duty required of a noble heir—breeding a son. Grey's daughter, Harmonia, was Bridgehampton's only direct descendent. Her personal wealth, inherited from her mother's side, was significant. Bridgehampton wanted that money kept in the family line, under the control of himself and his heir.

Who happened to be the Earl of Rudgwick.

Upon his arrival home from Portugal eighteen months earlier, the duke had paid him a visit and announced his place in the line of descent. By that time, it was clear that Grey was too ill to remarry and father a healthy child.

Rudgwick had to marry some time and produce an heir, and his own estate needed an infusion of cash, so he'd agreed to the dutiful betrothal to the placid and very young girl. And then, after the betrothal ball had been held and most of the contracts signed, he'd met Lucie

Macbeth in the same week that news had arrived of Bonaparte's escape, and the army mobilized again.

"It's high time to set a wedding date. After the wedding, you may chase whatever—"

"Duke. Not here." Bridgehampton hadn't noticed the flash of Harmonia's eyes, quickly shuttered.

Did he think every young girl wanted to hear her grandfather tell her fiancé he could chase other women? Harmonia was young; very young. She'd been fifteen at their betrothal, and she was barely seventeen now. She was too young to marry then, and too young to marry now.

And if he was correct, Harmonia was having her own second thoughts after meeting the dashing Lord Jeremy Bolton. As the son and brother of a duke, Jeremy was perfectly suitable for her, and he could use the money she'd bring to a union. With two nephews and two brothers ahead of him in the line of inheritance, he'd never be saddled with the duchy of Northam. Like any younger brother, he needed to make his own way.

"Not here, sir, and not now." He took his mother's elbow and gestured toward a chair. "The play will begin soon."

Bridgehampton moved to the second row and helped Mother into the chair next to his own. His manner with her was courtly and as close to considerate as possible with Bridgehampton.

And why not? Mother had kept her figure, and she looked exceedingly well tonight. They were of an age, those two, and Mother was the soul of patience with the duke. Egad... He must have a word with her. He couldn't bear having the man as a stepfather.

He made his way to Harmonia. "Are you comfortable, my dear?"

She nodded.

"Will you excuse me for a moment? I shall return directly."

Bridgehampton started to rise. "Where are you going?"

"Paying my compliments to the necessary," he murmured. "When Jeremy returns, he may have my seat."

Leaving Bridgehampton spluttering, he found his way to the lower floor and an usher, spoke with the man, then waited in the back, his gaze straying to the glowing upper box where Lucie sat chatting with a hovering Jeremy.

He turned away, swallowing a ridiculous spurt of jealousy. He'd been hoping his affable friend would turn his attentions on Harmonia and relieve him of this great burden. He'd been hoping they'd find themselves smitten. As he himself was with Lucie, and as she was, would be, *must be* with him. Must be because there was no other woman but Lucie for him.

What was a tangled web but a challenge to be unraveled?

He watched the usher wending through the pit and disrupting conversations. Finally, a cropped-haired man of middling age craned his neck around. Their eyes met and a smile lit the wrinkled face, and then he was shuffling over the feet of drunken young bucks and clerks from the City, making his way to the back.

He stopped a few feet away and saluted. "Major Lord Rudgwick. A pleasure to see ye looking so hale."

He'd forgotten Hyde was hard of hearing. His voice would carry to the stage, perhaps even up to

Lucie's box. He glanced up at her. She was still conversing with Jeremy. "Where's your officer, Hyde?"

"Up in a box, the one that be. The old one sent me off on a mission, he did."

Rudgwick chuckled. Colonel Macbeth had put a firm hand in place for his daughter. Not that she'd listen to Hyde. "Is the old officer well?"

"Much recovered, he is, and happy as a lark with his lady. Out fishing and stalking game when he ain't chatting up the crofters and counting Lord Menteith's cattle and sheep, and when he ain't running down to Edinburgh to wrangle the Commissary Court over those boys."

Rudgwick had met both Hyde and Macbeth on the Peninsula, where the men had served with the Highlanders, and then encountered them again in London in March of the previous year. Called up with the Highland Regiment for Waterloo, both had been injured again. They'd all three convalesced together in Brussels.

The boys Hyde mentioned must be Macbeth's late cousin Banquo's sons. Macbeth and another cousin, the Earl of Menteith, had taken charge of the two boys after Banquo's death. Rudgwick didn't remember much of the circumstances, having been half out of his mind from either pain or laudanum when the subject was discussed in Brussels. He recalled that Menteith remained in France, tracking down his mother's property and honeymooning with the French Comtesse he'd married in Brussels, and would be no help to Macbeth.

"Are Banquo's boys giving the colonel trouble?"

"Naught but the usual. 'Tis their father's failure to leave a proper will causing the trouble."

Bloody wills, settlements, and other paperwork. He'd had his fill of the lot.

He pointed at the balcony. "And your present commander is also well?"

"Oh, aye, healed up." Hyde's bushy brows furrowed. "Mostly."

Healed up? This was news. "Healed up from what?"

"Riding accident." Hyde tapped his head at the temple.

Behind Hyde, the curtain rose. He glanced up and saw that Jeremy had vanished from Lady Walby's box, and Lucie sat stiffly in profile, her gaze directed toward the stage. Every serious rider took a spill now and then. How serious a fall had she taken?

He willed her to turn and look at him and felt the force of her resistance like the cut direct. Not that he, a respected earl and officer, had ever been cut by society.

He shook his head. He was being ridiculous. "Do you remember my house in Knightsbridge, Hyde?"

Hyde nodded.

"Come and see me tomorrow morning, or as soon as you are able."

Hyde's eyes lit. "The commander be wanting a horse."

"Is that so?" He extended his hand.

Hyde blinked and matched him with his own left hand, while saluting him with his right. "Tomorrow then, milord."

He left Hyde to make his way back to his seat and trotted up the stairs. Thank goodness, his legs were still in good repair.

Jeremy met him at the top and walked with him. "You're a sly one," he said. "When you told me of the family you stayed with, you didn't say the daughter was so fetching."

"But not more fetching than Lady Harmonia?"

Jeremy blinked. "Dankworth is here, oozing his usual charm."

The hair on his neck quivered. Lionel Dankworth was an old school fellow, a bit older than him, a bit younger than Jeremy's brother. Dankworth had been younger than Grey as well, but the two men had been thick as thieves in their carousing.

He was unctuous, and unsavory, and he'd had an interest in Harmonia's substantial dowry. Rudgwick might not want the girl for his own, but he'd never let Dankworth have her. "Then let us hasten to our box so we don't encounter him."

"With him around, you must not let Harmonia out of your sight."

He eyed his friend. "Or yours."

Jeremy's face colored.

Rudgwick stopped him outside their box. "I'm relying on you, Jeremy. You're a gentleman and a friend. I know when you're with her, you have her good interest at heart."

"There's no need to warn me off. I'd never poach...er dishonor either of you."

He laughed. "Come. Lady Sneerwell and her man, Snake, beckon us to watch their scandalous love plots."

"Where love plots are involved, there's no avoiding scandal," Jeremy muttered.

He hoped not, but it was likely that truer words were never spoken.

***

Lucie fixed her gaze upon the stage through the first two acts, though the comedy poked at her temper. The scandal mongering in particular reminded her of all she must make herself ignore whilst setting a foot into London society, and wasn't that ridiculous? Her parents' divorce had occurred over twenty years ago. Navigating society had been easier in Brussels, where impending battle had broken down some of the social barriers.

"This is a silly story," Lady Fiona murmured.

She made herself smile, and then laugh. The play was delightfully mocking, and she'd so far enjoyed the company. Lord Jeremy Bolton was another handsome young man, and his conversation had been refreshingly cordial. "And grateful I am to be here and to see it."

"All's well that ends well."

Her gaze caught the opposite box where Rudgwick sat in the front row with his fiancée and Lord Jeremy. The duke and Lady Rudgwick sat behind them.

Rudgwick's gaze strayed from the stage and met hers. Her vision narrowed and focused, a fog descending upon the rest of the theater. At the back of the box the curtain moved, and a shadow appeared—a man. She blinked, and he stepped into the box on stealthy feet.

Her chest tightened, fear pounding against her ribs. She wanted to shout, but all she could manage was a gasp. She wanted to jump to her feet, but she was frozen in place.

In a flash like a whirlwind, the shadow rolled forward, tangled with Rudgwick, and then pushed him over the balcony. Her heart locked itself around a cry. Her eyes fluttered. The floor of the box fell away.

Pain shot through her wrist with a sharp pinch, and she opened her eyes wide. Rudgwick was still seated. His dark gaze still drilled into her.

"Lucie." Lady Fiona's whisper cut through her confusion. "We are almost at the interval. Shall we order refreshments?"

Oh, Hades. She'd all but cried out. But for Lady Fiona's quick thinking, she would have. "Aye, my lady. I would like that."

As her breath calmed, the stage curtain closed, the rich hangings swaying in time to invisible pulls on a hidden rope.

Rudgwick was still seated, still watching her. That had definitely been a vision, quite different than the usual one involving Major Lord Rudgwick.

Who had the shadow been? A man, for certain, and one dressed as a gentleman to boot. He'd put her in mind of her late cousin, Giles Banquo. But Banquo was dead. Her cousin Malcolm and his wife Marielle had watched him die and had seen his body into the grave.

She agreed to Lord Grallon's offer to fetch ratafia and laughed politely over Lady Walby's critique of the actors.

Visions...the Sight. Dear God. Papa had lived with this knowing, or almost-but-not-quite knowing. He'd seen danger for Mother, and not taken action until it was almost too late.

But... danger to Rudgwick? What did she know really? The attacker's face, his hair color, none of those could she guess. What she did know, almost certainly, was that whoever the man was, he meant to harm Rudgwick.

Lifting her gaze, she saw that Rudgwick had stood and was helping his lady to her feet. He glanced back at Lucie, as if unable to look away for very long.

Fear niggled at her, and her neck prickled insistently. He could fend for himself, but he ought to be warned, and not in a letter that someone like the duke might pick up and read. Nor would she convey it through Hyde.

Somehow, she must warn him, without inviting a stay for herself at Bethlehem Hospital.

CHAPTER THREE

A Prime Mount

Only the tips of Harmonia's fingers touched Rudgwick's right coat sleeve, and he fought to keep her distaste for his stump from rankling. The fact was, he needed his good hand free. The crowd leaving Covent Garden and the riffraff of the streets shoved up far too closely despite the best efforts of the duke's footmen.

The duke flanked his granddaughter's other side, a footman led the way, and Jeremy followed behind with Mother.

Rudgwick craned his head around, and spotted a red head in the distance, one wrapped up in pearls. The duke's carriage inched forward in the queue of coaches. He'd deposit the ladies with the duke and go back and speak with Lucie.

Another face bobbed into view. He exchanged a quick look with the duke. They were both of one mind about Dankworth.

Bowing over Harmonia's hand, he wished her good night, and turned her over to the duke's footman, who whisked her away, the duke following close behind.

"What a crush," his mother said, looking around.

"Hurry on, Mother. The duke will see you home. Jeremy and I will return home later."

"We will?" Jeremy asked. "*Uh-oh*. Dankworth has changed course." He stepped out to block the man who'd veered toward Harmonia.

"I'll just see you into the carriage, Mother, and then there's someone I would speak with."

Smiling, she glanced back at the knot of ladies from Lucie's box.

Shouts erupted around them, and an urchin whipped through the crowd heading straight for Harmonia. Dankworth dodged around Jeremy and rushed toward her as well.

Before either could reach her, the duke's strapping servant all but tossed Harmonia into the carriage, and the duke clambered in after her.

Rudgwick snatched at the lad. His prosthesis landed like a club but didn't stop the lad's forward movement. He lurched again and snagged a skinny arm, just as a lady grabbed the other.

A red-haired lady, one wrapped in a fine, bronze-colored shawl the same shade as her eyes. Her chest rose and fell with the exertion, drawing all the male eyes to her bosom.

"*Pffft*," she said. "Ye little mutton-headed fool."

"What's afoot, Rudgwick?"

Dankworth had joined them.

"My dear girl," Mother said.

He'd abandoned Mother in the crush, and she'd hurried to join them.

"So happy to see you," she said. "What have you caught here?"

The crowd milled around, feasting their eyes on a story they could share at their late-night suppers. Somewhere a tattle sheet scribbler's pencil would be flying.

"My lady." Lucie curtsied, still clutching the lad's other arm.

"I'll take him, miss." Dankworth had moved nearer and was eying Lucie far too closely.

***

The sandy-haired fellow offering her help was dressed as a gentleman, and he was acquainted with Rudgwick having addressed him by name. Lucie had seen him walking toward the duke... or had he been heading toward Rudgwick's fiancée? And why had the lass been on the arm of a servant instead of her betrothed?

What the deuce was wrong with Rudgwick? He ought to have been looking after the girl instead of craning his neck after her. Aye, she'd seen him looking for her in the crowd, just as this wee bit of rabble tunneled past, taking Lady Fiona's reticule in passing.

She ignored the strange gentleman and held on to the skinny arm and felt Lady Fiona brush up next to her.

"I'll have the wee reticule, lad," Lucie said. "Honestly, my lady, have ye ever seen such a scrawny bag o' bones? Lad, ye'll not get more than a fine handkerchief and a few coins from my lady's purse. Her jewels are where they ought to be, around her neck."

Defiant eyes glared up at her. "I got nuffink."

The strange gentleman drew back a fist, the lad flinched and ducked, and Rudgwick's hand shot up and blocked the blow, holding like iron against the force in that fist.

'Twas his right hand, unclenched and unmoving, yet it otherwise looked very real. He had gained back his strength. And the look in his eye said the next blow would be his fist in the other man's jaw.

"No need for that," he said, with no heat at all in his tone.

"Give him to me. I'll hand him over to the Watch."

Rudgwick signaled to Lady Walby's godson, who came and nudged the sandy-haired man out of the way, then searched the boy's coats, pulling out a quizzing glass, a fob watch, a gentleman's purse, and Lady Fiona's beaded bag.

"Ah, there it is, my lady." Lucie handed the bag to Lady Fiona.

"Give him to me," the other man said.

Anger and fear snapped in the boy's clear blue eyes. "B-but...b-but..."

While Rudgwick frowned, studying the urchin, Lucie turned to face the lad, and Lady Fiona joined her.

Lady Fiona presented a coin. "I'll not let a child hang or be transported for stealing a handkerchief."

The lad frowned at the coin she pressed into his dirty hand.

"Ye're only encouraging him, my lady," Lucie said. "What he needs is a position with hard work, regular meals, and a steady roof over his head."

"A kitchen boy or stable lad," Lady Fiona said thoughtfully, and then shook her head at the boy's mulish look. "He's not ready, I fear."

Lady Walby and Lord Grallon pressed through the crowd and joined them. Whilst Lady Fiona recounted the tale of the theft, Rudgwick pulled the lad aside. Head bent and lips moving, he questioned the boy, or so it seemed to Lucie. The lad's head shook and bobbed, and then he slipped away. What was afoot here, besides a pickpocket working his trade?

Rudgwick straightened and turned to her. The angular jaw, straight nose, and curling dark hair were just as she remembered them. His eyes had cleared from the pain-wracked time after Waterloo, and what she saw in them now sent ripples of awareness through her.

"Miss Lucie Macbeth." The warmth of the greeting curled around her heart. "That was a valiant capture. You look very well. Are you?"

No, not with ye standing this close to me.

She looked around, wondering if anyone had noticed his intimate tone. The older members of the party still chatted. Lady Walby's godson stood with them, and the sandy haired gentleman was nowhere to be seen.

"I am," she lied. She must be. "And ye, Major Lord Rudgwick?"

His face broke into a smile that made her giddy, foolish girl that she was. "When I saw you in the box tonight, I thought of my invitation to escort you to the theater. I haven't forgotten your wish to see a London play. I've only just returned to Town, else I'd have made the arrangements."

There'd been no invitation from him. It had been more of a command.

When she'd found his mother attending him in the same hospital in Brussels as Father's man Hyde, Rudgwick had been addled from pain and the laudanum meant to quell it. At some point in their disjointed talk, she'd mentioned the theater, and he'd told her straight out he would take her. Foolish man. His mother's astonishment had cut through the hot, heavy June air of the room and reminded Lucie of her place. She set Rudgwick straight, else the poor lady might have fainted.

"I'd hoped, Major Lord Rudgwick, that when you eased off the laudanum you'd come to your senses."

His answering smile was wicked. "I fear I'm never sensible around you. Another time, I will accompany you."

He leaned close. "And if I become too giddy, you may keep me from falling over the balcony."

The vision flashed with a surge of panic, and she opened her mouth to speak, but Lord Grallon's servant appeared and told them their carriage was waiting.

And what would she have said anyway? Beware being pushed over the balcony? No, she must warn him without sharing all that she saw.

"What is it, Lucie?" Rudgwick whispered.

She shook her head, unable to gather breath to answer. As she followed Lady Fiona to the coach, she glanced back at him. His smile sent her heart reeling again.

That would not do. She needed to speak to him, privately, but not so privately as to put her heart in danger. She ought to have asked for a meeting— perhaps in the park on a morning ride.

Oh, but she couldn't make that request in front of his mother, while his fiancée was sitting a few feet away in the duke's carriage and Lady Walby and her godson were lingering.

She'd find another way. Hyde would help her. Hyde could serve as chaperon as well.

***

The next morning Lucie paced to the window again and looked out at the drizzle. A shiver went through her. Last year, she and Mother had been caught out on the rainy lanes of Chelsea. They'd wound up in perilous straits.

That would not be the case now, not in the morning, not even on a morning where the sun was hiding beyond gray clouds.

"Why not take a turn in my carriage, lass? You'll be warmer and drier." Lady Fiona Carlin spoke from her perch on the edge of a sofa upholstered in silvery damask.

Lucie battled more memories. On another evening last year, Father had sat on that very sofa next to Lady Fiona, his seemingly sturdy knees and legs bared under the plaid of his kilt.

He'd found his way to the seat after he swooned—actually swooned. He'd crashed straight to the carpet upon the first sight of his only child. There was something endearing about his reaction to meeting her. Up to that moment, Lucie had been prepared to hate him.

That night, Lady Fiona had fetched Hyde from the kitchens where he was biding his time while his master supped, and then Hyde and Lucie's cousin, Malcolm, Lord Menteith, had hoisted Father up and onto the sofa.

'Twas the first night Lucie and Finnley Macbeth met, and it was as if they'd known each other forever. She'd inherited his flaming red hair and, Mother said, his temper. It seemed she might now have his muddled ability to see trouble coming.

She shrugged off the memories and went to the hearth, where a low fire glowed. The fine wool of her dark blue riding habit kept the chilly air at bay, but it did nothing for the chill rising inside her. No vision like the one she'd had the previous night rose in her mind's eye, just a sense of an unsettling encounter, one that would shake up her world.

How could Father abide this curse?

He had carried on, mucking about as best he could, and so would she. "The sun is peeking beyond the clouds. 'Twill be a fine day to ride, and I'm too restless to sit confined in a carriage."

Lady Fiona harumphed. "That hat won't keep more than a spot of rain off your head. I wouldn't have you showing up in the park with wet locks looking like a wet—"

"Spaniel?" Lucie teased. "Or, given the color of my hair, an Irish setter? Or perhaps a fox?" She put her hands to her hips. "Yes, a crafty red fox out for some air."

Lady Fiona chuckled. "Yes, but beware the hunters following you."

"In their red coats, astride fine horses, with their hounds baying." She plopped down next to Lady Fiona. "I did use to love a cross-country dash on a fine horse, but I've never kenned the appeal of chasing after an animal one wouldn't put in the stew."

"Unless he had the chicken for your stewpot in his mouth?"

Lucie laughed and then sobered. "I thank ye for allowing me this freedom. I won't shame ye. Hyde would never allow it."

Lady Fiona's plump hand patted her own. "What's troubling you?"

She felt heat flooding her cheeks. *Ach*, her kinswoman was a cagey one. "Naught but a murky sense of...something. Trouble, mayhap. It's all no doubt the fault of falling off the horse and bashing my head."

Not any horse though; she'd fallen off Malcolm's stallion. Pegasus's leg broke when she'd pushed him too hard on boggy terrain. Her fault. Her fault entirely.

She swallowed a rising bile. After her head healed, she'd got herself back on a horse. It had taken every morsel of courage she could muster. "All will be well today. I'm feeling quite myself."

"A bit of fresh air will do you good, I suppose."

The sound of voices outside drew her to the window. Hyde had returned astride one of Lady Fiona's lazy hacks and was leading two horses down the drive.

She drew on her gloves. "He's here. No doubt he's been hoodwinked into taking a lazy mount." Hyde wasn't much of a horseman.

Lady Fiona rose and escorted her into the hall. "While you're riding, I'll be conferring with Cook about the supper for your ball. Are you sure you'll be fine with my selections?"

Lady Fiona, having had a childless marriage, seemed to be wanting to launch Lucie into a society she'd never be a part of. "Oh, madam, I'm ever so grateful for your generosity. Whatever you select will be wonderful." Nor would she likely be able to taste a morsel of it, being the center of attention at a ball that she'd never expected. In truth, her hopes had gone no higher than *attending* a few balls in London before making her way back to Scotland.

She was one-and-twenty now. Mother and Father had settled their differences and home was really a home now. After all the events of the previous year, much of her restlessness had abated. Settling down as the future heir of Calder and learning to manage her world would be enough—for now.

Plus, there was the matter of the unsettling and enticing visions of sensual abandon—with

Rudgwick, of all people. The sooner she took herself away from him, the better. She wouldn't lower herself to serve as his mistress. Not that he'd asked for that service.

He was, as far as she knew, a good man, one who deserved a warning to take care. He'd known something of Father's visions, and she didn't think he would laugh at her.

Or... knowing Rudgwick, he probably would laugh and go about his business. But at least she'd have fulfilled the obligations of this worrisome responsibility, and if he stumbled into trouble...

She couldn't bear the thought.

"It's a great pleasure for me to host a ball, and you are worth it," Lady Fiona said. "Now, have a care." She tucked a stray lock of hair behind Lucie's ear and turned her head.

Lucie dutifully kissed the older lady's cheek. "Do not worry, Lady Fiona. I shall be the soul of caution."

Lady Fiona's eyes took on a momentary glaze and then her lips relaxed into a smile. "All will be well."

Mother said their elder kinswoman was also afflicted with the Sight. Lady Fiona had seen something just then—and there was, drat it, no time to ask her about it. Or rather, Lucie wouldn't take the time. She trotted down the front steps and found Hyde adjusting the girth of the saddle on one of the horses.

As she stepped closer, a ray of crisp, golden sunlight broke through the clouds, flooding the horse in bright light. The coppery red of her coat—for this was a mare—sparkled as brightly as Lucie's own hair must be doing. Her mane had been brushed to a gleaming blond, and the lady's saddle atop her was hand tooled with a design as fine as the lines of the beast herself.

Heart pounding, Lucie walked all around the horse, examining her with eyes and hands. It was *that* prime mount, wasn't it? 'Twas a moment before she could catch her breath and speak. "This horse—"

"Fetch you a good one at the stables, you said." Hyde made a show of cupping his hands to help her mount. "An' it took a while to find one trained to a side-saddle, so we'd best be off and ride before the rain starts again."

Lucie would rather ride astride, but Hyde had insisted cavorting about in trousers would shame Lady Fiona and himself.

"And I may keep her the month?"

"Aye."

"And the cost?"

He turned away. "Is not yours to bear."

"What do ye mean?"

"Did not ye hear Lady Fiona say ye're to be her guest? Stop fashing and let's be off before the heavens decide to open again. Likely to pour later this morning, and I don't wish to be out catching my death." He made a great show of coughing.

The mare caught her eye, cast her a long look, and dipped her head.

"Very well," Lucie said, nodding back. She stepped onto Hyde's laced fingers and popped into the saddle.

*Trained to a side-saddle...*and yet, it *was* the same horse. How had the mare ended up at a livery stable? Or...

A vision rose up from nowhere, flooding her senses. A man, dark-haired and handsome. The feel of his lips, the touch of his tongue twining with hers, his arm drawing her close, his body, long, lean, and hard, pressing against hers. Heart pounding, the world started to tip, more memories flooding her. Brussels; the Duchess's ball; the distant cannon; the frantic farewell.

That kiss. He'd been deadly serious, raw with need, torn by his duty.

Blasted duty.

She blinked and saw Hyde, seated atop another fine horse, this one a dark-maned bay gelding. He watched her, concern in his eyes.

Warmth flooded her cheeks. That had been no more than a memory, hadn't it? Stirred by the sight of this horse, so like the one Rudgwick had ridden the night of...

No. It couldn't be the same one. And she wouldn't think about that horrible night. She wouldn't think about anything except a brisk ride on an astonishing horse, and perhaps at the end of it, a chance to speak briefly with Rudgwick and warn him. She would do that. She would be direct and to the point and there'd be no mincing of words.

CHAPTER FOUR

A Warning

"I say, Rudgwick," Jeremy exclaimed. "Isn't that Athena? And the lady..." He broke off and laughed. "You're a sly one. I thought you'd trained the mare up for Harmonia." He looked over and frowned. "See here. Do you mean to make Miss Macbeth your mistress?"

Rudgwick sighed. Jeremy had lowered his voice, and the rain, overcast skies, and early hour had kept the crowds thin. Still... "No. Ask me that again, or spread that rumor about, and I'll thrash you to a pulp, one-handed though I may be. And you know I can do it."

He'd kept his voice low as well. None of the other riders were paying any heed to their conversation. They were all fixated on the straight-backed woman attired in royal blue perched on an equally majestic horse. A tiny afterthought of a hat sat atop her head like a nesting bluebird perched in her glorious hair, a long feather raised as a warning.

"But Athena—"

"Deserves a competent rider. She would carry Harmonia hither and yon. She'd stop for a nibble at every patch of green. She'd come back to the mews when the oats called, no matter where Harmonia wanted her to go."

Jeremy was silent. He knew the truth of that better than anyone, having taken on the task of accompanying Harmonia on rides during her Yuletide visit to Rudgwick Abbey.

"You had a much longer conversation with her than I did last night, Jeremy, how did you find the lady?"

"Miss Macbeth?"

"Of course, Miss Macbeth."

"Rather pensive, actually. Solemn. One might almost say, troubled."

Rudgwick had a long visit with Hyde that morning. He'd been one of the search-party looking for Lucie when she went off riding and didn't return home. He'd been the one to put down the horse. Someone else had pulled the unconscious girl from the bog and brought her round. When she was able to travel, Hyde brought her down to Edinburgh where the Colonel and his wife were staying with Lady Fiona in the newly acquired townhouse the lady was refurbishing. Lucie had seen a physician there, and later, one in Bath. Her head was healed, and she was riding again, but she wasn't entirely herself, Hyde said.

She was having, in Hyde's cryptic words, *spells*.

Which explained her demeanor the night before at the theater. She'd been suffering a spell, one so alarming he'd wanted to leap over the pit into her box and hold her. He'd had to restrain himself from going to her.

"Grallon told me about her parents' scandal," Jeremy mused, the ass.

So, the gossip had started already. Well, there would be more.

"Were you invited to her birthday ball?" Rudgwick asked casually. They were still a distance away from Lucie, but had almost caught up to Hyde, who held his mount back, following Lucie, watching the watchers. Social rank be damned, Hyde would not stand on ceremony should some one of the gentlemen misbehave.

The slavering fools. Let one accost her and he'd be on top of them before Hyde.

"The birthday ball for Miss Macbeth? I've never been so surprised, but I assumed my godmother submitted my name so there'd be enough gentlemen. Sent my regrets and tossed the invitation into the grate. Surely you're not going to attend?"

He nodded. "We will most assuredly attend."

"We? You don't mean to escort Harmonia? Bridgehampton won't have it."

He doubted Harmonia had been invited, and truth to tell, he'd just as soon not have her on his arm for that occasion. "I mean to escort my mother. We owe Miss Macbeth's family a deep debt of gratitude. Macbeth and his cousin, Menteith, had let a very comfortable villa in Brussels before the battle. They welcomed us like family, and we stayed several weeks with them."

Lucie had found him and rescued him at what was a very low time for him, perhaps the lowest in his life. He'd awakened from a lengthy fever missing a hand and remembering the horror of losing part of it in battle and the rest of it under the surgeon's saw.

Lucie had told the world she was looking for Hyde, combing the many improvised hospitals after the battle, but she'd been looking for him as well and she'd found him, and Mother with him. Without her, he might have succumbed to the fever he'd been battling on and off, as well as the dark cloud of self-pity. A man might function quite well with one leg, as Lord Uxbridge was learning, but to lose one's strong hand set one back almost to infancy.

A challenge, certainly. One he'd spent the autumn and winter addressing. The duke had expected him to alight from his ship and proceed directly to the altar. They'd had a row over that, as they'd had over his service with Wellington. There would be a bigger row when he told the man he wouldn't marry his granddaughter.

He pressed a knee into his gelding's side, saluted Hyde as he passed, and eased up next to Athena, who cast the intruder a haughty look until she recognized him, nickering and swishing her tail. Lucie's posture never budged.

"Lucie," he said. "Miss Lucie Macbeth."

She turned a knowing gaze on him, not at all surprised, and smiled, as she'd done that day in Brussels when she'd found him in a sweltering bed on a hot June day. That was better than a nicker and tail-swishing. The smile stirred his blood and chased away the chill of the day.

"Major Lord Rudgwick. I owe ye much thanks. She is lovely."

"Isn't she, though?" He leaned close. "And as I told you once before, you may call me Tristan."

She shook her head. "Hyde didn't tell me the horse's name."

"Athena."

"A goddess. She is that. How long may I borrow her? Hyde would not say, nor would he tell me how much the debt will be. Ye may have to wait on payment."

"As you well know, the debt is all mine. And as I well know, you've been coveting a ride on this horse for over a year."

Not as much though as *he'd* been coveting a ride... Oh Hades, Macbeth would run him through if he could read his thoughts.

Rudgwick had been riding Athena the night he'd met Lucie, the night she'd set out on a mission to rescue her mother clad in a fetching pair of trousers and men's coats. He'd seen her attraction to both the horse and himself, and if the way to her heart was through the horse, so be it.

"Don't tell me you'd forgotten Athena."

She laughed, and the sound made his heart leap as if he was a green boy chasing his first skirt.

"Only now and then, when I had occasion to think of her." She craned her head around. "Is your fiancée riding with ye today?"

"There is only my chaperon, Lord Jeremy Bolton."

The smile left her, and she frowned into the distance. "I would not cause harm to your reputation, Major Lord Rudgwick."

"Nor I yours. The world will learn that your father is my good friend. That your parents and cousin..." *and you, most especially you*, "helped me when I most needed it. Not every member of the *ton* is cruel and cynical."

She turned a cool gaze on him, nodded and then, seized by some sudden emotion, closed her eyes a moment too long. When she opened them, she steered Athena to the side of the path, reining up and catching her breath.

He moved his horse beside hers. She'd gone pale, her chest rising and falling as she gulped breaths, and her eyelids fluttered. Macbeth had suffered a spell just like this the night his wife's carriage was attacked. Perhaps the Sight had shown him a threat to his daughter, and that was the real reason he'd written asking for Rudgwick's help.

Hyde rode up on her other side, a hand ready for her should she need it.

She shook herself, licked her lips, and turned a solemn gaze on Rudgwick, her topaz eyes shining, before glancing back at Hyde. "When ye met up with Major Lord Rudgwick this morning, did ye tell him?"

"About the crack to your head, aye, Miss Lucie."

"And?"

Hyde shrugged. "And the spells, what I know about them, which is naught."

There'd been no rancor in her tone, and Hyde's replies were matter-of-fact.

She frowned past him, and he saw Jeremy approaching.

He shook his head and Jeremy reined up, staying back.

"Thank ye," she whispered. "I'm not wishing to be carted off to Bedlam. But, aye, let me get straight to it. There's danger ahead for ye, Rudgwick. Or there might be. What sort or from whom, I can't see. I only know, ye must have a care." She swallowed. "Promise me ye'll have a care."

Her face had gone pale, the freckles standing out starkly, but her mouth firmed in a way that reminded him of a soldier watching the enemy's advance. He wanted to sweep her off her horse into his arms. He wanted to tell her that all would be well, that he'd look after her.

But he couldn't do that, not yet anyway, and she wouldn't appreciate his pity.

"You must tell me more."

"I don't know more."

"Everything you've seen. The smallest detail."

She shook her head and straightened her back, regal and ever so stubborn.

"What was it you saw last night at the theater?"

Her chin came up and fear flashed in her eyes.

The sight made his breath catch. Lucie Macbeth showing fear? He wanted to lift it from her proud shoulders. To hell with the duke and Harmonia. Lucie needed him more.

"What's happened?" Jeremy nudged his horse closer.

A drop of water fell from an overhead leaf onto Lucie's nose, and she wiped it away, along with that spell of stark fear, finding her impertinent self again, to his great relief.

"I was telling Miss Macbeth she must wear a larger hat," he joked.

She grimaced. "Against the rain and for the sake of my dreaded freckles. It is a pleasure to meet ye again, Lord Jeremy." Her gaze lifted and sharpened.

A sandy-haired man approached, his confident swagger evident, even on horseback—Dankworth again. This was the second time within twenty-four hours. Rudgwick wondered if the encounters were purposeful.

Lucie cleared her throat. "I bid ye farewell. Have a care, Major Lord Rudgwick, sir."

"Do not ye fash," he teased. He still needed to offer the help her father had requested with Banquo's solicitor. But it wasn't a subject he wanted to broach with Dankworth nearby. "I believe the heavens are about to open again. Jeremy and I will escort you home."

"Don't be silly. Hyde is with me."

"Aye, Major, milord," Hyde said, from her other side. "I'll see her safely home."

Hyde was a sturdy fellow. A determined villain with enough henchmen could overpower one man, but Rudgwick reminded himself that in the middle of the day on busy streets, such an attack wasn't likely.

"Good man, Hyde. Miss Macbeth, you must hurry home. And be advised, my mother plans to pay you a call. Perhaps I'll join her."

That news sent color into her cheeks.

"Your mother is very kind." She patted Athena's withers and said in a lower voice. "And just who *is* that man approaching?"

"No one you want to know."

She looked up at him through her lashes, but the look was assessing. He couldn't expect Lucie Macbeth to flirt. "Aye. We're of one mind there. Good day to ye, Major Lord Rudgwick." And then she turned Athena and trotted off. With a quick salute, Hyde followed, closing the gap to follow more closely.

"What was that about?" Jeremy asked.

Rudgwick eyed his younger friend. He'd known Jeremy for ages and trusted him. Oh, there'd been a youthful spell of chasing women and running up debts, but Northam had drafted Jeremy to assist with diplomatic endeavors in Flanders and Paris. Returning to England in late autumn, Jeremy had paid a call at Rudgwick Abbey and stayed. Now he was lodging at Rudgwick's house in Knightsbridge.

Jeremy was a welcome guest, one who'd spent considerable time with the placid Harmonia. She displayed signs of life around him, thus tormenting her grandfather who deemed him a scapegrace. Which he wasn't, at least not anymore. Besides his diplomatic service, he'd done work for Sir Thomas Abernathy at the Home Office, a fact Rudgwick had learned from Sir Thomas himself.

And having done that sort of work, Jeremy would understand the need to keep secrets. But Rudgwick wasn't quite ready to tell his friend about Lucie's message. Jeremy might wish to know what she knew and how she knew it. She wasn't wishing to be carted off to Bedlam, she'd said. That was just the sort of tactic Bridgehampton might attempt. Though the duke had more honor than his late villainous son, Grey had learned some of his ways at the feet of a master.

"In point of fact." He brushed at a drop of rain. "You interrupted us just as she was about to tell me something interesting."

Jeremy studied the approaching Dankworth, his face carefully devoid of emotion. "The duke won't like it," he muttered without much conviction.

Was the pull between himself and Lucie that obvious?

He laughed. Yes. Mother had seen it immediately in Brussels. The duke sensed it.

He'd best have a care, for Lucie's sake. And he must also keep in mind Harmonia's reputation.

Dankworth was almost upon them, so he held his tongue.

"Rudgwick. Bolton." The terse greeting came with a sly, yellow-toothed grin.

Oh yes. Dankworth had noticed Lucie.

"And *who* was that? Saw her last night at the theater. Prime bit of muslin. Yours, Bolton?" he asked, his gaze fixed on Rudgwick. "I saw you visiting her box last night."

His hand fisted. Jeremy, being a true friend, stepped in, saving him from the sort of confrontation that would stir up rumors and bring the wrath of Bridgehampton down upon him before he was ready. Oh, that would come, but he'd prefer to have a complete plan in place. What that plan would be, he wasn't yet sure. Like Wellington, he had to study the maneuvers of his enemy, the duke, allow for the moods of his questionable ally, Harmonia, and account for the vagaries of terrain and weather, like these supposed threats and the quest after Banquo's estate.

"Don't be an *ass*, Dankworth." Jeremy wisely smiled and infused his words with good-natured humor. Grey had been bloody ruthless in duels, and Dankworth had always served as his second. "She's a young lady friend of my godmother. A respectable one. Heiress to a Scottish barony."

Dankworth's eyes lit. "Rich?"

Dankworth's expression conveyed humor, Rudgwick decided. He probably knew all about Lucie, yet he probed anyway.

"Who knows?" Bolton brushed at a drop of rain.

Dankworth turned that sardonic grin on Rudgwick. He schooled his expression and gazed back, steeling himself for what might come. For what would *certainly* come, sooner or later, because he wouldn't suffer this fool for very long.

He'd spent months in the country, fighting the pain that rose again and again as the stump healed, training his weak hand with knife, fork, quill, and most especially his sword and his pistol. Let Dankworth hint that Lucie was *his* "prime bit of muslin". He'd take his chances on the field of honor.

The rain pattered harder, quickly becoming a downpour and dripping off the brim of his hat. He sat, waiting. He'd fought through worse downpours in the Peninsula and at bloody Waterloo.

Dankworth chuckled and saluted. "Another day, my lords," he said, and rode off.

They turned their horses toward the gate. "What's he up to?" Jeremy mused.

"I don't know."

"Stirring up a duel? That would have been Grey's tactic. Has he a grudge against you?"

Undoubtedly.

Where had that certainty come from? Perhaps he'd been touched by Lucie's fanciful fears. "I barely know the fellow."

"Last night, Dankworth was walking toward Harmonia when that boy crossed our paths." Jeremy glanced at him. "You spoke to the lad."

Rudgwick shook his head. "Odd, wasn't it? I wondered if the target was to be Harmonia and the rescuer Dankworth. The little thief had nothing to say."

"Dankworth will know of Harmonia's dowry. He doesn't have a chance with the duke though, not even if you were to break off your engagement."

"Very true." Dankworth undoubtedly held a grudge over Harmonia. The girl's dowry came to her through her maternal grandmother, and it was substantial. Should she not marry, it would be hers at five and twenty, eight years in the future. The duke was one of the tightfisted trustees, plotting to keep control of it until he could hand it over to the husband of his choice, the heir to the Bridgehampton title.

That he was Bridgehampton's heir was not commonly spoken of. If he'd died at Waterloo, the next in line was a married, middle-aged cleric. Unless the duke found a way to make the man a widower, Harmonia would marry someone else and her fortune—much needed by the Bridgehampton duchy, he suspected—would depart from the control of the incumbent duke.

"I say, Rudgwick. I heard Dankworth's name brought up in Whitehall. I don't remember by whom."

Sir Thomas Abernathy had his offices in Whitehall. He'd written to Sir Thomas upon his arrival in town and hadn't received a reply. "Come along then. Let's pay Sir Thomas a call."

CHAPTER FIVE

An Appointment Interrupted

Lucie set a faster pace on the ride back to Chelsea, as much as was possible on the crowded wet streets. The damp air helped clear her mind, though the cobwebs seemed thicker than ever. She'd done her duty and warned Rudgwick. Not that she was sure he'd listened and would take care.

The man had a warrior's heart. The mere loss of a hand wouldn't keep him hiding in his rooms from the danger she sensed around him.

Who was this Lord Jeremy? He'd been quite civil with her at the opera, and his godmother adored him. But the other man who'd approached on a horse—the frank look on his face had raised her hackles.

"Hyde," she called, and he nudged his mount closer. "What do ye know of Lord Jeremy?"

"Not a thing, miss."

"And that other fellow riding over to talk to Rudgwick—do ye know him?"

"No. Saw him last night when I came to fetch you to the carriage. Didn't like the looks of him, though."

It was no wonder Father had sent Hyde along to play nursemaid. He had good instincts. Not that she'd tell him that. He'd puff up and think he could bully her.

"What did ye think of Lord Jeremy?"

"Like I said, don't know him."

"Aye, but what did your gut tell ye?"

"Weel... horse was a fine one. May have been Rudgwick's. Fit enough; he's not a slack-about, stuffing his face like the Regent." His brow furrowed. "Got some wear on his boots."

She forced a laugh. Perhaps, despite his inheritance, Lord Jeremy was pockets to let. She ought to have paid such close attention, but she'd been far too focused on Rudgwick, both this morning and at the theater. "I'd like to know more about both men—Lord Jeremy and the other one. Ask around for me. Visit the mews where Rudgwick stables his horses." She leveled a look at him. "When Rudgwick isn't there."

"Miss Lucie, his lordship did ye a good turn, and yet ye'd send me to snoop on his friend. I can't—"

"Then mayhap I'll visit the mews."

"Mayhap ye should ask one of the ladies. Or ask the Major himself."

She gritted her teeth and set Athena into a faster pace. She didn't intend to spend any time with Rudgwick, but if she could ferret out who was likely to harm him, she'd meet him again and warn him.

Fine if Hyde didn't want to help her. She'd puzzle this out herself.

"Mr. Stephenson has still not replied to my letter." Nor had he received her when she'd visited his office. "Mayhap I shall sit on his doorstep tomorrow until he agrees to see me."

Hyde grunted.

"Ye don't need to grunt. I know fully well what the problem is—I'm a woman, and a young one at that."

"And Scottish," Hyde said helpfully. "Need a gentleman's help."

She eyed him. Hyde owned a good set of coats, but when he opened his mouth, he'd be caught out as less than a gentleman.

"Aye, not me, Miss Lucie. What of Lady Fiona's man of business?"

"Traveling. And his clerk..." She shuddered. The solicitor's clerk was a pompous young fellow who would expect to do all the talking.

"His lordship might be willing to help." Hyde's sly smile told her who he meant.

Two could play at being sly. "Lord Grallon?" she asked.

He pursed his lips until he could hold them still no longer and a laugh burst forth.

"*Rudgwick?*" She forced an equally exuberant laugh. "No. Who else do we know of Father's acquaintance who may be in town, Hyde? Someone who won't be shocked when I call without an introduction."

Hyde rubbed his jaw where a gray scruff sprouted. He'd departed the house too early to shave, the bounder, and gone off carrying tales to Rudgwick.

"There be Sir Thomas Abernathy, if he's in town."

She remembered Sir Thomas, a bald-headed, serious man. She'd met him last August when he came to dinner at Lady Fiona's.

"Do you know where to find him?"

"As it happens, I do, miss."

Early the next day
Whitehall

"Wonder what the old man wants of us," Jeremy mused, as he and Rudgwick dismounted and handed the reins to a waiting servant.

"Curious, isn't it?" Rudgwick said. Sir Thomas Abernathy had not been in when they'd called the previous day, but his clerk had handed over letters he'd been about to post to each of them requesting this meeting today.

They found their way through the labyrinth of offices into a waiting area, where a clerk told them Sir Thomas would be available in a few moments.

Rudgwick paced the length of the room and back. They were early, and even an earl had to wait sometimes, yet he bristled with impatience.

The duke was right that he'd been rusticating too long. The warning delivered by Lucie had piqued his curiosity, and this call to arms by Sir Thomas—for surely it would be that, as well as Colonel Macbeth's request that he aid Lucie, were just what he needed to break out of his funk.

Mother would call on Lucie later today, and he would accompany her. Perhaps then he could broach the subject of her father's request with her.

"Did she go through, then?" The whispered question came from one of the clerks who'd deposited a file on Sir Thomas's secretary's desk.

"Yes."

Rudgwick paused in his pacing and exchanged a look with Jeremy.

"Who *was* she?" the man murmured.

At that moment, Hyde strode in, wearing a fine set of coats that made him look like a gentleman.

Lucie was here.

Rudgwick strode past the secretary's desk and opened the door to the inner office before the man had a chance to jump from his chair.

"I have visited twice and..."

Lucie turned astonished eyes his way. Sir Thomas, looking not at all surprised, dipped his head in welcome.

"Ah," he said. "You are here, and right on time."

"Indeed, sir, and happy to find the two people who've brought to me to London together in one place."

Lucie stood. "*He* was your next appointment? I see. I will—"

"No, no, my dear," Sir Thomas said. "Be seated, please. Is Lord Jeremy here, Rudgwick? You may fetch him as well. I believe you can both help."

***

Lucie remained standing, watching the two handsome noblemen swan in and intrude on her visit with Sir Thomas Abernathy.

Oh fine, they'd had an appointment, so she was the intruder, but, nevertheless. Having been shut out of Mr. Stephenson's office again that morning, she'd had Hyde direct the coachman to Whitehall, on the remote chance that Sir Thomas would be in and would have time to see her.

But devil take it, Rudgwick, of all people was *here*, and what did he mean the two people who brought him to London were in one place? She'd had nothing to do with him.

Unless it had something to do with those visions? Good heavens, did having the Sight mean one could send messages, in her case, unknowingly? In fact, against one's will?

They'd shared one kiss, that was all. The scenes popping up in her cracked head had more to do with the past, for when she was honest, that kiss had been earth-shattering, what with passion all mixed up with the terror of the coming battle.

It was the past, not her future. She refused to lust after an affianced man. She, Lucie Macbeth, was stronger than that.

A drop of perspiration slid down her back under the too-heavy gown, her pelisse and shawl. With the men crowded in, the room had suddenly grown wretchedly warm.

"Do be seated, Lucie." Though humor flashed in his eyes, Rudgwick managed to sound bored. "Lord Jeremy and I won't take our seats until you do as well."

"I hear you've inherited an estate in Norfolk called Thornview Farm." Sir Thomas, who was back in his chair, addressed Lord Jeremy, who in turn, launched into a description of the estate, his yacht, and what he called his and Rudgwick's recent repairing lease, a few leisurely weeks spent traipsing all around Norfolk. Lady Walby said Lord Jeremy's brother was some sort of diplomat; perhaps diplomacy was a family gift, as the younger man's soothing soliloquy completely defused her anger and stirred her curiosity.

Norfolk had been Banquo's home. What was Sir Thomas up to?

She seated herself, and both men sat down.

Sir Thomas braced himself on his elbows. "I assume you are all acquainted?"

Everyone nodded, and he went on. "Let me review what you may not know: Colonel Macbeth is attempting to settle the estate of his late cousin, Giles Banquo, on behalf of the man's two sons. While Macbeth deals with the courts in

Edinburgh, he's requested his daughter's assistance with a London solicitor who was handling some of Banquo's business affairs. The solicitor has made himself unavailable to Miss Macbeth. Do I have the facts right, my dear?"

Blithely sharing her business with two other visitors was not what she'd had in mind when she called on Sir Thomas. It was irritating, in fact, no matter how kindly he addressed her as *my dear*.

She unclenched her teeth. "Yes. I've politely asked for an appointment and, that request going unanswered, I've been twice to see him."

"Colonel Macbeth is a friend," Rudgwick said, "As is your mother. As are you. I am at your service, Lucie."

Oh. Under his steady gaze, the room grew still warmer. Her shawl slipped down, and she glanced at Sir Thomas. She'd hoped for *his* help—a threatening letter from the Home Office might suffice. Had he planned all along to foist Rudgwick upon her?

A buzzing started in her head, her heart pounded harder, and heat swirled around in her belly. Heaven help her, she wouldn't mind Rudgwick's help, though she *should* mind.

The vision of him reared up, and she quickly studied the polished front of Sir Thomas's desk. Even in this stuffy government office with two other men present, Rudgwick's tug on her heart—and other parts of her person—was powerful.

And that thought roused a flood of annoyance. How dare he pop in during her private conversation with Sir Thomas crowing about the two people...

"Major Lord Rudgwick, what did you mean when you said you'd found the two people who brought you to London in one place."

He blinked.

"I invited Rudgwick to London," Sir Thomas said.

"Quite right." Rudgwick had recovered his aplomb, and now he leaned forward, speaking only to her as if there were not two other people in the room. "And your father wrote, asking me to assist you with Banquo's solicitor."

No. Anger rolled through her, flooding her cheeks with heat, and sparking a moisture behind her eyes. Father didn't trust her to see to the matter herself. He *would* bring in Rudgwick.

How could he not have seen the way Rudgwick looked at her? And she was only human, a child of scandal, and not just her parents' divorce and all the trouble it had wrought; her Aunt Charmaine had died unmarried in an ill-begotten childbirth.

Rudgwick watched her, his eyes darkening. The room fell away and the distance between them shortened, and her breath quickened with a mixture of anger and smoldering desire.

Lord Jeremy cleared his throat. "Sometimes a title will open doors. I will be happy to lend my brother's name to the cause."

"Your father wrote to me as well," Sir Thomas said. "Did he not describe to you the difficulties he was having with this man Stephenson?"

She took in a breath and blinked away the shimmering edges of the nagging vision. "Aye, sir. He did."

Father's wounds, suffered during the battle of Waterloo, had not yet totally healed. In fact, he'd carry some of the pain for the rest of his life, and she mustn't be angry with him. It wasn't his fault that she was a woman, and a young one at that.

"I have clear instructions on what my father needs and how to proceed," she said. "But perhaps a noble boot to the door will help. If ye're free tomorrow, Lord Jeremy, will ye accompany me?"

"No," Rudgwick said. "The request was made to me, and the honor will be mine."

Fierce words stated in an affable tone, yet it was clear he'd brook no objections. Still... "But your fiancée—"

"I owe a great debt to your family."

Ah. It might only be that. Mayhap she'd been letting her imagination get away with her. Rudgwick's kiss had been heartfelt but, facing death, he might have kissed any young lady he came across. She'd seen that in the men who swooped in to help her mother and her when they'd long ago found themselves nearly destitute. Men were like that.

She rose. "The sooner, the better, please, Major Lord Rudgwick." With her birthday ball looming, she had busy days ahead.

***

Lucie's frown and primmed lips shouted displeasure. "Of course," he said. "I'll send a note this afternoon and confirm."

She said her farewells. Rudgwick escorted her to the door and held it open for her. In the anteroom, Hyde spotted them and came out of his slouch to attention.

On the other hand, he'd best force Lucie's hand before she could drum up an objection. Lady Fiona might have another gentleman to call on for help.

"Excuse me, Sir Thomas," Rudgwick said. "I'll be right back."

He pressed his hand to Lucie's back and steered her toward Hyde. The waiting room was otherwise empty. The secretary had stepped away.

The blue gown Lucie wore was not the sapphire blue riding habit he'd seen her in at the park. "Is your carriage waiting?" he asked.

"Aye, Major," Hyde said. "Lady Fiona's rig is just outside."

"Wait for me there. When I have finished with this other business Sir Thomas has, we'll go back to that solicitor's office this afternoon."

Her lips thinned even more.

"Unless you have other appointments."

"It's Lady Fiona's at home day and she'd like me to be there." Her frown deepened, her regard for Lady Fiona evident. Finally, she shook her head. "But no. She'll ken this is more important."

CHAPTER SIX

A Good Left Hook

Rudgwick watched her leave, waiting for the glance over her shoulder. When the door closed on her—and his disappointment—he chuckled. She was a proud girl, and not as rash as he'd once thought. Definitely not rash about matters of the heart. She wanted help, but not from him. He would help the prickly girl anyway—in fact, the gauntlet she tossed was irresistible.

He returned to the office and found both Sir Thomas and Jeremy watching him. Jeremy had that *the duke won't like it* look about him. Sir Thomas's expression was, as usual, inscrutable.

"Is this solicitor of the late Banquo a person of interest?" Rudgwick asked. "The reason you called me to London?"

The corners of Sir Thomas's lips turned up. "As a matter of fact, he is. Quite a felicitous coincidence, Lucie appearing this morning. I hadn't planned it in case you were wondering." He rubbed his hands together. "She has pluck, yet I don't like the notion of her wandering into that particular office on her own."

"Did Macbeth know of the possibility of danger?"

"Perhaps not at first, else he wouldn't have asked for her help. I'm astonished that he did so; given the association with Giles Banquo, one might assume the worst."

"And what is the worst?"

"Though the war has ended, we haven't closed certain investigations. Banquo was involved with military provisioners. He also had connections with smugglers. It's believed he might have diverted and sold equipment and arms to the French or was in league with those who did. One wonders what that solicitor is holding or what he knows."

"And besides assisting Miss Macbeth, how may we help?" Jeremy asked.

"There is a connection to Norfolk. You have an estate there now and are well-situated to investigate. We'd like to find out what the connection is, and who else might have been involved."

Rudgwick's gaze locked with Jeremy's, his mind sorting through the possibilities.

"Might one of those involved be Lionel Dankworth?" his friend asked.

Jeremy had taken the words from Rudgwick's mouth, but Sir Thomas's assessing gaze raised another question. "Was Grey involved as well?" he asked.

"We haven't found evidence yet." Sir Thomas said. "It's an open question: Dankworth, Grey and perhaps others? I have been reticent about discussing the matter with you, Rudgwick, because of your pending nuptials."

His pulse pounded, inciting a pain in his stump. Jeremy had gone very still. He felt both sets of eyes on him.

"Bridgehampton." He fell back in the chair. He'd thought the duke's opposition to Rudgwick's service in Brussels had been a personal matter. Would the duke have opposed the renewal of hostilities because he supported Bonaparte? Would the duke have committed treason?

His mind worked through the cascade of consequences for such villainy and came down to the self-interested one: Bridgehampton would be stripped of the title, and Rudgwick would be spared the dukedom.

Unless of course, he himself was, as a future grandson-in-law and heir presumptive, somehow implicated. And, oh Hades, if that were the case, Mother would be smeared by the scandal, and Harmonia. His sister and her husband as well.

"We have no reason to think Bridgehampton was involved," Sir Thomas said. "It's far more likely he's worried what evidence might surface."

"Blackmail?" Jeremy asked.

Was the duke being threatened over Grey's villainy? If the Bridgehampton budget was already tight, extortion would certainly give him a need for more funds.

Sir Thomas shrugged. "Let's start with that solicitor. When will you visit him?" He unearthed a file from the small pile on his desk.

Rudgwick stood. "Right now. If he's dodging Lucie, he'll be off his guard, not expecting her to return the same day. If that file in your hand is for us, Jeremy, you review it. I'll meet you back in Knightsbridge this afternoon."

"What of Miss Macbeth?" Jeremy asked.

"She's waiting for me in her carriage."

He escorted the coach like an outrider, needing time to think as well as to avoid the dangers of a carriage ride with Lucie Macbeth. Alone in an enclosed space, he might not be able to keep his hands—that is, his hand—off her.

He scoffed at himself. He knew his way around women two-handed, but that was before. He'd not bedded a woman since the loss of his hand—in truth, not since his betrothal to Harmonia.

A man could do many things with only one hand, and he wanted to do all of them to Lucie Macbeth. But there was her honor to think of, her father's honor, Harmonia's honor. And his own, of course. Blasted honor.

The carriage traveled into the City and turned onto a side street, pausing before the sort of tall, narrow, nondescript building that would house dark, dank warrens of offices. The lengthy list of names on the building's sign confirmed the notion. His own solicitor had a whole floor to himself in a far better establishment closer to Parliament.

He dismounted, handed over his reins to Lady Fiona's groom, and went to open the carriage door.

"I say, Rudgwick. Is that you?" The greeting came from behind him, but he recognized the voice. Lucie peered out through the closed glass of the coach.

He turned, blocking her. Too late, judging by the grin on Dankworth's face.

"Seeing an out-of-the-way solicitor to set up *carte blanche,* hmm? I knew at the park there was something afoot."

Anger shot through him. There was no Jeremy here to smooth over the situation, and he opened his mouth to issue a challenge when the carriage door slapped open and hit his backside.

Lucie hopped out, straightening her skirts. She handed him a small document case. "Major Lord Rudgwick, will ye carry the colonel's papers? Let's see to business and be done. I don't wish to miss your mother's call today." Before he could speak, she turned away and beckoned Hyde from his perch, whispered something to him, leaned closer when he shook his head, and whispered something more. Then she slipped her hand around Rudgwick's stump.

She'd given him time to regain his composure. Before he lost his hand, he'd been the cool head in the Regiment, persuading the hotblooded asses to turn their wrath on the French and not each other. He'd been a whole man then. And dammit, he would be again, but it was foolish to think a duel would get him there sooner.

He dipped his head to her. "I'm at the colonel's service, miss." They passed Dankworth without another word and entered the stale-smelling hall where she dropped her hand. Light from a glass transom illuminated her fierce glare.

"Ye'll tell me now who that was." She'd gone pale with her anger, her freckles in stark relief.

"Lionel Dankworth."

A hissing breath escaped her. "I know what *carte blanche* signifies. I may have to kill him. Or someone."

"Allow me the honor."

"Honor? *Pffft.* It might be yerself I have to kill. Come, Stephenson's rooms are on the third floor."

He swallowed a chuckle and followed her.

The worn beadboard lining the walls shed flakes of brown paint, and the stairs and floor creaked and echoed under his boots. She led him to a door near the landing and went in.

The clerk there, a reedy looking fellow with thinning hair and a permanent scowl, remained seated. "I told you, miss" he said. "Mr. Stephenson cannot see you."

The insolent fellow deserved a crack in the nose—his wooden hand might work nicely for that; it was a weapon he hadn't yet tried.

But Rudgwick would start the battle with courtesy first.

He juggled the document case and dug in his pocket, retrieving a card, and handing it over, causing the man to spring from his chair like a jack-in-the box.

"I am Rudgwick," he said. Redundant, given that the man held his details, yet he infused the words with all the starchy dignity of the five Earls of Rudgwick who'd gone before him. "The lady's father, Colonel Finnley Macbeth, is a close comrade and friend. Kindly announce us to Mr. Stephenson."

"I c-cannot, my lord."

"Cannot, or will not?"

"He's not available."

"Ye said that the last time I visited," Lucie said. "Both times. And that after I'd written requesting an appointment, without the courtesy of a reply."

"He's been away these last several days, on business. We don't know when to expect him."

"Is that so?" Rudgwick asked. "Does he not have a partner who is handling clients in his absence?"

"There's only the head clerk, Jones and myself."

"And where is Jones?"

He glanced over his shoulder at the closed door to the inner office.

Rudgwick offered Lucie his arm. "Shall we?"

She nodded, and he led her to the door.

***

"No." The clerk hurried around them and blocked them.

Inwardly seething, Lucie accepted the document case. She would allow that Rudgwick's title and arrogant proclamation of it had induced a bit more courtesy from the weaselly assistant. Oh, his self-assured noble lordliness was on full display. Yet, on the street, she'd seen him wavering over his answer to that wretched man who'd all but called her a whore. True, she was nothing to Rudgwick, so she shouldn't expect him to defend her honor. Yet it had rankled; had all but pierced her pride.

"Will you move?" Rudgwick asked, sounding bored. "Or shall I move you?" Three breaths passed before his hand shot out, capturing the other man by the neck and tossing him aside.

Seizing the moment, Lucie opened the door and rushed in. A bushy-haired head lay on the desk, attached to a thick neck covered in wrinkled linen, wide shoulders under a worn dark coat, and a pair of beefy arms. A bottle of spirits and two empty glasses stood nearby surrounded by untidy stacks of paper.

"Don't think to call any bully boys," Rudgwick called to the choking assistant. "Now get out." She heard the door close while she found the only chair—other than the one currently occupied by the body attached to the head—and set down her case. Then she surveyed the room, spotted a glass pitcher filled with water on a sideboard, and fetched it.

"You'll drench one of the lovely contracts he's working on," Rudgwick said.

"Needs must. He's drooling on them anyway. Or... There are boxes on those shelves over there. Shall I just have a look?"

He waved her toward the wall of shelving and its pressed board boxes. "While you look there, I'll poke around through the dribbled-on contracts."

Heart pounding, she stepped up to the shelves. The boxes held labels; she ran her thumb over them. 'Twould be too much to expect some organization here, but in fact, it wasn't all higgledy-piggledy; it seemed Stephenson's clerks had some knowledge of the alphabet. She found a grouping beginning with the letter B and searched.

No Banquo.

Unless the Bs were misfiled, which seemed a distinct possibility in a slipshod office like this. She moved on and came to a box marked Bridgehampton.

She glanced over her shoulder. Jones was still fast asleep. Curiously, not snoring or spluttering. Might he be dead? Surely not.

She opened the box, removed the few pages within, and sidled over, slipping them into her case. Rudgwick raised an eyebrow, and she gave her head a little shake.

He gestured toward the desk, his fist loosely coiled. "Take that pile."

He was pointing with his entire prosthesis; the hand was partially rounded in a semblance of human relaxation. Not unlike the rest of him. Rudgwick projected an air of calm confidence, even while tossing a clerk aside. Although she sensed that, underneath, he was a tightly coiled wire ready to spring. He must have been fierce in battle when he exerted himself.

She flipped through the small stack on the corner. There were leasing agreements and marriage contracts, and dun letters for debts.

One stack remained under Jones's hand. Rudgwick whisked it away. Not quickly enough.

"The devil." Jones lumbered out of his chair with a belligerent shout and teetered over the desk. He was better fed than the other clerk, built more like one of the bully boys who roamed the streets extorting protection money, enforcing rough justice, and occasionally engaging in illegal bouts of pugilism. She knew about that aspect of London society from Hyde's tutelage.

"*You.*" He bellowed. She dodged back from the flying spittle. Not that he was spitting at her, precisely. He was still insanely foxed, and his lips weren't yet working properly.

"Though ye and I have never met," she said, "I suppose my hair has given me away. Yes, it is I, again, along with my father's associate, Major Lord Rudgwick."

Jones's eyes flared.

"The *Earl* of Rudgwick," she added.

"You ought to have taken a moment from your busy diary to see Miss Macbeth when she called before," Rudgwick said. "I do believe we have something here, my dear."

Rudgwick handed her a sheaf of papers, more to free his good hand for punching, she suspected, but she stepped further away and scanned the lines. One name jumped out at her: that of her father's late cousin, Banquo.

Oh my. This was something; at least there was a reference to Banquo in the letter from—she glanced to the signature—Stephenson. The writer had been unavoidably delayed by bad weather in Suffolk but could be reached at the Blue Boar in Yarmouth, where he would be seeing other clients. His visit to May, Falton, and May in Norwich would be necessarily delayed as well.

"That ish private correshpondensh." Jones came around the desk and made a grab for the paper.

Lucie snatched her case from the chair and dodged away.

"Gimme tha."

Rudgwick's hand shot out—his good hand— and clipped Jones in the jaw. The oaf went down, hitting the desk as he fell and pulling the pile of wills, contracts, and dun notices with him. She stuffed the letter in her case and picked up the pitcher.

"Come, Lucie."

"But we haven't questioned him."

"We'll come back when he's sober."

Jones groaned.

Mayhap Rudgwick was right. Jones was too muddled for a proper questioning. She'd return another day with her blades and maybe even a pistol.

She allowed herself to be led to the anteroom, where she straightened her skirts, looking around. The desk had been cleared. There'd been papers there before, some document the clerk was working on.

"Where did he go?" she asked. "To summon a Runner?"

"I doubt they'd want legal authorities nosing about in here. More likely he went to get some street muscle, since the office muscle was three sheets to the wind. Best we retreat to fight another day."

"I'd let go the lot of them." With a boot to the behind on the way out. For certain, Father wouldn't be retaining Stephenson's services.

On that sentiment, the hall door opened. The head that popped in was young, but already squinty-eyed and attired in coats that hung a bit loose.

The man eyed her curiously, but when his gaze landed on Rudgwick's splendor—the custom-made coat, tight buckskin breeches, and shiny Hessians—he squinted harder. "I beg your pardon. Where is Loomis?"

"Is that his name?" Lucie asked. Better evasion than a straight answer.

Rudgwick leaned his way and said in a stage whisper: "Popped out to the privy."

"Ah."

"We're waiting to be called," Rudgwick said. "Is there a message for Loomis?"

"There's just this." He held up a letter. "Left downstairs at Mr. Halliburton's by mistake. Mr. Halliburton is my employer. I expect this is the letter from Norfolk they've been waiting for." He cleared his throat, sending his Adam's apple popping. "My employer, Mr. Halliburton, would never leave his clients unattended for so many days. If you're in need of services—"

"We shall certainly consider Mr. Halliburton if Mr. Stephenson continues to prove unsatisfactory," Rudgwick said. "Leave that if you wish. I know Loomis will be back shortly."

After the briefest consideration, Halliburton's man plopped the letter on the empty desk and took his leave. When the door closed, Rudgwick slipped the letter into his waistcoat.

"Better I hold it," he said.

She scoffed. "Because no one will subject an earl to a patting."

His lips quivered. "I might enjoy a patting from the right patter. But if anyone touches you, they'll regret it."

She didn't deign to blush at that remark, at least she hoped she hadn't. She listened until the thin walls conveyed the shuddering and snapping to of a door closing somewhere in the stairwell, and then reached for his arm.

Without speaking, he escorted her down the stairs and out through the front door to the waiting carriage. Lady Fiona's groom opened the coach door and lent Lucie a hand.

"And where is my horse?" Rudgwick managed to sound both bored and dangerous.

She'd best rescue the poor groom. "Hyde has taken it," she called over her shoulder. "Ye'll ride with me, Major Lord Rudgwick. Hurry, then, before Loomis returns."

With a shake of his head, he climbed in behind her, settling across from her in the rear-facing seat. The carriage pulled out into the London traffic.

"Hyde will see no harm comes to your mount. Though I noticed it wasn't the best of your stable."

***

Rudgwick eyed her a long moment. The gelding wasn't the best of his stable, but he was a good-natured mount that even a foot-slogger like Hyde would be able to handle, and she'd seen that. "You sent him to follow Dankworth."

Her chin shot up. "Aye."

"Well then." He shifted, squashed himself next to her, and watched as her color rose. The itch to touch her must have shown in his eyes. He wished he had chosen the other side instead of sitting to her left.

"You've a fine left hook," she said.

"Thank you."

Her gaze went to the hand resting upon his right knee. "May I..." She looked up through her eyelashes. "May I touch this hand?"

The unexpected request made his breath tighten. "You may touch any part of me you wish."

Her gaze dropped and her color rose while her fingers settled over the clump of wood. She slid her other hand under and lifted the false hand, studying it closely, letting the pad of her thumb slide over the glove covering the hinged knuckles in a way that sent blood pounding through him.

As if had been a real hand. *What the devil.*

"Should your left hook fail you, it might make a good club."

"I've wondered about that. Perhaps if it wasn't attached to what remains of my forearm?"

She looked up again and slid her hand up over the buckles and straps lying under his shirt and coat sleeve. Sometimes a touch sent his nerves screaming with pain. Now, it was desire that roared through him.

When she looked up again, he couldn't stop himself. He kissed her.

CHAPTER SEVEN

An Afternoon Call

His first kiss since the last one he'd shared with Lucie in Brussels. His first kiss as a one-handed man and all the awkwardness that might entail. With his right arm trapped by her, he set his left hand to her shoulder and deepened the kiss, reveling in her warmth and the unexpected welcome. When her lips parted for him, he pulled her to him, pressing into her breasts, relishing the feel of her, wondering whether she would allow him to—

She went very still. It took him a moment to notice and sit back.

Her golden eyes searched his. Her flushed, swollen lips thinned as he watched. He'd rushed his fences, but he couldn't apologize. He'd kiss her again if she'd allow it. *When* she allowed it.

"Major Lord Rudgwick, what *precisely* does *carte blanche* entail?"

Carte blanche. Dankworth would carry the tale of the solicitor visit to the club, twisting it into something ugly.

"Lucie, I would never... I respect you too much to..." He let out a long breath. "Your father will slay me."

"The father who sent ye to London to help me?" Frowning, she looked away. "Does Colonel Finnley Macbeth know something we don't? If ye recall, he has the Sight and..." She inhaled sharply and her blush deepened.

"What?"

She shook her head. "Would ye like to see what I took?"

He'd seen her slip something into her case, but he knew the distraction now was as purposeful as the question about *carte blanche*. She didn't want to talk about what her father might have seen... what she herself had seen. And that was a matter they still had to discuss.

"I didn't find Banquo's name. However, I did find a file for Bridgehampton."

Bridgehampton. He knew for a fact that Bridgehampton's solicitor was not Stephenson.

"Of course," she said, "it may be some lowly businessman or landlord with the surname Bridgehampton, and not the duke."

They had made good time and were passing Mayfair, where the duke had his grand townhouse and where he kept Harmonia under close supervision.

The file might contain a bargaining chip that would help him escape the marriage to Harmonia. But that would still leave the girl trapped by the old man.

Unless he would be able to help *her* as well.

"And what of the letter in your waistcoat?"

"We'll be to Knightsbridge soon. We may look at both the letter and your document there."

Lucie shook her head. "No. The duke might pop in at any time looking for ye, and then what will happen if he finds me ensconced with ye there? No, we'll go to Chelsea. Lady Fiona's counsel will be helpful. And there's also the matter of Norwich. Now that I have a name, I'll need to visit that bank."

"No, you won't. I'll go on your behalf. I'll leave tomorrow."

"Ye'll not. I canna leave tomorrow. I have the ball in two days."

"I'm going alone. You're not coming with me."

Her jaw firmed and then softened on a long breath, and she leaned back against the squab. "That's probably for the best."

Which meant, she expected to travel on her own anyway with Hyde as escort. It was just as well they were going to Chelsea. Lady Fiona would talk sense into her.

As she fell into an icy silence, he thought about the events of the afternoon. It had felt good to knock heads, the first time he'd had anything close to a real fight since Waterloo. Perhaps Lady Fiona would allow him a spot of her fine whisky to celebrate. She'd sent over a few bottles to Menteith in Brussels. Perhaps she'd raise a glass with him too when she heard...

"Two glasses," he said.

Lucie roused and frowned. "Loomis wasn't tippling. Someone else had been there, and not long before." Her mouth dropped. "Your friend, Darkworth."

"Dankworth. And he's definitely not my friend." Jeremy might have more information on Dankworth after reviewing Sir Thomas's file.

He'd keep that to himself. Lucie didn't need to know everything. It would be harder to protect her if she did. She was apt to take the matter into her own hands.

***

Lucie gave silent thanks that Lady Fiona did no more than blink before welcoming them as they entered the drawing room. Paul, one of Lady Fiona's jolly young footmen, straightened up from where he was clearing tea dishes, and left them to fetch a fresh pot and more cakes.

"I'm glad to see you had Lord Rudgwick's escort, Lucie. I'm sorry to say you've just missed our last callers, Lady Rudgwick and Lady Harmonia."

"Ah," Rudgwick said, reaching for a biscuit. "I didn't know Harmonia planned to join Mother."

"She was anxious to meet you, Lucie."

Rudgwick's brows knit together as he chewed and swallowed. "She said that?"

Well, why not? The lass wanted to meet the lady her fiancé was pursuing.

Lady Fiona smiled slyly. "She did. A very gracious young lady, she was. Told me all about her fond memories of Chelsea."

"Chelsea," Rudgwick said, bemused. "Fond memories."

"You know naught of them," Lucie said.

"No. Afraid I don't."

"Her mother's governess married and settled near Cheyne Walk," Lady Fiona said. "She hasn't been able to visit or correspond with her since her mother passed away."

"Why?" Lucie asked the question of Rudgwick, who avoided answering by biting into his slice of lemon cake.

"She didn't tell me," Lady Fiona said. "Do you know, Rudgwick?"

Lucie snorted. He hadn't bothered to get to know the girl he'd promised to marry. What lass would want a husband like that?

"His grace keeps a tight rein on her," he said. "Lady Fiona, Miss Macbeth and I have had an eventful morning. We encountered each other at Sir Thomas Abernathy's office—"

"I paid him a call after visiting the solicitor," Lucie said. "Hyde was with me the first time I visited Stephenson."

Lady Fiona raised an eyebrow. "The first time?"

"I escorted Lucie back for a second visit," Rudgwick said. "We secured some documents we'd like to review with you. Are you expecting more callers?"

Paul entered just then with a tray.

"Have your tea and tell me about it, and then we'll move to my study."

Lucie waited for the door to close on the servant, and then, while Rudgwick plowed his way through finger sandwiches, seed cakes and biscuits, she told Lady Fiona about being turned away from the solicitor's office, visiting Sir Thomas, and returning with Rudgwick to Stephenson's. Rudgwick's influence—she omitted the choking and the punching— allowed for a more productive visit with his two clerks.

"Miss Macbeth neglected to tell you that she allowed Hyde the use of my horse."

She ignored his sarcasm. "He ought to be returning soon. He's following a friend of Major Lord Rudgwick's, who we encountered leaving the office."

"Lionel Dankworth, my lady. And, as I told you, Lucie, he is not a friend."

Lady Fiona wasn't acquainted with him, nor did she know the family or remember seeing him in the crowd outside the theater. When Rudgwick had cleared the platter, she escorted them into the cozy room she called her study. It was a bright yellow space, more of a book room for her small collection, and also the place where, when she didn't have houseguests, she retired of an evening.

She settled them around her writing table.

Rudgwick drew out the letter they'd purloined. "The papers, Lucie?"

She rummaged in the document case she'd carried with her and found the letter they'd retrieved from the desk. "First the letters, sir."

After a long look, his lips quirked. "Do you promise to let me see what else you have there?"

"Of course."

She passed Lady Fiona the open letter Rudgwick had pulled from under Jones's big paw. "You'll see that Stephenson is in Norfolk. It appears that Banquo had an account at a bank in Norwich, May, Falton, and May."

Rudgwick cracked the seal on the other letter.

"You have an unopened letter?" Lady Fiona shook her head. "No, do not tell me how you obtained it. I take it this will give the results of his visit to Norwich?"

"We hope." Lucie slid her chair closer and read over Rudgwick's arm.

When Major Macbeth's daughter next visited, Jones was to prepare legal documentation authorizing Stephenson to represent her at the bank. On no account was he to discuss details of the Banquo estate with her, including the name of the bank holding funds and other items for Banquo.

Lucie passed the letter to Lady Fiona. "A statement from you authorizing his representation? It seems to me it's your father's man of business he should be writing to."

Of course. Stephenson thought her an easy mark. "He's pawning me off. He wouldn't have told my father anything. But why?"

"Did Colonel Macbeth know of this bank?" Lady Fiona asked.

"I don't think so. He suspected Banquo might have assets in Norfolk since his wife's family lived there and his boys were in school in Norwich. 'Twas only recently he learned Stephenson's name. Mayhap from Sir Thomas, do ye think? Stephenson has been ignoring his letters, thus Father asked me to pay him a call."

Rudgwick frowned down at the letter, his disapproval evident.

"There's not much for the boys as it is. Father didn't wish the added expense of a London solicitor. And he said the experience would be educational for me."

Rudgwick's lips quirked. "And he knows you're a valiant lass."

Heat rose into her cheeks. She'd judged him wrong. He hadn't been thinking ill of Father.

Lady Fiona looked up from her reading. "What did Sir Thomas say of this Stephenson?"

"He said Father wrote to him about the man. Otherwise, he said nothing."

Rudgwick cleared his throat. "He said a bit more after you left the room, Lucie. May I have both your promises to keep the matter confidential?"

"Of course," Lady Fiona said, and Lucie nodded.

"Stephenson is a person of interest to the Home Office. Sir Thomas was concerned about Lucie visiting the man without proper escort."

"Why?" His failure to meet Lucie's gaze told her he was leaving something out. And then she remembered... "Banquo was a provisioner during the war. He was corrupt. This man was part of it. And..." She pulled the Bridgehampton papers from her case and set them on the table. "So, perhaps, was the duke as well."

She flipped through the pages, taking a closer look. This time, Rudgwick looked over *her* shoulder. Two columns for dates and amounts trailed over the pages, going back years.

"Even viewing that upside down," Lady Fiona said, "I'd surmise that's a record of payments to Mr. Stephenson."

"Increasing amounts," Rudgwick mused. "Stephenson is not Bridgehampton's solicitor, at least not his regular one."

"Is Bridgehampton a common surname?" she asked Lady Fiona.

"Perhaps," the lady said. "Probably. But look at those amounts; who would have the wherewithal to pay that much? Someone very wealthy."

"Blackmail." Lucie drummed her fingers on the tabletop. "I must visit that bank in Norwich."

"It's too dangerous," Rudgwick said.

"I must. Come with me, if ye wish, but I must go myself. It's what Father would wish for."

"I'm sure he wouldn't, and I can't allow it."

Oh, that spiked her temper. Before she could speak, Lady Fiona reached for her hand.

"Forgive me, Lord Rudgwick," Lady Fiona said, "but neither you nor I can allow or disallow Lucie visiting this bank since she is of age. Best would be to have Finnley Macbeth visit him, or Macbeth's solicitor. But it might smooth the way to have Lucie pay a call. Perhaps, like Sir Thomas, the banker had an inkling of something amiss with this solicitor." She tapped her chin. "These two men, the banker and this solicitor, must not know each other. Puzzling, if Stephenson has been doing business with the banker."

"Perhaps the banker is corrupt as well," Rudgwick said, "and interested in retaining Banquo's money. He would thus be a danger to Lucie."

"That is a possibility. Lucie, we will leave two days after the ball. I'll accompany you. We'll take Hyde and some of my men. You may come as well, Rudgwick, if you wish." She smiled. "I doubt we'll be able to keep you away."

Rudgwick shook his head and stood. "And where *is* Hyde?"

Unease threaded through Lucie. If any harm came to Hyde, Father would be heartbroken. And the horse... she couldn't have the loss of another horse against her account.

"Lady Fiona, might I borrow one of your mounts?" Rudgwick asked. "I'm to meet Lord Jeremy, who might have more information. We can both ride on into town and see if we can trace Hyde."

"I can go as well," Lucie said.

"No." He took her hand and rested his false hand atop it. "If I find him, I'll send him home."

The warmth and strength in his true hand sent feelings through her that she ought not to indulge. She mustered a breath. "Do that, Major Lord Rudgwick. Tell him I'll wait up to hear his report."

He blinked and then grinned. Lady Fiona's presence must have reminded him that he'd been holding her hand much too long. He wished them both farewell and hurried off to the stables.

***

The next day, Lucie stepped into the carriage and settled herself next to Lady Fiona for the short journey to Knightsbridge, where they would repay Lady Rudgwick's call.

Every nerve in her body thrummed. Hyde had appeared late the previous night with little to report beyond that he'd waited outside a tailor's shop, a gentlemen's club, and a bawdy house. She wasn't sure she trusted those were all the details, which might have to do with Hyde's arrival home on Lady Fiona's mount, the one Rudgwick had been riding. Under questioning, he admitted he'd stopped on the way at Rudgwick's stables. He claimed he'd run into Rudgwick on the outskirts of Knightsbridge and followed him to the mews.

Rudgwick, Hyde said, had been out and about on his own, without even the escort of Lord Jeremy or a groom.

She gripped her gloved hands in her lap and tried to quell a rising disquiet. Oh, Hades, she was fast approaching a ninny-headed panic. Strange, because in all the hubbub and excitement of the day before, she hadn't felt a bit of this... this foreboding of danger to Rudgwick, and this time, unlike the night at the theater, with no picture of what was to happen to him.

With her gaze turned toward the glazed carriage window, she watched as the market gardens and terraced homes blurred and faded, and transformed into another closed space—a bedchamber, a simple one. An inn room, perhaps; impersonal, clean, the bed barely wide enough for two.

Her heart pounded, heat rising within, joined by a chill that rattled her nerves. She wasn't alone in this room. Arms were braced on either side of her, and she looked up into eyes of the darkest gray.

"Lucie." Lady Fiona's calm voice penetrated the vision.

Penetrated—oh heavens. She shut her eyes. She'd seen naughty drawings and knew what a man looked like. This one was as bare as the day he was born, but a man, oh, fully a man.

Easing in her breath, she fought the tingling pleasure that warmed her insides and pooled somewhere in her nether regions.

"Will you let me help you?" This time Lady Fiona's voice, her offer of help, her clear understanding, settled the air around them, and she was able to breathe again.

"You're having visions." The lady's hand settled over Lucie's knotted fists, untangling and gripping one of them.

"Not all the time. Not yesterday. I don't understand... Mayhap I need to see to Father's business, and then proceed home sooner than planned." The original plan had seemed a good one—spend the spring and early summer in Chelsea with Lady Fiona, and then accompany the older lady to Edinburgh, where Lady Fiona had a second home. She'd best leave sooner if she wanted to preserve both her wits and her maidenhead. Or at least, not give away the latter to a man certain to marry someone else.

But the temptation of Rudgwick...

"Will you tell me what you're seeing?"

"I..." She let out a long breath. She couldn't share the visions of a naked Rudgwick making love to her equally naked self. She wouldn't have shared them even if they'd done the deed in fact. The other, though...

"I sense trouble. Danger."

The older lady's thumb made a calming sweep over the back of Lucie's hand as she pondered the words. "Danger to Rudgwick?"

How perceptive she was. Mayhap that was merely the wisdom of age, and nothing supernatural. "At the theater, I saw... 'twas so real, Lady Fiona." Panic flared in her, the need to act, and she gulped in air.

"Tell me more."

Lucie swallowed a mad surge of moisture, cleared her throat, and felt the older lady's warmth wrapping around her person in a comforting swaddle. "I saw a man rush into the box where Rudgwick was seated. He caught Rudgwick unawares, and they tussled, and then he pushed Rudgwick over the balcony rail."

The panic of that moment swamped her, the powerlessness, the grief...

The hand on hers squeezed encouragingly.

"He was so like Giles Banquo, yet I couldn't see his face, his hair, his eyes. Just a dark smudge of chilling evil. Not even anger. Nor hatred either, come to think of it."

That had been unlike Banquo, her father's cousin, and Malcolm's as well. Banquo's evil heart had embraced the lingering grudge he bore for the two men. Banquo had died a year earlier. Malcolm and his lady, Marielle, had witnessed his death, and Malcolm had seen his body into a Suffolk grave. She knew for certain Banquo was gone.

This person, if she wasn't raving mad, and there really was such a person, wasn't Banquo.

Nor was the person one of Banquo's sons. Fleance and young Giles had disavowed their father's murderous schemes and were under her father's care. Though they resembled their father in looks, their characters were wholly different. She'd long forgiven them their bad blood. They were like younger brothers to her now.

"Not Banquo, but a man with a similar mantle of darkness," Lady Fiona mused. "A chilling evil, though."

"That is worse, is it not?"

"Cold or hot, murder is murder. Though the madness of anger is perhaps more within reach of our understanding. Did you warn him of this that day at the park?"

She'd not told Lady Fiona of her meeting with Rudgwick, yet the lady knew of it. Hyde was reporting on her. Hyde, her nursemaid.

The thought lifted her mood. She wasn't alone. "Aye. He promised to take care. And of course, he wanted to know the whole story, but there were too many people around to speak more of it. Not that I know much more than that."

"Rudgwick is an affable fellow, but I suppose every man of wealth and authority has garnered a few enemies in the course of his life. What do we know of his character, really?"

The question startled her. She didn't have to question Rudgwick's character. He was an honorable man, aside from the hopeless longing he raised in her. And perhaps that came from *her* lack of character.

"Father trusts him." Probably because he didn't know about the kisses.

Lady Fiona smiled as if she'd just read Lucie's mind. "Lady Rudgwick said he's worked very hard at overcoming the loss of his hand. Said he won't hear of being pampered."

Proud he was, and valiant. "I saw that yesterday and was glad of it. I'd never imagine him to be the sort to play the victim."

"And he certainly doesn't. Is there anything more you can tell me?"

She bit her lip. "No."

Lady Fiona's lip quirked. "I see."

Heat rose in Lucie's cheeks. Lady Fiona really *did* see.

"I've had my share of visions, Lucie. They're usually an apprehension of an event charged with strong emotion, not always of danger and doom."

"But they don't always come true." She hoped. Though Father's visions—of danger to Mother, of the battle at Waterloo, those *had* come true.

Her visions of Rudgwick must not. She must not allow the one, and she must prevent the other.

"They don't always come true the way we expect or fear. But there is some truth in them always." The carriage rolled to a stop. "Now. We have arrived. We'll have a pleasant chat with Lady Rudgwick and then visit the shops and the dressmaker. What say you?"

Lucie pasted on a smile and allowed the groom to help her out of the carriage. Lady Fiona's plan to help her enjoy her stay had included not just the upcoming ball, but a great deal of shopping. She had more gowns now than she'd ever had. No trews, though, and she might have liked a brand-new pair.

She stared up at the familiar façade that gleamed white in the light of day and looked around. The terraced homes, though expansive and generously proportioned, were nevertheless squashed side by side with each other in a tight row. Unlike Lady Fiona's home, a visitor would have to traverse the house to get to the garden beyond.

"Lovely," Lady Fiona murmured, joining her at the foot of the stairs. The door opened and a man appeared.

'Twas the butler himself, attired in his dark coats and starched neckcloth. He trotted down, greeted them both by name, and took Lady Fiona's arm.

He'd been expecting them, and he'd recognized Lucie, just as she'd known him immediately. The last time they'd met, on that rainy March night the year before, he'd been attired in a work smock tending to some household chore when Rudgwick escorted her mother and her through the door. And before she and Mother departed Rudgwick's townhouse, this butler had engaged in a heated row with the housekeeper. Despite the sturdy construction and solid walls, the voices had carried all the way from below stairs to the hall where Lucie and her mother had awaited the carriage meant to carry them home. This butler had survived that altercation; the housekeeper, and an insolent maid who'd insulted Mother and herself, had been dismissed that very same night by Rudgwick himself.

Now, though she saw recognition in the butler's eyes, he kept his expression otherwise carefully neutral, as any good servant should.

Nerves rattling still, she took in a quelling breath and followed the butler and Lady Fiona up the steps just as she'd followed Rudgwick escorting her mother a year earlier.

Inside, Lady Rudgwick herself greeted them in the hall. 'Twas an honor, and a clear declaration of their welcome.

She pulled Lucie close for a kiss on the cheek. The few lines on the older woman's face appeared to be from laughing, not frowning, and her affectionate kindness was reassuring. Perhaps Lucie could get through this visit without disgracing herself.

There were likely to be other callers, of course, this being Lady Rudgwick's at-home day.

What Lucie wanted—and in truth most feared—was a quiet moment with Rudgwick himself. To learn everything Hyde had told him. To make sure he hadn't run off to Norfolk without her.

The visions, though... *ugh*. She didn't want to spend an afternoon in company with his mother, Lady Fiona and him, sitting nearby smiling and chatting, while she fought hard not to imagine him naked.

She swallowed a chuckle. If she kept on this way, it would be Bedlam for her.

Armed with that spot of humor, she followed the ladies into the drawing room.

CHAPTER EIGHT

The Duke Arrives

Rudgwick's townhouse was tastefully decorated, the work of his mother, no doubt, as he'd been away fighting the French. This room hadn't been altered since Lucie first visited last year. There was the sofa upholstered in pale brocade, the one she'd avoided sitting on in her wet trousers. The Axminster carpet that had borne her wet boots still stretched underfoot. And the window seat: it was now cluttered with pillows, as if someone had made a habit of perching there, watching the passersby. Did Lady Rudgwick still keep extra shawls under there? She'd borrowed one for Mother.

They seated themselves and the same butler supervised the delivery of the tea tray by an unfamiliar footman. Perhaps Rudgwick had replaced more servants than the housekeeper and maid.

"How good of you to call on me." Lady Rudgwick smiled.

"How kind of ye to make us welcome, madam." Lucie accepted the cup handed to her. Rudgwick's mother had been startled and stiff at their first meeting in the hospital in Brussels, and shortly thereafter, when her son dragged her along to attend Malcolm's wedding, both of them uninvited, she'd moved like a woman in a trance. A well-bred woman, of course, saying the most exquisitely polite and correct things. She'd been courteous, yet formal, even after she and her son moved into the villa they'd all shared. It had only been when the Macbeths packed up to leave that she'd shown her true warmth.

And of course, Lucie knew why. The poor lady had been holding her breath in fear that her son would seduce her.

Or vice versa, a sad but true fact. She might as well admit it. The spark she felt for Rudgwick burned steady and true when they were apart; when they were together, the attraction was a bonfire that threatened to scorch her common sense.

She couldn't fault Lady Rudgwick for her legitimate concerns. Rudgwick had made a promise; he'd committed himself to Bridgehampton's granddaughter. For whatever reason, the promise was made, and the fact that Lucie had come along later didn't relieve him of his duty to see it through.

Lucie knew that and stood by it. As the daughter of a man who'd divorced his wife, she'd lived through the scandal that came with a failure to honor a sacred promise. She'd never inflict that pain on another woman or child.

Oh, she understood—now—her parents' failings, and she forgave them both, and loved them. But it wasn't true that all was well that ended well. One still carried the pain.

In Brussels, Father'd had a frank talk with Rudgwick's mother. He'd had a frank talk with

Lucie as well—which made his request for Rudgwick to help her all the more puzzling.

Perhaps he'd even talked to Rudgwick, though she couldn't be certain about that. In any case, the secret kiss they'd shared at the Duchess's ball had not been repeated in Brussels. She'd avoided the handsome bounder, and there'd been no private chats. No hints at familiarity.

It had made her heart ache, yet she'd shoved down her longings. She and her parents had traveled back to Lady Fiona's in Chelsea, and once Father had recovered more, they'd gone home to the Highlands, Father's first visit there in twenty years. It had been glorious in its own way, and she'd pushed the memory of the handsome cavalry officer with his dark hair, and his fine twinkling eyes, and his hint of a smile to the back of her mind.

Mostly. Out of sight hadn't meant totally out of mind; the visions stirred up by the blow to her head in the accident proved that. The longing for Rudgwick had reared up inside her in new and more terrible ways.

The lady asked a question about the birthday ball, and she inwardly shook herself and joined the excited Lady Fiona in the conversation. Lady Rudgwick would attend the event. Her son as well. She'd conveyed that news the day before.

With so many of the *ton* sending notes to accept their invitations, and with Rudgwick an engaged man, he'd be no trouble to her at the ball. The *ton* would be watching, and he'd behave himself, as she must as well. Nor would it be possible that those visions would come true—Lady Fiona's bedchambers were far more luxurious than that sparsely furnished room where the Sight had imagined her and Rudgwick together.

"Your new ball gown sounds lovely. Are you pleased with it?" Lady Rudgwick's question nudged her out of her woolgathering.

"Yes, madam." She glanced at Lady Fiona. The gown was an unnecessary extravagance, yet it made her older kinswoman happy to dress her so she must allow this one last expense. "I'll be wearing white like a proper girl of the *ton*, though in truth, it's more of an ivory to complement this." She gestured to her hair. "And Lady Fiona has said we will powder these." She traced a finger over her cheek and the bridge of her nose.

The two older ladies laughed.

"Only if you wish, dear girl," Lady Fiona said. "I find no fault with them."

Lady Rudgwick smiled fondly. "My daughter has as many freckles. She used to lament terribly over them, but her husband says he finds them charming."

Lady Rudgwick's daughter, Lady Emily, had married the year before.

The lady blinked, probably remembering that Rudgwick found Lucie's freckles just as charming.

Best not go down that path. "How is your grandson?" Lucie asked.

"He's not a bit colicky, Emily says." The lady beamed. She'd been present for the birth of her first grandchild in February and had only come up to London a few days after Lucie and Lady Fiona. "A fine healthy boy he is. Emily did well."

A tap at the door brought the butler. Lady Rudgwick scanned the card he presented, and her mouth firmed.

She settled her face back into a pleasant mask and nodded.

A young lady appeared in the doorway, a young lady with the same dark-haired, blue-eyed, creamy-skinned beauty as Lucie's mother, Greer, the sort of beauty that never spotted or wrinkled, or sagged at the jaws, the sort of beauty that lasted into middle age. Lady Harmonia Haughton entered with the Duke of Bridgehampton hot on her heels.

Their hostess stood and went to greet them, leading them in and making introductions.

Too startled to speak, her emotions a jumble, Lucie made her curtsey and sat down again. Neither visitor had cut them, but neither had they so much as uttered a good day. The girl told Lady Fiona how happy she was to meet her again, at which the duke pinned Lucie with a steely gaze, like a hunter lining up his shot on his favored prey after a morning of careful stalking.

His obvious dislike roused a chuckle which she quickly squashed.

Had their hostess told him of their planned visit? Or had he set watchers on Lady Fiona's house. Or perhaps he had a spy among the servants and had learned that Lady Harmonia had paid a call on Lady Fiona with Lady Rudgwick. Why had Lady Rudgwick brought her yesterday? It wouldn't serve her interest to provoke this powerful duke, would it?

Lady Harmonia tipped her head, her blue gaze impassive. Carefully so, Lucie would judge. She was a girl well in control of her emotions. "Lady Rudgwick said she met you in Brussels, Miss Macbeth." Curiosity lurked under the lass's inbred haughtiness.

Two could play that game. She herself had not been so carefully bred, yet she'd learned to look down her own freckled nose at gossips and snipes.

She nodded. "Yes."

The young lady's lips quivered, and Lucie immediately relented. Lady Harmonia was young—very young. And skittish. And who wouldn't be, living under the thumb of the great white-haired oaf watching the both of them.

"I was in Brussels with my mother and father, Colonel and Mrs. Macbeth, and my cousin Lord Menteith, and his lady. 'Twas, in truth, a fraught time."

"Very fraught," Lady Rudgwick said. "By the grace of God, your father and your cousin survived."

Lucie blinked away the memory of the long day spent riding with Mother and Marielle scouring the battlefield for Father, Malcolm, and Hyde. The carnage and fear had been too horrible. "And your fiancé, as well, Lady Harmonia. Any man was lucky to have come through that battle."

Curiosity sparked higher in the young lady's eyes, but next to her, her grandfather stirred, and she closed her mouth quickly on a question.

"'Twas quite a balmy place, Brussels, do ye recall, Lady Rudgwick? Father was ever so happy to return to the brisk, clear air of the Highlands."

The two older ladies took that cue and launched into a discussion of the weather which was proving to be cooler and wetter than normal. All the while, Lucie felt the resentful gaze of the old man upon her. After greeting his hostess, he'd not spoken a word.

And why would a duke deign to speak to Lucie Macbeth? Lady Fiona, however, deserved courtesy, if not for her social standing, then for her dignified demeanor and her advanced age. She was older than the duke, if Lucie might hazard a guess.

She watched Rudgwick's fiancée over the rim of her teacup. She'd been unable to resist a scant bit of gossip about the girl. Lady Harmonia's father had married young, at his father's behest, of course. After Harmonia's mother's death, the marquess had refused all other matches and tumbled into the life of dissipation that led to his death. Bridgehampton couldn't be terribly old. His hair was white and his face craggy from frowning, but he might not yet be sixty years of age.

It was a wonder he'd never taken a young bride for a second attempt at an heir. What might that mean? Had he loved his son's mother that much? Had he suffered an injury that impaired his ability to breed? He didn't seem the sort to give up on anything so important as the quest for an heir.

She sat mulling the matter and watching young Lady Harmonia, who, under the steely gaze of her grandfather, was snatching occasional glimpses of Lucie from under her dark lashes, while the two older ladies steered the conversation along.

***

"You ought not to do this, Rudgwick. Or at the very least, you ought not to involve me."

Jeremy had been nagging him ever since they'd left Angelo's and he'd announced the plans for the rest of their day.

"You think it's highhanded of me, asking you to make yourself useful?"

"The duke won't like it when he finds out." Jeremy adopted the gloomy tone he used when speaking of Bridgehampton. "And you know he will. He's probably bribed half your servants to report on you."

"If you learn which ones, you must let me know."

"So you can send them packing?"

"I might. Or I might merely send them down to the country. Or perhaps I'll bribe them to feed the duke the information I want him to hear."

Jeremy laughed and shook his head.

They passed the toll gate and Rudgwick spurred his horse. "When your brother returns, we shall find a way for you," he called over his shoulder.

Jeremy might not know what he meant, but he intended to play matchmaker. If he couldn't devise his own plan sooner, Northam, a skilled negotiator and plotter, would help him when he finished this diplomatic mission. Together they'd find a way for Jeremy to win over Harmonia to the idea, and then Bridgehampton.

Rudgwick only needed to stay away from the altar for as long as it might take.

They rode on in silence until they reached the mews behind Rudgwick's townhouse.

Rudgwick knew Jeremy's protests and gloomy air were false. Though he would never admit it, he was hiding the same sense of excitement Rudgwick himself felt. They were about to spend a few moments with the women who filled all their thoughts and dreams. At least he hoped that was the case.

The duke wasn't the only one bribing servants. Rudgwick had bribed Harmonia's maid, who'd sent word that morning that Harmonia would be calling on Mother. This on a day when he had it on good authority that the duke was expected at some meeting that involved the Prince Regent.

He needed a few moments alone with Lucie. More than a few moments, in fact. A lifetime. But that would have to wait.

Mother and Lady Fiona would not object to Rudgwick and Bolton escorting the ladies for a stroll about the square and a breath of fresh air. At present, it wasn't raining. Once past the eagle eyes of whichever of his servants Bridgehampton had bribed, they would switch partners.

Jessop, his butler, met him in the hall.

"Callers?" he asked.

"Yes, my lord. If you would like to change, your valet—"

"No." Lucie wouldn't mind the smell of horse. "Come, Jeremy."

He pushed through the sitting room door and his heart plummeted. Bridgehampton, the wily old campaigner, had outmaneuvered him again. Perhaps Harmonia's maid was accepting bribes from the duke as well.

Schooling his face into careful aplomb, Rudgwick greeted the ladies, and gave the duke a curt bow, noting the triumphant gleam lighting the old man's face. It was as much happiness as Bridgehampton ever displayed, and always at someone else's cost.

If only he knew of the visit to Stephenson's office the day before. Or perhaps... perhaps he did. Perhaps Loomis ran to tell him.

He seated himself on the sofa with Harmonia, as an engaged man ought to do. And because it allowed him to look directly at Lucie. Jeremy plopped down his handsome self next to Lucie.

"You've been riding." The duke's tone bore an accusation of ill breeding. *The pompous ass.*

"Yes. Spent the morning at Angelo's. We just rode back from there. Why take a carriage on such a fine day?"

Lady Fiona's kind eyes twinkled. "I fear we've already conducted a thorough review of the weather, Rudgwick."

He chuckled and plated a biscuit from the tray. His arm and hand were almost limp from the morning's practice, and he juggled the plate, steadying it with his prosthesis and righting it before the biscuit slid off. He felt Harmonia tense next to him, and he breathed out a silent curse.

"If this cold weather continues, there will be worries about the crops."

Mother had jumped in to save his dignity. Of course, she had. It was the sort of pitying thing she'd been doing since Brussels, and it riled him. She'd tracked down the prosthesis maker, James Potts in his Chelsea shop, and had him send his best man off to Cambridgeshire for a fitting, and then she'd badgered her son to wear the blasted thing. Sometimes, he wished she would cease and simply allow him the indignity of his stump. But he would master this, dammit. He would.

He lifted his gaze and saw Lucie's frank open stare and the curiosity there. But no pity, as he saw in Mother's face, or the blinkered distaste Harmonia couldn't quite hide.

He'd lost a hand at Waterloo, but so what? So many men had lost more than that. He didn't wish to discuss his impairment or be the center of everyone's solicitousness and attention.

And to hell with Bridgehampton. He'd follow through on his plans for this day.

Having finished the biscuit, he set away his plate. "Since it *is* so fine a day, I propose that Lord

Jeremy and I escort the ladies and take some air. What say you, Harmonia? Miss Macbeth?"

"Ye haven't asked Lord Jeremy if he's agreeable," Lucie said. "I'd say that's high handed of ye, Major Lord Rudgwick."

Jeremy smiled on her. "It would be my pleasure, Miss Macbeth."

Ever the gentleman.

Jealousy sparked in Rudgwick, and he wondered if Harmonia's sudden twitch signaled she was feeling the same emotion.

"A capital idea," Lady Fiona said. "You young people take a stroll while we chat before the rain starts. Surely you can't object, duke?"

Bridgehampton must have been wearing his customary scowl. Lady Fiona was a bold one, spiking the old man's cannon. Rudgwick had noted the man's disdain for the lady, or more precisely, the duke's absence of cordiality toward her.

With Mother adding her support, they outmaneuvered the duke, and the outing was arranged. Jessop had a footman fetch bonnets and wraps, and then they stepped out onto the street, Harmonia on his arm, and Lucie on Jeremy's.

They turned a corner, passed the entrance to the mews where more servants might be watching, and stopped. He glanced back. No followers, that he could see.

Jeremy nodded.

"We shall switch partners," Rudgwick said.

The corners of Harmonia's lips lifted with as much happiness as the poor girl ever displayed.

Lucie, however, was frowning, her color starting to rise. "Major Lord Rudgwick—"

"No, Lucie." She was beautiful, even more so when she was animated by an impending snit. He shook his head. "No scolds." He took her hand and set it on what remained of his right forearm, and they followed the other couple. "We are doing Harmonia and Jeremy a kindness."

That brought a quizzical look, and she glanced toward the younger couple. They were inclining their heads toward each other, ever so slightly, both having been well-trained to avoid public displays of affection. A person who didn't know them wouldn't see the regard they felt, but he did. He'd noted their rising attraction when Mother brought Harmonia to Rudgwick Abbey for a visit at Christmas. Fortunately, that time, the duke's presence in London had been required by the Regent. Rudgwick had faithfully begged off from company, allowing Jeremy and Harmonia a great deal of time together in the afternoon and evenings, properly chaperoned by Mother, of course. She'd noticed as well, and though they'd never discussed a plan to end his engagement, she'd signaled her support.

Lucie wouldn't know any of that, of course. "Don't be alarmed," he said, keeping his voice low. "I'm not going to kiss you again." Not today, anyway. "I completely forgot in the excitement of yesterday to ask you for more detail on the warning you gave me."

She looked away. "I know nothing, really. Oughtn't we to be talking about Mr. Stephenson and your..." She waved a hand. "your friend Darkworth."

Whatever thought had passed through her head just then had caused her to pale. He was not about to be distracted by her diversion.

"Then tell me that *nothing*. Tell me what you sense. What you *see*."

Her lips thinned in a grimace. She didn't seem right. Certainly, a different girl to the one he'd accompanied yesterday.

"Lucie, at Salamanca, Wellington anticipated Marmont's moves so effectively that some in the Highland Brigade whispered he had Second Sight."

"I don't."

He stopped and turned to face her.

She closed her eyes and let out a sharp breath. "Very well. I don't *know*... anything, Major Lord Rudgwick. I've been... barmy, at times since I cracked my head."

Her lip quivered. He so wanted to take her in his arms.

"I want to hear more about that injury, but first, tell me everything you know about this threat. Help me, Lucie."

She glanced toward the other couple, who had walked on, too far ahead and too engrossed in each other to overhear. "At the theater, I saw someone at the back of your box. That is, I saw the shadow of someone lingering and peering in after the play had started. I'm certain that was real. But later." She swallowed, her eyes lighting with a strong emotion. "Come. They've gone too far ahead."

Perhaps she needed the break from his scrutiny. Perhaps it would be easier to talk while they walked. He tucked her hand over his arm, and they stepped out again.

"And?" he prompted.

"A man... Oh Hades, Rudgwick. A man... a man rushed in, scampered past the others, ran straight to ye, and startled ye so that ye barely had a chance to fight back. He overpowered ye. He pushed ye over the balcony."

Her face had gone pale under a shimmering glow of perspiration, and the hand on his arm trembled. She was afraid for him. He'd never thought the feisty girl capable of so much fear.

The gooseflesh shivered down his back. He hadn't made it through so many battles without listening to instinct—his own and that of his valiant comrades in arms.

"What did he look like, Lucie?"

"That's just it: I don't know. How could I have seen so much and not that? 'Twas a man, of a similar height to ye, strongly built, finely attired. A gentleman, not a ruffian or servant. The rest was a cloudy, dark smudge." She gulped in a breath. "He put me in mind of Giles Banquo."

Her hand jerked, the squeeze on a still-sensitive nerve sending a jolt of pain up his arm, and he gasped.

CHAPTER NINE

Another Vision

Lucie quickly dropped her hand. "I've hurt ye."

"No. That is, not much. I have phantom pains from time to time, all perfectly normal. Don't concern yourself; the stump is healed." He took her hand and placed it again on his arm and they continued walking.

"If a squeeze on it causes pain, ye won't be using it as a cudgel," she said, lightening the mood. "Do ye think I'm mad?"

"Mad?" He smiled down at her. "Mad, bad, Lucie Macbeth? If you save me from an unseen, unknown enemy, I'll be eternally in your debt."

She frowned.

"Lucie, I've been in several battles. You're not mad."

"I almost called out that night at the theater. If it weren't for Lady Fiona... she knew, that is, she sensed my... my disquiet and stopped me in time."

"Is there anything else? Are you having other visions? Other premonitions?"

Her gaze skittered to the pavement ahead of them. "No."

She'd omitted something there. That single stark word had been a boldfaced lie. "No?"

"That is, nothing about danger to ye."

"To someone else?"

She shook her head. "Who would want to hurt ye, Major Lord Rudgwick?"

"I suppose I've made enemies. Most men do. Will you promise to tell me the rest of your visions? It may help me to sort this out. Perhaps there's a connection you're not seeing."

Color rose in her cheeks. Her eyebrows rose with the cocky impudence that meant she was feeling more herself. "Ye've completely forgotten to tell me what ye've learned about Darkworth. I'd know that. And I promise to tell ye of any suspicions of harm to your person."

"Now you're equivocating. Why do I sense there's something important you're not telling me?"

She turned to face him. "No. Nothing important. Now what did ye learn yesterday about Darkworth from Sir Thomas?"

"Dankworth, not Darkworth, though I suppose that suits him better." The file Jeremy - reviewed contained bits and pieces of information about a ring that had operated out of Norfolk, selling munitions and other supplies to the highest bidder. "And there was nothing of any use." Dankworth's name was mentioned, as well as the late Banquo's and Grey's.

***

He was lying. Perhaps his friend would be more honest.

Lucie quickened her pace, forcing him to match her steps, ignoring the question, determined to catch up with Lord Jeremy and Lady Harmonia who'd paused at a busy street corner. "We must switch partners now," she called.

Lady Harmonia glanced up at Lord Jeremy, who nodded.

"I should like to walk with you, Miss Macbeth," the girl said in a voice that was both cultured and sweet, not at all haughty, and, Lucie sensed, not false either. "Will you mind? We had no chance to speak earlier."

Drat that. 'Twas Lord Jeremy she wanted to walk with and question, not this lass.

"I fear this path is not wide enough for four abreast, my lady."

"I believe that's the idea, Lucie," Rudgwick said kindly. "Go ahead. We shall follow behind like your loyal footmen."

No one flinched at his use of her Christian name, not Lord Jeremy, or Lady Harmonia. And he'd said that they were doing his friend and his fiancée a favor, letting them walk ahead just the two of them.

Perhaps Rudgwick had been correct, and if so, the blasted Sight hadn't bothered to show her that the seemingly placid, obedient, consummately well-bred girl was more inclined to her fiancée's friend. What use was a gift if it only showed temptation and danger?

And that Rudgwick knew, and he didn't mind? Oh, what a recipe for a jaded, cynical life and much unhappiness. Lady Harmonia would do her duty to Rudgwick by producing the necessary heir, and then take up with his friend, who'd in turn betray his own wife if he bothered to marry at all.

The ways of these English nobles made Lucie's skin crawl. The sooner she put annoying thoughts of Rudgwick behind her and went home to Scotland, the better.

Lady Harmonia drew close and linked arms with her.

Lucie's heart raced and emotions rushed through her: elation, certainly, that Rudgwick and the girl had no romantic bond, but also a simmering anger, the bad temper Mother said she'd inherited from the Macbeths, a reflexive reaction to all sorts of trouble.

'Twas astounding: Lady Harmonia with a tendre for Lord Jeremy Bolton. Yet here the girl was, engaged to marry Rudgwick. And Rudgwick would marry and breed with her, whilst pursuing another would-be lover. Herself.

And what was she supposed to do? Simply give up her dignity, her honor, her*self* and go along with it?

No. She'd told him about the danger. Forewarned, he could fight his own battles, marry his wife, and she herself would shake off those other foolish visions. She'd had one ardent suitor, the eligible Jamey Paisley, heir to the neighboring laird, a thought that made her shudder. Father didn't know it, but Paisley had tried to force a marriage. As if his brutish attempt on her virtue would win her heart.

But there might be other men, worthy men, men who didn't pale next to her memory of Rudgwick. She would take herself to Norfolk and then home. Lady Fiona would accompany her with servants who would protect them.

"You've had such a life of adventure," Lady Harmonia said. "I have so wanted to speak with you."

"What do ye mean, a life of adventure?" Lucie took in a breath and tried to curb her waspishness. The girl was so closely guarded by her odious grandfather that all she would know was the duty she'd been groomed for. She'd never don trousers and go off for a wild ride in the country, in London, or anywhere else. "Truly, my life was boring until I came to Town last year. Although, I suppose being a child of a scandalous couple, well, there was that. Is that what ye mean?"

Lady Harmonia scoffed. "My father's scandalous life surely trumps anything your parents might have done." She patted Lucie's arm.

Patted it. This child. And who would have expected her capable of scoffing like a fishmonger wheedling after an extra penny?

"How old are ye, Lady Harmonia?"

"Seventeen. Just turned. Grandpapa arranged the engagement to Rudgwick when I was fifteen." Her mouth moved in a grimace. "Can you imagine?"

Lucie couldn't. Her temper eased. Fifteen, seventeen; either age was young for marrying, in her opinion. Though if a lass was in the grip of a true passion as her own mother had been with Father... but that youthful ardor had led to years of heartache.

Remembering Lady Harmonia's regard for Lord Jeremy, she managed to hold her tongue. If the girl was truly in love with another man, what the deuce was wrong with Rudgwick? Why not release her? Why carry on with the match?

"Tell me about Waterloo. You saw the battlefield, did you not? Grandpapa tries valiantly to censor what I read and what I hear. Lady Rudgwick, however, and Jeremy tell me some things. And, having been sheltered, I've been known to listen at keyholes upon occasion."

They heard the rattling of passing carts and carriages and the clip-clopping of horses, but behind them the men were silent. Lucie wondered if they were craning their ears trying to eavesdrop. "Doesn't Major Lord Rudgwick tell ye things about his own adventures? He fought in the Peninsula as well."

"No." Another scoff. "He's very courteous, but he mostly treats me like an empty-headed child. We talk very little, and Jeremy says he won't speak to him at all of his injury or the battles. Will you tell me about Brussels and Waterloo?"

Lucie flinched, the memories swimming in grief and worry, like the bodies they'd seen mired in mud in the aftermath of the battle.

"I beg your pardon. If the subject is too disturbing..."

"In fact, it's the stuff of nightmares, Lady Harmonia." Lucie'd had a few of those, but nothing compared to what the soldiers who fought there must be experiencing. Mother said Father's spirits had been, strangely, much improved after the battle, despite his terrible wounds. Hyde had healed well and never spoke of the battle either.

And Rudgwick—he'd had the worst of the three, looking every day at the end of his arm where his hand should be. Did he experience terrors at night?

The small hand pressed her arm again, and she shook off her woolgathering. "In Brussels, leading up to the battle, there were many parties and fêtes. The men drilled during the day and danced the nights through."

Society had been laxer there, more easily navigable by such as the Macbeths. She'd made a sort of a come out then, had been welcomed at parties, routs, and balls. Rudgwick had arrived in Brussels weeks after them, but he was busy preparing for battle. Yet in the evenings he'd stalked her. Oh aye, he had. She'd dodged him—dodged the pull between them. Sweet heaven, she'd been avoiding her own baser instincts, hadn't she?

He'd finally trapped her at Lady Conyngham's ball, and they'd danced one glorious waltz together. She'd expected to dodge him again at the Duchess's ball, but he didn't appear.

Until he *did*, descending the steps of the villa, dusty, distracted, having just delivered a dispatch. He'd pulled her out of sight for a private moment.

She shook off the memory of their kiss. "After the battle, when my father and my cousin, Malcolm Comyn—Lord Menteith he is—and our man Hyde didn't return and we could learn no news of them, we took horses and went to look for them—my mother, Malcolm's fiancée, and I."

"Your mother went out? And took you along?" The girl pressed her free hand to her chest. "Onto a battlefield?"

"We are Highlanders, my mother and I. Mother is strong, and so is—though she is French nobility—so is Marielle, having escaped the Terror when only a child. And we weren't the only ladies out scouring the battlefield for their men." She blinked back sudden moisture. "In truth, 'twas dreadful."

"My maid smuggled in newssheets, and I read of it: mud, dead horses, bodies—some dead, some gravely wounded, and scavengers stealing the purses and clothing from them, sometimes even teeth."

Lucie swallowed a sudden bout of nausea, and the girl paused.

"I do beg your pardon, Lucie. May I call you Lucie?" Harmonia's blue eyes widened, and Lucie saw honest sympathy there. "No one tells me anything. And I have no friends—no true friends, only the silly girls sanctioned by Grandpapa. Perhaps *we* might be friends."

She managed a smile. And how was that to be possible? "Your Grandpapa would never allow a friendship, and after ye wed Rudgwick..." She'd never put herself between the girl and her husband. "I'll be leaving very soon. But yes, ye may call me Lucie."

"Thank you. Will you tell me more? Were the newspaper descriptions correct?"

"Aye." She shook her head. The smell, the heat, the scavengers... Dear God, she and Marielle had beat off a woman pulling the boots from Father's feet.

The girl looked at her, her face open and frank. "I don't love Rudgwick." She stopped and gripped Lucie's hands. "But I know that you do."

Heat flooded Lucie's cheeks and swelled her tongue. *Don't be silly, of course I don't love him.* The words stuck in her throat and wouldn't come out.

Because they weren't true? Of course, they were. She didn't love Rudgwick. She merely felt an attraction, a carnal tug. She admired him and his horses. That was all.

"Good day to you, Rudgwick. Lord Jeremy."

The voice came from behind them. A rider had reined up, his horse tapping its hooves from side to side in annoyance.

An icy chill passed through her. The man, Dankworth was here, calling a pleasant greeting to the men. No mention of *carte blanche* this time, not in the presence of a duke's granddaughter.

Lady Harmonia froze and then snapped around and dragged Lucie farther down the street, passing a few doors before slowing her pace.

Lucie eased the girl to a halt and faced her. Lady Harmonia's face had gone blotchy, as though she was torn between fear and angry loathing. When she lifted the girl's hands, something of that sensation crept into her own veins. "Do ye know that man?"

"Dankworth." Tension laced Harmonia's voice. "A friend of my late father."

"Ye don't speak to him?"

"I don't. He is the one person Grandpapa and I agree upon wholeheartedly. My father attempted to arrange my betrothal to him."

"*What*?"

"Grandpapa stepped in and stopped it. Thus, the betrothal to Rudgwick."

Rudgwick had saved Lady Harmonia.

The sound of an approaching horse sent a chill up her spine.

"*Ugh.* Since the season started, he is suddenly everywhere," the girl said. "He even tried to approach me at the theater a few nights ago. Grandpapa hurried me into the carriage before that could happen."

The man had been at the theater. Aye, Lucie remembered. She'd seen him there as well.

Her chest tightened around a scant breath, as a gray mist descended around them, muffling the sound of the approaching rider, and wrapping them both in a protective blanket, together, yet strangely apart.

Lady Harmonia's blue eyes widened. Her hands tightened with Lucie's, and a dark shape formed behind the girl. A black-clad arm snaked around the girl's waist, and her hands were ripped from Lucie's grip.

The girl kicked, thrashed, and opened her mouth in a soundless scream as the mist parted and she was tossed over the withers of a waiting horse, joined by the dark shadow, and they rode off into the mist.

"Lucie." A masculine rumble reached through the haze. Hands squeezed her own. Other hands gripped each of her elbows.

She took in a trembling breath. Rudgwick had one elbow, Lord Jeremy the other, and Lady Harmonia held both her hands.

She blinked and breathed in the scent of men's shaving soap and a light lady's perfume.

"Is he gone?" she whispered.

Lady Harmonia exchanged a look with Lord Jeremy, who released Lucie's elbow and joined the girl.

"He's just moved on down the street." Lord Jeremy glanced back and then tensed. "And here comes the duke's coach."

"Drat." Lady Harmonia sighed. "Are you well, Lucie?"

The mist had lifted. Sudden sunlight sparkled off the girl's earbobs, the dark lacquer of the approaching coach, and the gold of its escutcheon.

"Lucie?" Rudgwick murmured.

Oh, Hades. That had been another vision. One that didn't involve an erotic encounter with the man who'd just moved his arm about her waist. Unlike the action of the dark shadow in this latest vision, the movement was caring. In fact, it was melting her insides.

She inwardly shook herself and stepped out of Harmonia's hold and Rudgwick's embrace. "Don't fash about it. I'm fine."

The coach had stopped. A liveried groom was approaching, and the duke looked out from inside, too much on his dignity to call out.

Lady Harmonia reached for her hand again. "Perhaps we will meet again soon."

The sadness in the girl's voice poked at her own sense of loneliness and stirred a sudden protective urge. "I should like that. In fact... Lady Fiona is hosting a birthday ball for me tomorrow night." Had Lady Fiona invited the girl? She doubted it, but never mind. "I should love for ye to attend."

"My grandfather—"

"May come as well. Will certainly do so if ye plan to be there." She managed a smile. "How entertaining that might be."

CHAPTER TEN

A Proposal of Sorts

Harmonia laughed, actually laughed, a tinkling, foreign sound. Yet, Rudgwick sensed, the laugh was authentic. Why would it be otherwise since the girl wasn't one to giggle out of nerves or politeness?

In fact, this was the first time Rudgwick could recall hearing his fiancée laugh. Though he couldn't say that he'd ever been listening closely. He'd teased her a bit from time to time, but he'd never made her laugh. Theirs was not, after all, a love match.

And come to think of it, Lucie's laughs had been rare as well. He *had* paid attention to her. She'd chuckled over Athena in the park the other morning, and the memory still made him giddy.

She'd been recklessly cheerful the night she'd gone out to rescue her mother, and so very brave then, as well as later that night, but she'd never laughed until that morning she'd visited his bedside in Brussels, when he'd offered to escort her to a London play. And that laugh, when it came, had been most assuredly false. Even in the fog of pain and laudanum he'd heard that.

He couldn't recall any others. What a poor suitor he was, unable to inspire true mirth in both his fiancée and in the woman he loved.

He caught sight of the duke's glare framed in the coach window.

"I'll have Mother approach the duke and offer you my escort to Lucie's ball, Harmonia," Rudgwick said. "And now, I'd best hand you to your grandfather."

Harmonia sighed and her face settled into her stoic mask. She curtsied to Jeremy, kissed Lucie on each cheek, and took Rudgwick's arm, the whole and intact one. As usual, she said only what was required for politeness, a toneless thank you, and let him hand her into the carriage. He saluted the old man with his false hand and watched as they pulled away.

Jeremy and Lucie passed by behind him, returning the way they'd come, his friend taking long strides to keep up with Lucie's brisk pace.

He hurried after them and caught up. When he slipped her hand over his arm, she stiffened and tugged, setting some space between them, yet she was too much of a lady to otherwise start a row in the middle of this Knightsbridge street, blast it.

Despite the excitement yesterday, Lucie's spark had dimmed since Brussels. He wanted to know why. Something had happened since then. Was it the accident and her injury, and the spells plaguing her, or was there something more?

What had she said to his mother in Brussels, when she'd declined his offer of escort to the theater? That she was from a disreputable Scots family and that his family was well above hers.

Had someone spurned her during her visit to London last autumn or now?

The last bit about social standing was true; his family was well above hers, at least in the eyes of Society. Perhaps the first bit about her parents' scandal had once been true, twenty years earlier when her father and mother divorced. But Colonel Macbeth had redeemed himself, not just by his subsequent twenty years of valorous service to the Crown, but also by his faithfulness to his lady over that period.

He saw that, and Mother did also. Bridgehampton did not, but it wasn't to his benefit to see Lucie as anything but a nonpareil. Her very existence was upsetting his plans to safely keep his granddaughter's inheritance under the control of the Dukes of Bridgehampton. What had the man been about to say at the theater? *After the wedding you might chase whatever...*

Bridgehampton had completed that sentence when he'd proposed the alliance between Rudgwick and Harmonia, mincing no words. He had no expectations of faithfulness on Rudgwick's part, though he hoped he'd be more discreet than his own son.

Bridgehampton had assumed that Rudgwick was just like Grey, a philandering fool who dipped his wick anywhere and everywhere.

It was rumored that, until his marriage, the duke himself had led a rakish life, and thus he suspected the worst in young men.

He'd surely made enough inquiries to know that Rudgwick, though no monk, wasn't like Grey at all. Rudgwick was like his father, a man made to be faithful to the woman he married. And Lucie wasn't some bit of muslin. She was a lady, dammit, a stubborn and headstrong one, certainly, but also a brave and true one. Not easily won. Not compliant. A woman who'd fight for the people she loved.

That night in his drawing room, the first night they'd met, the attraction between them had been deep and strong. Only the presence of her mother had kept him from reaching for her. But from the moment Lucie learned of his engagement, she'd made certain to keep her distance, and when he came too near, she'd pushed him away.

He knew she still longed for him. He and Harmonia weren't yet married—so why wouldn't Lucie fight for him? She'd been hurt by her parents' scandal, but she was not out of his reach, nor was he out of hers.

Except of course, for the matter of Harmonia. Lucie wouldn't cause hurt to another young woman.

And something had just happened between her and Harmonia. They'd talked with some intimacy, and then Lucie experienced one of her spells, and then she'd made Harmonia laugh.

Jeremy nodded to him over Lucie's head and slipped back, following behind them.

Rudgwick glanced down at her. The brisk stride had brought her color back, her cheeks glowing a lovely shade of pink over jaws clamped in some stubborn emotion—hurt, perhaps, or pride. Despite the courtesy she'd extended Harmonia, the smile accompanying the invitation to her birthday ball had not reached her eyes. The duke's condescension bothered her—the duke's condescension piled atop his own attention, which she was desperately pushing away.

Damnation, he wanted her. He *would* have her, honorably or dishonorably, he didn't care—however she'd allow it.

Oh, hell, who was he fooling? Himself, certainly if he thought he could convince her to become his mistress. Besides, she'd suffered too much in her young life for him to dishonor her. The only way he could have her was if he were free.

For now, they would be friends. She needed a friend, someone to go on adventures with her, someone who would understand the need to occasionally knock heads.

"Now tell me," he said briskly, just as he might have spoken to one of his men reporting the enemy's movements. "What did you see just then?"

Her breath quickened.

"You're not going to faint." He kept his tone even, as he would have when soothing a skittish horse he was training for battle. "Not while you're walking so briskly. One minute you were looking at Harmonia, and the next you were off somewhere else. You quite startled Harmonia, I think. Not that startling Harmonia is such a bad thing. And you know, that's the first time I've ever heard that child laugh."

She halted and looked up at him. They'd reached the front step of his house, and a carriage was drawing up. Seated next to Lady Fiona's coachman was Hyde, who tipped his hat to him. Behind him he heard the front door open.

Her gaze searched his. "She *is* very young, isn't she?"

"What did you see, Lucie?" He heard Mother's and Lady Fiona's voices approaching. They didn't have much time.

"Ye must both have a care. Ye must see that she's safe."

"From whom? From what?"

"When ye marry—"

"I'm not going to marry her. I'm going to marry you."

Her color rose, and then drained from her. "Don't be a nodcock. I'm going to Norfolk, and then I'm going home. I'm going to get through this blast..." She took a deep breath. "blessed birthday ball, and then I'm leaving."

"You're not the sort of woman who runs. You're not a coward."

She swiped a hand over her face, her fingers framing the sparkling red curls struggling out from under her small bonnet. His own fingers itched to yank the head covering away, pull out her pins and watch the hair cascade to her waist as it had that night in his parlor.

Her fingers pressed at her temple, and he remembered her injury, wondering whether that lovely stretch of pale skin and shimmering hair was the part of her head that she'd cracked in the accident.

"Lucie?" Lady Fiona's hand touched her arm. "Are you well?"

She nodded. "Aye."

Liar. "No, Lady Fiona. She's not well. She's had one of her episodes. She won't tell me what she saw."

"Ah." Lady Fiona's gaze appraised him and then she nodded to Hyde, who opened the coach door.

"Is all well?" Mother asked, joining them.

"Quite." Lucie's mouth went hard around the word, her back straightened, her face settled into a tight mask. "Thank ye, Lady Rudgwick, and good day to ye." She dipped her head. "Major Lord Rudgwick." She nodded to someone over his shoulder. "Lord Jeremy."

He'd completely forgotten that Jeremy was present.

Before she could turn away, he shoveled her hand up with his prosthetic one. When he kissed the back of her glove, the lovely pink rising in her cheeks stirred his blood again. "Fear not. I shall heed your warning, my love."

Her mouth dropped open and she scoffed.

"Go on, Lucie. I shall be right along." Lady Fiona shooed her over to Hyde, who helped her into the carriage. Hyde closed the door, climbed onto the back of the coach, and signaled the coachman to proceed down the street a few doors.

A perceptive man and a good friend to Macbeth and his ladies.

Lady Fiona touched his arm. "I heard everything you said, young man." There was no accusation in her quiet voice. No alarm either.

"The whole street heard," Mother whispered.

"Very true," Jeremy muttered. "The duke won't like it. Not that I would tell him."

Rudgwick huffed out a breath, and then laughed.

"It *is* a pretty puzzle." Mother bit her lip and the small lines between her eyebrows furrowed. "The duke is a stumbling block, and Lucie is not an easy girl. Her father told me."

"Did he, Mother? You discussed... *this* with Macbeth?"

"Of course, that first day in Brussels when he invited us to lodge with them. I am your mother, and he is her father, and your attraction was as plain as day. And I am glad to hear you use the word marriage, because it was clear to me that if you dishonor her with any other proposal, he will hunt you down and make you regret it."

He nodded. "Of course." He'd expect no less from a proud Scots baron and soldier.

His thoughts had, of course, gone first to the notion of taking Lucie as a mistress, as soon as he realized he wanted her and couldn't have her in marriage because of Harmonia.

When had that been? Not Brussels—by then he'd been head over ears with Lucie. Had it been when he first saw her riding astride the night of the riot? Or was it that same night when she'd ripped off the man's cap she'd been wearing to reveal her hair? Certainly, by the time he'd tracked her down at Lady Conyngham's ball in Brussels; he'd never wanted a woman so desperately after merely one waltz.

He'd been on duty the night of the Duchess's ball—the night before battle—and so had been unable to attend, hating the thought of dying without seeing Lucie one more time, without telling her how he truly felt. And then, as luck had it, he'd been delivering a dispatch when he'd spotted her in the courtyard, waving farewell to her father, who was returning home for a few last moments with his lady before changing and gathering his weapons.

He'd pulled Lucie around the back of the building and showed her exactly the depth of his passion. Well, not exactly, and certainly not thoroughly. If he'd been any less of a gentleman, he would have taken her against the brick wall that very night. He would have done his very best to plant his seed, knowing that if he died the child left behind would be raised by a strong woman.

It was the instinctive, dishonorable brutishness of soldiers. He'd resisted it. Barely.

"You must think of Harmonia's tender feelings as well," Jeremy said.

Both ladies turned on him with appraising looks. Lord Jeremy Bolton, a noted man about town, actually blushed.

For his own part, Rudgwick had never thought of Harmonia as someone who had tender feelings. "You're right. Perhaps you might help me there, Jeremy," he said. "As you did at Rudgwick Abbey."

"I would never try to divert Harmonia's attentions—"

"I know." He waved away Jeremy's oft-repeated disclaimer. "You're a true and honorable friend."

"What do you mean to do, Rudgwick?" Lady Fiona asked.

There'd been no accusation in the older lady's question, only sympathy and perhaps, *perhaps* a hint of a willingness to help.

"Lucie is troubled," he said. "Why? Do you know, Lady Fiona?"

The lady pressed her lips together. "She sees a danger to you."

"She's told me something of this. You must assure her I can see to my own safety."

"She did say she's warned you."

He nodded. "But I fear there's more she's holding back. I'd like to banish those worries. She can't think straight until then." He couldn't either.

The lady eyed him shrewdly and then smiled, her eyes kind. "How perceptive you are. I will see what more she'll tell me. Shall we still see you tomorrow night?"

Lucie's birthday ball would be her official London come out. "I will be there. And I will still accompany both of you to Norfolk. You should know that Lucie just invited Harmonia, so you might as well plan for the duke's attendance, as well."

Lady Fiona's eyes sparkled. "Perhaps the duke's presence is just what Lucie needs." She smiled. "We'll have a spectacular crush, and the scandal sheets will be agog. I shall send Lady Harmonia an invitation when I arrive home today."

Mother's startled look transformed into a smile. "I believe you are right, Fiona. If you and my son can persuade her to return to London after your business in Norfolk, Lucie will find a place in Society, if for no other reason than the *ton*'s curiosity. And then her natural spirit and charm will win the day."

Rudgwick shared a look with his mother, astonished at the praise. Oh, he knew Mother was on his side, but he'd had no idea she had such regard for Lucie.

"I will do what I can to lift her out of this black mood," Lady Fiona said. "Now, we are off to the dressmaker to see to the new gown she claims not to want." Her soft glove touched his cheek. "My dear boy, you must help her by attending to those dangers she's seeing."

"And leave Bridgehampton to me," Mother said.

The clouds had moved in and as they watched Lady Fiona's carriage drive off, a drizzle of rain fell upon Mother's cheek. He hurried her into the hall, reviewing the events since they'd left the house for their walk.

Lucie had not shared everything that troubled her. And whatever she'd seen with Harmonia had been equally unsettling, so much so that, but for his and Jeremy's steadying hands—and Harmonia's as well, he supposed—Lucie might have swooned right there in the street.

They almost hadn't reached her in time. Blasted Dankworth had appeared from nowhere for a chat. Just come from visiting a farrier in Knightsbridge, he'd said, but it was uncanny running into the blackguard yet again. Dankworth had been looking around for an urchin to hold his reins, a signal he might dismount and irritate them further.

The ladies had surely heard Dankworth's greeting, and it was just then that Lucie'd had her episode.

The footman closed the front door behind Jeremy and Mother dismissed him, leaving the three of them alone in the hall.

Rudgwick touched his mother's arm. "I told Harmonia that you would convey the invitation to Lucie's ball and convince the duke to attend. Shall we call upon them today?"

"Not today, I think. Let him receive Fiona's note today and fume a bit." She lifted her cheek for a kiss and smiled at Jeremy. "As for you, Jeremy, I fear the duke is plotting more matchmaking. After you left, he questioned Fiona about Lucie's prospects and mentioned quite pointedly that you, sir, are in need of a wife. But don't fret. You must continue your kindness to Harmonia. Rudgwick has been assuming that she's too young to marry. However, *I* was her age when I married Rudgwick's father, and I will tell you, Harmonia is not too young to marry *for love*. She will do quite well in a love match, and her dowry is more than sufficient to maintain a respectable household for a duke's son."

With those parting words she left them.

"Close your mouth," Rudgwick said.

Jeremy blinked and smiled at him. "She's a handful, your mother is. I quite like her. Though I don't have any idea how she plans to bring this about." He waved a hand. "Whatever *this* is that she's planning."

He laughed. "Oh, you *know*. Mother is planning two weddings." His own and Jeremy's.

Jeremy grimaced. "Perhaps. What the devil was that business of Miss Macbeth seeing things?"

He glanced around. No servants were lurking, but he didn't want any unnecessary gossip, and besides, he didn't know who might be in the duke's pay.

"Come, let's have a drink and I'll tell you."

He closed the door to his study, a compact room at the back of the house where he could look out on the garden. Or rather, where Mother had been able to look out on the garden when she managed things for him while he was off fighting. She'd been hopeful enough of his safe return to have decorated the space to his masculine tastes, with a mahogany desk, a sideboard well-stocked with his favorite spirits, and burgundy upholstered armchairs near the hearth. It was a comfortable refuge for him.

He had Jeremy toss another shovel of coal into the fire, and they propped their boots on the fender, drinks in hand.

"Damnably chilly weather for April," Jeremy said. "Now tell me."

"You've heard of the Second Sight."

"Of course. Superstitious nonsense if you ask me. Never tell me Miss Macbeth thinks she has it?"

He shrugged. "I would never tell you that. *She* would never tell you that. Perhaps what she's experience is merely a strong intuition. But yes, she *sees* things. Her father did as well."

"He told you that?"

"Not directly. There are too many men in the army jockeying for rank and ready to destroy a competitor's reputation. It was his lady who spoke to me forthrightly. He'd had visions of some dangerous events before they occurred." Like the wild March night when Greer Macbeth's carriage was attacked, and when later, both she and Lucie were abducted by their cousin, Banquo. The night Greer had ended up in the Thames with a would-be murderer. He hadn't spoken of those hellish events with Jeremy, nor anyone else but the parties involved and Sir Thomas Abernathy. "And Waterloo; he had a vision of that battle before it happened. Was it his intuition? His soldier's instinct? Second Sight? Whatever it was, the man survived twenty years of hard-fought battles." He tossed back his drink. In his own five years battling the French, he'd seen the value of having eyes in the back of one's head. "What difference does it make what you call it? He's not some barmy Scotsman, Jeremy."

"No, I suppose not. Would have saved civilization a heap of dead soldiers and..." Jeremy glanced at Rudgwick's new right hand resting upon the arm of his chair. "Missing limbs, if someone with those abilities had moved Bonaparte to the hinterland sooner."

Rudgwick tamped down the flare of irritation he always felt when someone mentioned his injury. At least Jeremy never coddled him as if he were some blasted invalid.

"Getting back to Miss Macbeth, you're saying that this morning, and the other morning at the park when she went glassy-eyed and looked ready to keel over, she was having visions?"

"Visions, spells, episodes—she had a head injury last autumn and since then she's had these...occurrences."

And they were getting worse, according to Hyde.

"Triggered by the injury? Hmm. She's never experienced them before?"

Hyde hadn't known whether she'd had them before. He'd been with her father fighting the French, and like Macbeth, hadn't met Lucie until last year.

"She had one at the theater the other night."

"Really? When? She certainly didn't make a scene in the box. She looked fine when I spoke with her. Did she tell you about it?"

"Yes." But she hadn't needed to tell him—he'd been watching her instead of Lady Sneerwell and her man, Snake. He'd seen the horror come over her, right there in the theater box. "She says I'm in danger."

She was afraid for him, as Macbeth had been for his lady. The notion that she worried about him gave him hope.

"Who might be threatening you? Have any vengeful Frenchies snuck into England? No wonder you've been working so hard with that left sword hand."

He took a swallow of brandy. Vengeful Frenchmen weren't likely to be a problem. Most of the French were as sick of war as their British and other European counterparts. The French had paid an equally terrible price at Waterloo, and many laid the blame on their erstwhile tyrant, Bonaparte.

Jeremy took his silence in stride and went on with his own musings. "Miss Macbeth and Harmonia seemed to get along well."

Perhaps that was true at the end, but he'd seen the flare of anger in Lucie. "Do you think so?"

"Yes. You didn't? Well, you're better acquainted with Miss Macbeth, aren't you?" Jeremy smiled slyly, for once not protesting about dishonor to Harmonia.

"I didn't notice any tension until Dankworth appeared."

Jeremy's mouth dropped and his feet hit the floor. "*Dankworth*. Visiting a farrier in Knightsbridge. What rot."

"Pity that Sir Thomas's report didn't have more on him."

"I've made some more inquiries about Dankworth," Jeremy said. "Discreetly, of course." He recounted what he'd heard about Dankworth's past—a distasteful one, given that he'd managed his cousin's Caribbean plantation, and his prospects as that man's heir. Apparently, there would not be as much wealth in slavery as Dankworth might have hoped for.

"There *is* someone who might know more about Dankworth," Rudgwick responded.

"Let's go and talk to him. Or her? Is it a woman?" He laughed. "Shall we have to pay a call on a Cyprian? I confess, I haven't been straying that way much since..."

Since he'd met Harmonia. Rudgwick laughed, silently finishing the sentence. "I quite understand, Jeremy. And no, it's not a Cyprian. It's Bridgehampton."

He'd not told Jeremy about the file Lucie had retrieved from Stephenson's office. "You recall that eighteen months ago, Grey was arranging Harmonia's marriage to Dankworth."

Jeremy jumped to his feet and began to pace, raking his hand through his unruly hair. "I wondered about that. Was it payment of debts?"

"Maybe. I don't know. The duke had Grey on a tight leash. The duke proceeded to have himself appointed her guardian and—"

"Arranged a betrothal to the Earl of Rudgwick, heir presumptive if Grey kicked up his heels without issue."

"Yes. An imminently prudent match." *Then.*

Hades. It would still be prudent, given what he'd learned about his father's debts. Bridgehampton had bought up all the reckless mortgages on the Rudgwick properties.

Father had been a loving husband and a kind father. He'd rarely frequented gambling dens. His weakness had been modernizing his homes, particularly Rudgwick Abbey and the massive Mayfair townhouse they'd had to sell upon his death. With a sinking feeling, Rudgwick had realized that he'd have to marry someday anyway, so why not a union that would save the earldom and the people under his care from financial ruin? The duke hadn't even needed to voice that argument.

Rudgwick had agreed to the betrothal on the understanding that he would still serve in Horse Guards and the wedding would be delayed until Harmonia was at least seventeen, preferably older. The duke had grumbled about the latter condition and agreed to the former, knowing that Bonaparte had been defeated and exiled to Elba, and Rudgwick's duties were likely to be no more than ceremonial nonsense.

"Grey must have been furious he was thwarted," Jeremy said. "It's a wonder he didn't have Dankworth abduct Harmonia and cart her off to Gretna Green."

"Grey might have taken her there himself for the nuptials, but she was already living with Bridgehampton. The duke wisely increased his guard on her. She still never goes anywhere unattended."

"Yet he allowed her to visit Rudgwick Abbey last winter without him."

"Mother convinced him that people were whispering about Harmonia's lack of concern about her fiancé."

Jeremy smiled. "The injured war hero."

When he rolled his eyes, Jeremy laughed.

"And your mother knew I was there? Your mother is devious. I suppose I must be honored that you trusted me with Harmonia's protection during her visit while you were swanning about the Abbey encased in your black cloud."

"It wasn't a black cloud." He *had* been self-absorbed, alternating between a determination to master his handicap, flares of selfish anger at the loss of his hand, and the nightmares that plagued him. And Harmonia, had, quite frankly seemed wholly uninterested in him, happy to go off with the fully intact Lord Jeremy. "At least, it wasn't a black cloud *all* the time. I appreciated you taking her off my hands. Or..." He laughed. "My *hand*. You formed an attachment and she welcomed it."

Color rose in Jeremy's cheeks. "I would never betray you, Rudgwick, or dishonor Harmonia."

That again. "I don't see it as a betrayal."

Jeremy's jaw worked. "She's seventeen. She needs Bridgehampton's permission to marry."

"I wouldn't object if you whisked her off to Scotland. Pour me another drink?"

His glass disappeared and came back topped off, and Jeremy settled back into his chair and propped up his boots again.

The otherwise shiny Hessians showed some wear at the toes. Jeremy was another lordling short on cash.

"Grey is dead," Jeremy said. "There's no danger of her father snatching her up and handing her over to a brute. So why won't the infernal man release you to marry someone else?"

It was a fine question; one he'd pondered since dancing with Lucie. Since kissing her.

"I suppose for one thing, if Harmonia is the duchess and produces an heir, it will keep the bloodline intact."

Jeremy waved a hand. "Most of the *ton* are related if one looks back far enough. And anyway, we are not horses or hounds."

"If not that, then it must have to do with her dowry. He's been very crafty in arranging matters to his benefit. Before the engagement, he bought up the notes on my father's mortgages."

Jeremy's eyes widened. That was a fact Rudgwick had never shared with him.

"He may have overextended himself there. He holds a far-flung array of properties, much more than I do, and if he's like the rest of us, at least a few of them are a drain on his coffers. Harmonia, when she marries, will have buckets of money coming to her from her maternal grandmother. It will be Harmonia's husband's, and if that husband is the next Duke of Bridgehampton, well, he would like to keep the money propping up the dukedom."

"Is the current duke embezzling her trust?"

"There are trustees preventing that." He'd met with those trustees before signing the marriage contracts.

"If she doesn't marry, does the money come to her when she reaches her majority or are there other safeguards?"

"There are no other safeguards." He'd asked about that as well. "If she doesn't marry, she'll receive the money on her twenty-fifth birthday." For his part, he'd been inclined to wait until Harmonia had the freedom to make her own choice.

He'd been more than willing to delay marriage, to offer Harmonia the protection of their engagement for a much longer term...until he'd met Lucie.

"And she'll be an even greater target and need more protection from fellows like Dankworth."

"How wonderful it would be to see Harmonia settled in a happy marriage to a man who is not a fortune hunter," he said. "Whether or not he needs her money."

Jeremy turned his gaze to the glowing coals. "With Bridgehampton's blessing."

It wasn't a question. Rudgwick knew Jeremy had standards. It would be up to Mother to persuade Bridgehampton to approve the union, and failing that, up to him to persuade Jeremy to elope. And of course, Harmonia must be persuaded to play her part. That would have to be Jeremy's task.

"With Harmonia's blessing, that being far more critical. As my mother said, this is a pretty puzzle." He set aside his tumbler, grasped the thumb of his fake hand and began ticking off points on each wooden fingertip. "The duke halted Grey's plot with Dankworth, and Grey is dead.

Harmonia is underage and needs Bridgehampton's permission to marry. Even if she were one and twenty, she wouldn't choose Dankworth. I have observed that she blooms in your presence, Jeremy. And most important of all to me as her soon-to-be jilted fiancé, you appear to be head over ears in love with her."

Jeremy colored deeply under the dark scruff of his afternoon beard, right up to the disorderly dark locks that were so like his own. They were of a similar height and coloring, and in fact had sometimes been confused for each other at public houses and inns and even at some society events. Both had, after all, been gone from Town for a number of years, Rudgwick fighting, and Jeremy first at university, and then off doing whatever Sir Thomas or his brother commanded.

"And you are head over ears with Miss Macbeth." Jeremy laughed. "Damn, but we're getting maudlin."

Rudgwick stood. "And the cure for that, my friend, is action."

He'd been following that cure since his return home to England. When the nightmares of battle plagued him, memories of the random piece of shrapnel that blew his saber from his right hand, he shoved them aside, picked up a pen, or fork, or a sword. He'd lost his hand, not his manhood, and sometimes a man needed to wage battle. He had an obligation to protect Mother, to defend his good name, to free Harmonia. And, dammit, he had an obligation to Lucie as well. She was his. She must be his. He'd fight for her, no matter what it took. He wanted her in his life, by his side, in his bed. He wanted to crown all that glorious hair with a countess's coronet, and someday, that of a duchess.

"Perhaps we're looking too high for information." He went back to his desk and pulled a piece of paper from the drawer, and a pen from the holder on his desk. He held the pen over the inkwell. Writing left-handed was still awkward, but there was another problem. He had no idea whether Hyde could read.

He dipped the pen and scratched out a note to Lady Fiona.

CHAPTER ELEVEN

The Star and Garter

While Madame herself fussed around Lucie, one of her seamstresses held the pin dish. Lady Fiona circled around her, wisely offering only compliments when Madame achieved just the right draping and fit.

Lucie had thought the vermilion gown was exquisite and made her look like a lady, but this gown was even more transformative. After the last round of pinning, Madame led her to a pier mirror for approval. The gown of ivory, trimmed with gold braid and fringe, made her look like a Greek goddess, Persephone perhaps. She'd once seen an illustration in a book.

She caught Lady Fiona's eye, and they both laughed. Making her elderly kinswoman happy warmed her all the way to the delicate slippers Madame had designed for her. She couldn't regret her sojourn with Lady Fiona.

Oh, she'd hoped that by one-and-twenty, with Calder to manage while Father and Mother ran the Menteith holdings, she'd be more independent, more self-reliant. The accident, her injury, this visit in London, had upset her plans. She knew, though, from watching Mother's experiences and hearing the little Father had shared of his time in the army, a body couldn't plan out everything. Very little was entirely under one's control.

Her feelings for Rudgwick, for example, and the way he kept popping up in her life, and her dreams.

The blasted man was strong enough to take care of himself, even with only one hand. Mayhap he wouldn't marry Lady Harmonia, but once this business in Norfolk was settled, once she herself had returned to Scotland, he'd forget all about Lucie Macbeth.

"Are you happy with the gown?" Lady Fiona asked, as they settled into the coach.

"Yes." She grasped her elderly kinswoman's plump hand. "Ye're very generous, my lady. I wish Mother could be here to see it."

"You'll take it home with you."

"I will. And treasure it always. It's very dear. As are ye."

The twinkle in Lady Fiona's eyes shone brighter and a tear leaked down her cheek.

"Never say I've said something to upset ye, my lady. Not for the world would I trouble ye."

"Tears of joy, child. I'm so glad to see you smile, especially after such a morning as this one. And the birthday ball—you can't know what a pleasure you're allowing me." She dabbed at her eyes with a lace-trimmed handkerchief. "Lord Rudgwick said you invited Lady Harmonia to the ball."

Tension tightened Lucie's shoulders. They were back on to the topic of Rudgwick. She wasn't certain at all how she felt about him, not after Lady Harmonia's revelations, and she'd like to think more on those before Lady Fiona's probing commenced. "Do ye mind?"

"Not at all. It's a fine idea. She and the duke are most welcome."

Lucie nodded and turned her gaze to the window. The skies had darkened, clouds heavy with moisture settling over their path, the air cold enough now for spring snow. It had been a half-hearted joke about the duke's attendance making the ball more interesting, meant to soothe the young lady's concerns. Yet the possibility of crossing swords with the old codger raised Lucie's spirits. Let him dare to attend the ball and cut the person being fêted—herself.

Likely though, he would behave, and his presence would also make Rudgwick behave. There'd be no heated waltzes. No stolen kisses.

"We might as well clear the air with the duke," Lady Fiona said, "especially as Rudgwick means to break off the engagement... and marry you."

That wee tension in her neck jolted through her entire spine, pounding with hot pain in the part of her head that had cracked.

Arrgh. Lady Fiona had been working her way to this, just like her mother might have done. She closed her eyes against the sudden onslaught of boiling ardor, an improvident act, because there he was, raised above her, the dark hair of his chest brushing against her bare breasts, his lips dipping to meet her own. Her insides pooled and heated into a raging desire that gripped her beyond her means to resist and she opened all of herself to meet him.

"Lucie." The crackly voice broke the vision into shards of colored glass. Lady Fiona's smile broadened. "Fate can be hard to resist, lass."

"Madness as well." She pressed her gloved hands against the flaming heat of her cheeks. "But resist, I shall." At least for now. Truth be told, she mightn't be able to resist forever. Not if she stayed near him.

What was she to do about this business in Norfolk? They mustn't be alone else... sooner or later, if he beckoned, she might come, no matter the betrayal.

She caught her breath, thinking about Lady Harmonia. This was how it was done amongst the nobility. The girl didn't love Rudgwick. He said he wouldn't marry her, but of course he would. They'd pledged themselves. They'd signed contracts. They'd celebrated with a grand betrothal ball.

I'm not going to marry Harmonia. I'm going to marry you. A man could wear a woman down with words.

She wouldn't be worn down.

"Lady Fiona, after we visit Norfolk, I'd like to leave for home earlier than planned. Would ye mind? Perhaps ye might journey with me and spend the summer in the Highlands?"

"And what if Rudgwick follows you there?"

Oh my. The lady did see things. Lucie closed her eyes and then opened them when the vision threatened again, blinking it away like a cow fighting off midgies.

"He's in danger, you said. Do you not want to stay and help him?"

She took in a great breath, remembering the sight of Lady Harmonia being thrown on a horse. In that vision, neither Rudgwick, nor Lord Jeremy, nor Bridgehampton had come to her rescue.

One determined villain could thwart a bevy of guards, as well she knew. Was she meant to be the lass's protector as well?

"Oh, Hades, Lady Fiona. What am I to do?"

Lady Fiona was right. She couldn't just run off and leave Rudgwick and his fiancée in peril. Yet if she stayed, she might be ruined.

Warmth unfurled again. Eyes still open, he appeared again, smiling down at her on the white sheets of that simple bed, disheveled dark hair framing his eyes, his face pebbled with dark scruff. Closing her eyes made no difference.

She'd certainly be ruined. She knew that as surely as she knew the freckles on the back of her hands. She would have him. She would feel him, his flesh upon hers, in hers.

***

Later that evening

The Star and Garter on North Street bustled with a late evening crowd of men, gathered around for their evening pints after the day's toil. The room quieted as they entered, the regular patrons assessing them and then resuming their rumbling chatter.

Rudgwick scanned the room and led Jeremy to a table still littered with the empty glasses of departing customers. They settled into the chairs, and he begged a third one from a nearby table, while a boy cleared the dishes and they waited for Hyde.

He knew the inn, having stopped here upon occasion in past years, but it wasn't a regular haunt. In the reply to his afternoon missive, written in Lady Fiona's hand, Hyde had suggested this location.

"He's late," Jeremy said. "Who is the esteemed fellow we're meeting?"

Jeremy had not waited up for Hyde the night before. "You saw him at the park with Lucie, as well as today on Lady Fiona's coach."

"The fellow in plain coats helping Miss Macbeth into the carriage?"

"Yes. Hyde's a Yorkshire man who served with the Highlanders. Came out of the army with Macbeth to serve as his valet. More than his valet. More like a major-domo." A blissfully unpolished one. "Or, if you will, his Man Friday. Hyde went back into the King's service for Waterloo."

"Ah. I believe that's your Man Friday just arriving now," Jeremy said.

Rudgwick glanced to the door and smiled. An answering grin appeared on Hyde's battered face, and he came to stand beside their table.

"No salutes," Rudgwick said, forestalling the arm that was moving up. Jeremy, this is Hyde. Hyde, this is Lord Jeremy Bolton. Now sit down, man."

"Aye, milord, sir." Hyde didn't budge. "Shall I fetch us all pints first?"

"Yes. If you would. And meat pies." Rudgwick handed him some coins.

Hyde grimaced at them as if he would object.

"Don't argue with him," Jeremy said. "We're here at his behest, and he likely has more blunt than either of us."

With a chuckle, Hyde jostled his way to the bar.

"Sensible fellow. What's he doing in London if he's Lucie's father's man?"

"Looking after her."

Jeremy scoffed. "She's certainly another woman who's a handful."

"Most women are, Jeremy. You'd know that if your mother had lived longer; if you had a sister." He studied his friend, deciding to poke him a bit. "Most women except Harmonia. Never puts a foot wrong, does she? Her name suits her."

"You say that as if it's a bad quality," Jeremy said. "You should be glad. After seeing the troubles Northam went through with his first wife, I'd not want a woman who turned my world topsy-turvy."

Jeremy's brother's first wife had been a harridan. Lucie was lively, but not a harridan. It was more a case of her setting his world to rights. He'd been in a fog, and she'd made things clear.

"I haven't met your brother's new wife. Is she more harmonious?" he teased.

"She's agreeable, somewhat plain, very rich, and she's given him heirs. If he's happy with her, I'm happy."

Hyde returned empty handed and drew out his chair. "Daniel's a good lad. He'll send over our drinks and pies."

"Sit, man," Rudgwick said. "What were your ladies planning to do tonight?"

"Stay in, what with the ball being tomorrow, and both are in good spirits, so says the footman tending to them at dinner. Most likely, Miss Lucie is reading to Lady Fiona while they have a whisky by the fire. Spent the afternoon at the dressmaker's." He quirked a lip. "Course I didn't venture in there, though I wouldn't have minded having a chat with the old girl who helped the porter carry out their packages."

The serving girl arrived with a tray and set out mugs and plates.

Rudgwick reached for his drink.

"Wait." Jeremy lifted his ale. "A toast to you both. I'm honored to be in your company. Heroes of—"

"Don't say it," Rudgwick ordered, leveling him a long look.

Hyde's lips pressed together; his gaze riveted on the steaming crust of his pie. Despite their difference in rank and station, he and Hyde had taken a few private moments to talk during their stay at Macbeth's villa in Brussels. No one understood the hell of that battle but the men who'd gone through it.

Nor could they understand how much they'd like to forget. If Hyde was like him, he'd landed in England and shoved all those steaming memories away, covering them like the crust on the meat pie, at least during waking moments. At night they broke through like live things.

He took a bracing drink of the ale, then poised his fork over the pie and stabbed the heart of it.

"Eat," he said.

Both men obliged him, and he forced himself to join in, concentrating on the mundane task of eating mostly one-handed. The right hand, with its moveable fingers, was still new enough to be awkward.

The pie was surprisingly good, and he finished it all without having to force himself as he'd often done the last several months.

When the boy delivered more ale and whisked their plates away, Hyde sat back and rubbed his stomach. "I thankee, milord. Good pies here. The major and I used to stop from time to time."

Major—now Colonel—Macbeth, wasn't a man to stand on ceremony or rank. "You're welcome and for God's sake, Hyde, lower your voice a bit. Is the colonel still well?"

"Aye." Hyde glanced at the next table and leaned in. "Had a letter from him today, Miss Lucie did. He's back in Edinburgh for a time tussling over Banquo's estate. I finally went north and saw those high hills last year. It's a grand manor the major...er, colonel...is managing for Lord Menteith. Miss Lucie's castle is not so grand, a crumbling old tower and more steps than a man ought to ever have to climb, but it's a fine place if you hanker after playing knight and damsel in distress."

"Lucie's not residing with her parents?"

"Doesn't plan to. Her da is thinkin' to give her a taste of managing, since she'll be the baroness someday herself. She'd be there now but for the accident. Had her down to a doctor in Edinburgh, and then Lady Fiona carried her off to Bath."

Hyde had revealed all that to him the other morning. He let him talk now, for Jeremy's sake.

"The colonel keeps a hand in at Calder. The missus had a steady factor runnin' things even before they came down to London last year." Hyde sent him a measuring look. "Don't reckon Miss Lucie will have to live at Calder all the time after she marries."

"Does she have a beau back home?" Jeremy asked.

"Would I tell you, milords, if she did?" Hyde's eyes twinkled. "Oh, all right, there's a laird's son after her, a braw fellow with good prospects. The colonel likes him well enough. Talk was they'd be married by Hogmanay, but..."

Hyde's voice trailed off and he studied his now empty pint. Jeremy raised an eyebrow.

Lucie married? To someone else? A suitor who was braw and probably whole. Did she love the man?

"But what?" Rudgwick asked.

Hyde shrugged. "Don't rightly know. She's a lively one, is Miss Lucie, and I'm not speaking badly of her. I own I think the world of the lass. 'Twill be a special man who wins her."

Rudgwick's breath returned. The fellow hadn't won Lucie over. He signaled to the barmaid to bring more drinks. "You think the world of her, yet I recall hearing you give her a piece of your mind once." *Damn and blast it*, Hyde had said, *this time you'll do as you're told.*

That had been his introduction to Lucie Macbeth.

Hyde shrugged. "All's well that ends well. Though I'd not repeat that particular night. Now, I did what you asked Major, milord. Would you like a report?"

A draft of cold air accompanied the lull of conversation in the taproom and Rudgwick glanced up. A boy had just entered, his cap pulled low, his bulky coats swallowing a thin frame.

"Damn and blast it," Hyde muttered, rising.

Rudgwick set a hand to Hyde's shoulder. "I'll go. Fetch another chair, Jeremy."

In a few strides he reached the new arrival. Eyes the color of warm honey peered at him through angry slits.

"You're late, boy." He signaled the barmaid to fetch a fourth drink, then set his new hand to the back of the bulky coat and steered through the curious faces to the table.

Jeremy's eyes widened and he pressed a hand down on a chuckle.

"'Tisn't a laughing matter," Hyde hissed.

The barmaid brought over four brimming glasses and eyed the boy.

Not fooled. Not fooled at all, as no one would be up close.

"Another pie?" she asked.

"What say you, *Luke*?" Rudgwick asked. "Are you feeling peckish?"

The answering glare made him want to laugh.

"Bring one," Jeremy said. "If you don't want it, er Luke, I'll have it."

The maid cleared the empty plates and glasses and finally left.

***

Lucie let out a breath, relieved that no one at this table would unmask her as a female, though the look on Hyde's face said he wanted to. Lord Jeremy was fighting the giggles, and Rudgwick... he'd rescued her after a fashion, hadn't he? He'd save the fussing for later. Hyde though...

She fixed him with a glare. "I looked for ye after dinner. They said ye'd gone out."

"You oughtn't to be out and about all alone. What're ye thinking?"

"I had to comb every horse in the stable waiting for ye. Good that Billy was drunk enough to tell me all."

"When I get my hands on him—"

"He's here now, waiting with the horses. Wouldn't let me come on my own." She leaned across the table and whispered, "Before ye go and box his ears, I'll thank ye to remember ye serve my father and me and not these lords."

Rudgwick cleared his throat. "We are all here to serve you. Hyde went back to Covent Garden to nose about in the pubs there."

The conversation at the next table stopped. The tavern wench arrived with the pie. Lucie poked at the crust and inhaled the enticing aroma of stewed meats and vegetables. On another night, it would be appealing, but tonight her appetite had failed her. She slid the plate over to Lord Jeremy.

The men at the next table stood and left noisily leaving them some measure of privacy if they spoke softly enough.

"Your man is pockets to let," Hyde said. "Owes every merchant in Covent Garden."

The hair on her neck prickled. "Banquo had rooms near Covent Garden. What else did ye learn that ye didn't tell me?"

"For our part in the nosing about at the club, the barest of facts," Rudgwick said. "He's gentry stock, heir to a baronet cousin with a holding near the coast. He spent some years in the Caribbean running that cousin's sugar plantation."

"That's what ye know. What do ye suspect?"

"That he's up to something."

"How? With whom?"

Lord Jeremy's fork paused. "That baronet cousin is in Norfolk, not far from Norwich."

"Where Banquo's banker is located." She took a drink of the ale. It was strong and more bitter than she liked. "And that's it? We accomplished more at the solicitor's office."

"That's all I know," Hyde said. "And now drink up and I'll fetch you home."

"We'll all fetch you home," Rudgwick said.

She raised a hand. "Hold there. If they were all engaged in smuggling or procurement fraud, or whatever, why would our man be pockets to let?"

"With Boney gone, the Home Office has increased coastal patrols," Lord Jeremy mused.

"It's a fair point," Rudgwick said. "Maybe Banquo squirreled the money away, and he can't get to it."

"The key will be at that bank."

"And if the banker will only speak with Miss Lucie," Rudgwick said, "she must have a care."

Her visions had been about danger to him, and—today she'd seen danger to Harmonia. She shook her head. "It's naught but a stall. The banker is probably in on it. Did Sir Thomas say anything about that bank?"

"He did not. There's very little more and we can't speak here." Rudgwick pushed back his chair. "We'll ride with you and tell you what we know."

A short while later, Lucie found herself back in her bedchamber. It had been a disappointingly brief ride and the information conveyed even slimmer. And tomorrow was the ball. She'd not learn a thing more until she made her way to that bank in Norwich.

CHAPTER TWELVE

The Birthday Ball

Despite arriving in the grandest of Bridgehampton's carriages, they had to wait their turn in the crush of humbler conveyances—even public hacks.

Across from Rudgwick, Bridgehampton's very silence was like a deep grumble. Lady Harmonia, seated next to the duke, was equally reserved, her gaze turned toward the window.

Next to him in the rear facing seat, Mother chattered away about her memories of visiting Chelsea as a girl, before so many of the market gardens had been transformed into terraced homes.

Lady Fiona Carlin's manor was on just such a transformed plot. Her home was not part of a row of homes, though, not a townhouse like his own, but a mansion set upon more than an acre of land, with its own stable and kitchen garden. The dwelling itself was probably larger than the duke's Mayfair palace.

Not that the old man would allow himself to be impressed. Mother had called on the duke, arriving during his blustering refusal to allow

Harmonia to attend Lucie's ball. She'd bullied Bridgehampton into accepting the invitation. How, exactly, she wouldn't say, except for mentioning that the duke shunning the daughter of a hero of Waterloo might remind the scandal sheets and caricaturists of the suspicions about Grey. Perhaps Mother had a connection at a scandal sheet and would plant the notion herself.

When their carriage finally inched up to the portico, a liveried footman appeared at the coach door, and was nudged aside by another man.

It was Hyde, and he opened the door, put down the steps, and swept a bow. Without the livery and half-wig the other servant wore, Hyde's dark coats made him look like a swarthy butler, one who was fighting an undignified grin.

Rudgwick climbed out, followed by the duke. Candles glowed in all the windows, and a gaily dressed crowd pushed into the hall, the gentrified gawpers craning their necks, impressed that Lady Fiona had secured such high-ranking members of the *ton* as guests, especially the duke. He was recognizable to anyone from the drawings of him and his son Grey that had appeared in London prints shops during the height of the marquess's scandals.

He could almost feel Bridgehampton bristling next to him.

"*Hyde*," Mother all but shouted, having dealt with the man's poor hearing in Brussels. "How nice to see you." She not only bestowed a smile on the servant, she held onto his helping hand after she exited the carriage, while the other servant assisted Harmonia. "You're looking well. I trust you are completely recovered."

The duke sent her a glare. She smiled back at the old curmudgeon. "Hyde was at Waterloo with my son." She released the bemused Hyde and took Bridgehampton's arm. "Well now, shall we make our way in, Duke?"

Rudgwick tucked Harmonia's hand over his arm. "We shall be expected to dance together tonight," he murmured. "And I hope that you will allow Lord Jeremy a dance or two." Rather than squeeze into the carriage with them, Jeremy had preceded them in a hack.

At the mention of Jeremy's name, she lifted her chin, and then nodded, never taking her gaze from the open doorway where a footman stood waiting to take their wraps and direct them to the ball room.

His heart lifted when he spotted Lucie. She was a goddess in gold-trimmed ivory; a wood nymph; a selkie. He wasn't one to rhapsodize over lady's attire, except when it enhanced their attributes. And this gown did. The vee-necked bodice lifted her bosoms like treasures on display. He wanted to grip the ends of the fashionably draped shawl and cover those two apples and then carry her off to a private room—preferably one with a bed. A sofa would do. Or, oh hell, he'd take her on the floor if need be. It would be him testing the weight of those apples and savoring them. She ought to be his—would be his.

If only he still had both hands. One luscious apple at a time, it would have to be.

He willed her to look at him, but she gave each person she greeted the full attention of those amber eyes, all emotion carefully masked.

Harmonia's hand squeezed his arm. "Lucie looks lovely tonight."

He glanced down at the chit. There'd been no hint of envy in that declaration. In fact, there'd been more warmth in her voice than he'd heard...

well, ever. And even without smiling, she appeared, somehow, happy. Happy to see Lucie Macbeth.

Hadn't she kissed Lucie goodbye yesterday? What was Harmonia up to?

"She does indeed," Mother said around the duke. She smiled back at them before preceding the duke, greeting Lady Fiona, and then moving on to Lucie. Mother chattered brightly, the kiss to each lady's cheek meant to send a message to the crowd gathered there and to Bridgehampton.

Lucie greeted his mother with an answering kiss and the slightest curve of her lips. Then her gaze moved to the duke. She dipped into a deep curtsey and lifted her chin, challenging him with her dignity.

Heart swelling with pride, he stepped back, following Harmonia. Lucie would manage the role of duchess quite well someday, providing whatever danger she saw for him could be forestalled.

Harmonia paid her respects to Lady Fiona with more of that uncustomary warmth. And like Mother, she grasped Lucie's hands, kissed her, wished her a happy birthday, and declared her admiration for Lucie's gown, and hair, and jewelry. The sort of feminine fribble he'd heard countless times between his sister and her friends.

"My dear Rudgwick." Lady Fiona beamed at him. "What do you think?" The question was delivered with a sly smile.

Harmonia was still speaking—more words than he'd heard from her on a single occasion, while Lucie accepted the friendship with more of that native dignity.

He'd seen her quiet, brave self-possession before, hadn't he? She'd been formidable that

March night, on horseback, in his drawing room, and in the battle with Banquo's men on the sloop. Once he convinced Lucie to throw in her lot with him, to be his countess, Bridgehampton's plots wouldn't stand a chance.

He leaned closer to Lady Fiona's plump cheek and murmured. "A future duchess ought not to show that much bosom."

With a low chuckle, Lady Fiona handed him off to Lucie.

When their eyes met, he was encouraged to see color creep into her cheeks, an appropriate response to one's intended. The only thing to add would be a smile. A laugh would be far too much to ask.

He swept a gaze over her, top to bottom and up again. "No trousers tonight," he teased. Though the drape of the clinging skirts outlined the shapely legs he couldn't help remembering.

"Good evening, Major Lord Rudgwick," she said. "We're so pleased ye have joined us tonight."

"Save me two dances, if you please, Miss Lucie Macbeth, Maid of Calder."

She blinked. "Your fiancée—"

"He's already arranged to dance with me," Harmonia said. "So you must say yes."

Lucie lifted her eyebrows, rendered speechless by Harmonia's smile—as was he, and finally dismissed them both with a nod.

He spotted Mother standing with the duke and led Harmonia that way.

"Trousers?" Harmonia peered up at him.

"I see that you are becoming friends with Lucie Macbeth. Upon occasion, she's been known to don trousers. That is all I will say. I don't tell tales about ladies."

"Grandpapa says she is not good *ton*, and I must stay away from her. He was livid, even after your mother brought him around to allowing me to attend tonight. But as the afternoon progressed, I could see he was plotting something. What? I hope he doesn't try to ruin the ball for her. Oh, look. There is Lord Jeremy." She dropped his arm and veered away from the path that led to her grandfather. Quirking a brow at his mother, Rudgwick hurried after her.

As the violin bow traced the first preparatory note of the opening dance, Lucie accepted the greeting of an older couple, friends of Lady Fiona, and they proceeded into the ballroom.

"Well done," Lady Fiona said. "That is the most tiresome part of the evening over with, and now we will make merry. Are your feet comfortable in those slippers?"

The delicate satin shoes, trimmed in faux pearls and paste topaz, were part of the ensemble, and dancing in them would be like waltzing barefoot. Lucie would have to be careful of clumsy partners. "Yes, and I am ready to dance."

She'd danced at local assemblies and parties at home, exuberant affairs, often with claret and whisky flowing. The balls in Brussels had been tamer. Though, according to the gossip she'd heard, even those were less formal than London balls.

There'd been no London season for her the previous year, as they'd had to leave so suddenly and hurry with Father to Deal and Ostend, and then on to Brussels with Father's Highland Brigade. When they'd returned to Lady Fiona's at the end of summer, most of the *ton* had escaped to their country estates, and so had they, moving on to the Highlands as soon as Father felt well enough to travel.

Perhaps if the dancing were as lively as a Highland ball, she would set a new fashion for the *ton*. Or perhaps not, and it wouldn't matter. She wouldn't be staying in London, after all. Her social future didn't depend on the careful etiquette of the night, nor was Lady Fiona likely to be offended.

The thought of being a bit more of herself cheered her. Her nerves had calmed part way through the receiving line, and she'd held fast by reminding herself she was acting a role. Oh, she knew she must continue to behave herself and avoid altogether shaming her generous kinswoman, who'd spent a fortune in coin for this birthday ball, her launch into London society. The flowers and candles created a glittering wonderland, and the gown transformed her into a different sort of girl than her true self, much the way donning trousers and men's clothing did. Both sorts of apparel made her feel daring. And they required a certain demeanor for the wearer to be taken seriously.

Particularly this gown. More than one gentleman's gaze had stuttered over the neckline. Especially Rudgwick's. The bodice revealed far more bosom than she was used to, yet it was the first stare of fashion. The deep décolletage, the revealing drape of the skirts, made her look older, more sophisticated, like a woman who'd enjoyed passionate kisses. She must stop blushing over it, else she might pass for one of the green girls, no matter that in truth she was as green as any of them where romance was concerned.

At that moment, Rudgwick turned away from his conversation with Lord Jeremy and sent her that almost-smile. Heat flowed up her neck and into her cheeks, and she fought her body's urge to shiver.

"Ah, here is Lord Grallon," Lady Fiona said.

She would have liked to dance with one of the younger gentlemen first, Lord Jeremy perhaps, though he'd confirmed his attendance late enough that she suspected he hadn't planned to appear. Rudgwick had probably twisted his arm.

Rudgwick wanted two dances, but she couldn't possibly lead off the ball with him. True, that would antagonize the duke, a worthy endeavor, but it might also shame Harmonia, and though she didn't quite know what the girl was about with all her warm friendliness, she wouldn't openly embarrass her, or Rudgwick's mama either. Since her arrival in London, Lady Rudgwick had been quite cordial, finally convinced, probably, that Lucie wasn't after her son.

And she wasn't. Truly she wasn't.

She accepted Lord Grallon's hand and they led off the dancing. Mercifully, beyond the merest courtesies, he didn't talk, and neither did she. If only her cousin Malcolm, Lord Menteith, had been in town, he might have partnered her for the first dance. His wife, Marielle would have required it.

Lord Grallon was as old as Papa, though he moved with less creaking and stiffness, having not been a soldier. He was fit enough though, lacking the usual paunch of men of his restrained disposition and age.

A widower, he'd been no more attentive the night they'd attended the theater than courtesy required yet had offered himself up as her first dance partner. Whether he was in search of a wife or not, she didn't know, but she must be wary. Her dowry was small, as were her breasts, truth to tell, compared to those of other ladies displaying their wares. But at one and twenty she was young enough to bear a passel of children, and this blasted red hair set some men to imagining things.

Rudgwick, dancing with Lady Harmonia, glanced her way, a smile glimmering on his lips. He was one of those fellows stirred by red hair. That night in his parlor, hers had leapt from all its pins and fallen around her. The startled look on his face, the way his eyes had darkened, and his mouth had gaped—well, 'twas good he hadn't revealed himself like that again.

Oh, Hades, he'd done worse than smolder and gape. He'd held her too close in their one waltz in Brussels, and then he'd kissed her like a man kissing the woman he loved before going off to battle. And two days ago, in the carriage...

The dance ended and she murmured her thanks to Lord Grallon. Rudgwick and Harmonia approached, with Lord Jeremy wending his way through the crowd to converge on them. Other young men appeared eager to take her hand.

"No, no," Lady Harmonia told them. "Miss Macbeth must dance with Lord Rudgwick next. Their families are old friends, after all." She turned an expectant gaze at Lord Jeremy, who took her hand and bowed over it.

Rudgwick's mouth quirked. He was too astonished to speak, she'd warrant, as was she.

He held out his hand as he'd done that night in Brussels, and she glanced at it. Clad in a white glove that matched his other, the prosthesis looked very real. Palm up, fingers curled, the false hand beckoned.

So much had happened since their last dance. So much had changed for him.

She'd thought him a rogue. Protective and manly of course, braw, courageous, not a fribble... but still, a rogue, and a man—a lord—who would wheedle what he wanted from a girl not of his class and send her away when he was finished. An unfaithful fiancé whose flirtation with Lucie proved he would become an unfaithful husband. That was how it was done in the *ton*, after all.

Instead of the country dance she expected, the violin squealed a long note that signaled a waltz. The music set fire to her nerves. She took the hand he offered. It was hard, with no life.

He'd sacrificed his right hand for his country. After the battle, when he'd joined them at their villa in Brussels, he never spoke of the loss. He'd sit stoically while a servant cut up his food, but she'd seen the glimmer of frustration, and the winces of phantom pain as the arm healed.

Otherwise, she'd avoided him. Except for that stolen kiss, they were never alone in Brussels, not before the battle nor after. He was unforgettable, and she'd always admire his handsome face, his braw self, and his horses. And of course, his heroism. All from the safe distance of her Highland home.

His left hand, warm, strong and alive, captured her right hand, and his false hand slid to her waist, the dead weight of it a reprieve from the heated touch she remembered from Lady Conyngham's ball.

Oh, but when she lifted her chin, his eyes glowed with a fiery intensity that seized her heart and set her blood to simmering. Battle-scarred and one handed, pledged to another girl, he was more unattainable male than ever, and her rebellious self wanted him.

And *would* not, *must* not show it. No matter what he said about marrying her, he was still pledged to Lady Harmonia.

As they moved together in the first steps of the dance, she grasped for a few words and decided to remain silent.

When she missed a step, he smoothly corrected them and smiled. Oh, his grin was knowing. He knew what he did to her. She managed an answering smile, as she might have done at home dancing a Scottish reel with a roomful of tolerant tippling Scots.

"Let me lead, lass," he said, affecting a Scottish burr.

Wicked man. He understood her too well, at least where this dancing was concerned. For the rest of it... Perhaps he understood the rest of her too well also.

"I suppose I wouldn't make a very good horse," she said. "I fear I'm not easily led."

"If you were a horse, you'd put Athena to shame."

How was one to answer that?

"Did you ever ride her in battle?" she asked.

"Indeed, I did. At Toulouse. I didn't take her to Flanders, though. I meant to send her down for breeding but decided to wait until her next season."

So many horses had died at Waterloo. "I'm glad you left her behind. Was she a good cavalry mount?"

"The very best. Beautiful, intelligent, and valiant. Like you."

Speechless, she concentrated on the footwork as he twirled her into an unexpected turn.

"It's not every day a girl is held up for comparison to a horse," she said finally, biting back a smile. 'Twas high praise coming from a cavalry officer and showed just how well Rudgwick understood her. "Ye must cease the flummery, Major Lord Rudgwick. I can see right through ye."

They turned again, and she found them suddenly closer.

"Good," he said into her ear. "Then you can see right into my heart and know that I love you."

Speechless—thrice in one dance—she managed to scoff.

He stared down at her, lips tilted in his usual enigmatic almost-smile. No one looking on would see anything different about him.

But he was right, she saw into his heart. What was she to do?

She quickly closed her mouth and adopted the air that went with this dress and this night, and the music mercifully came to an end. With a courtly thank you, he handed her over to her next partner, leaving her feeling shaken and bereft.

And that would not do. She threw herself into the next few dances, all with handsome young bachelors, including Lord Jeremy. Lady Fiona had invited the best of her friends, and curiosity had widened the circle beyond to their acquaintances—especially the unmarried young gentlemen. They would be seeking dowries, and she would disappoint them there. Not only were her dowry and future inheritance paltry by London standards, but she also wasn't seeking a husband to take them from her.

Still, they were mostly an affable bunch. There were courtly compliments from some, but no one else professed to love her. The only truly high-in-the-instep guest was the duke. He stood fixed on the sidelines, watching his granddaughter like a hawk, and shadowing Lady Rudgwick when she wasn't dancing. Lady Fiona had set a room aside for cards, and some of the older men, some of the older women as well, had trickled that way. He ought to have joined them.

A few late arriving gentlemen found their way to their hostess, and were, in turn, introduced to Lucie. They were more sons of the gentry and noblemen of Lady Fiona's acquaintance, friendly and fortunately not interested in marriage with one such as herself. But too respectful of Lady Fiona to display any other sort of interest.

And so, she was stunned when a sandy-haired fellow with beady blue eyes and a wicked grin stepped up and asked her to dance.

CHAPTER THIRTEEN

Stolen Kisses

They'd not been introduced but she knew who he was.

He introduced himself as Lionel Dankworth and repeated his request. She lifted her chin and held his gaze, the room slipping away, the air clearing as if it was just the two of them. He stood in a rising haze, the color dark gray, like smoke from a new fire, and her skin prickled with an awareness of danger.

If Rudgwick and Harmonia truly were in peril, this man had a part in it.

She wouldn't know anything if she sat back and let others lead. If Dankworth was testing her mettle, then so be it. She dipped her head and let him take her hand.

As it happened, the dance was another waltz. Where Rudgwick's hand—even the cold dead one—sent melting warmth through her, this man's touch made her muscles tense for battle.

Let him think he is leading, she reminded herself.

"And so, we meet again," he said, "though we've not been properly introduced before. How are you finding London?"

"We've not been properly introduced now," she said. "And my time with Lady Fiona has been precious."

"You are quite the equestrian. Do you ride in the Park every day?"

"I ride every morning but mostly in Chelsea."

Oh fie, that had been a misstep. She didn't wish to meet him on one of those morning rides.

"I was surprised to encounter you with Rudgwick. Are you particular friends?"

She felt heat rising in her face. He feigned a crestfallen look. "I beg your pardon. I didn't mean—"

"Aye. I know what ye've been meaning. My father and Lord Rudgwick are particular friends. They fought together in the Peninsula and at Waterloo and convalesced together in Brussels. Were ye safe at home during those troubles?"

His lips quirked in an infuriating way. "I confess, I've never been past Glasgow or Edinburgh," he said. "I didn't know the Scottish Highlands produced such beauty. And I'm told you'll inherit a Scottish barony."

The compliment was Spanish coin. His real interest was good British money. That was why he'd pursued marriage to Lady Harmonia.

"Where do ye hail from?"

"I'm heir to a baronetcy in Norfolk and spent considerable time there."

The hair on her neck rippled. Lord Jeremy had mentioned the connection to Norfolk. Banquo's boys, Fleance and Giles, had lived with their grandparents in Norfolk. They'd been at school in

Norwich. Their father had been on his way to Yarmouth when he died.

In for a penny, in for a pound. "Then ye might have known my father's cousin, Banquo."

He screwed up his face as if pondering the name, but his eyes glittered. Oh yes, he knew Banquo.

"I might have. It's an unusual name."

"He is dead this last year. My father and another cousin, Lord Menteith, are his sons' guardians. Though they're not young boys, mind ye, but almost men. Fleance will likely be Menteith someday."

"Is that so?"

"Oh yes. Father is sorting out their inheritance. With the confusion of the past year—Waterloo, ye know—it's a bit of a jumble." She forced a laugh. "Banquo left them well-provided for, and we've become close. I adore them both, but especially Fleance. I'm a year or two older, but that is nothing."

His beady eyes began to glow as he fell into the notions she was tendering. "So, all the fellows lining up tonight to offer their suit might as well stand down?"

It was hard not to laugh over him taking the lure. But she mustn't. Instinct told her they were headed somewhere unsavory because this oily fellow was up to no good.

She cocked her head the way she'd seen other young ladies do and gave him a saucy grin. "They'd best not stand down from dancing, sir. It's my ball and I expect to dance every set."

The music ended, and as he walked away, she felt an overwhelming need to bathe herself and wash away the slime.

There was no time for that though. As lines formed for a country dance, she accepted another young man's hand. From the corner of her eye, she saw Rudgwick stepping away from his partner and heading straight for Dankworth.

From his spot along the sidelines, the duke's glare burned into the two men, and she was astonished to realize she wasn't sure which man the duke hated more. The lights of the room started to tremble, and she snatched her gaze away from the old man and concentrated upon her next partner's beak of a nose and bushy brows, the turning, and the passing, and mustering a few polite words. She shut out the duke, the swimming lights, the gray clouds floating about in her inner vision and kept to the mantra: her dance partner, the turns and the passes, a few polite words.

Despite her efforts, her gaze strayed back to the conversation between Rudgwick and Dankworth. On the last promenade, she looked over and saw that both men had vanished.

When the country dance ended, she begged off from her next partner, Lord Grallon, and headed off toward the room at the back of the house set aside for the ladies' retiring room. Needing a moment to think, she prayed that no one else would be there.

All through the last dance, she'd fought the ache in her head. Oh, Hades, she'd been fighting a threatening vision—the smoking cloud around Dankworth and the burning eyes of Bridgehampton were likely all a part of Rudgwick's peril.

As she turned a corner into another passage, a hand reached out and grasped her arm.

"What—"

Rudgwick shushed her, towing her along further and through a set of French doors into Lady Fiona's conservatory.

The brazier in the small greenhouse had been lit by the gardener against a possible frost. The glass-enclosed room was otherwise unlit, but the night was not a particularly dark one. Shadowed moonlight filtered in, backlighting clouds as they floated past the bright orb.

Rudgwick pulled her into his arms, and she didn't resist.

She smelled of lilac and sweet verbena, and his body ached for her. He wanted to take her home to his bed and make love to her.

But first he wanted to shake her.

"You ought not to have danced with Dankworth," he said.

She stiffened and he locked her against him.

"Aye. Ye're probably right, Major Lord Rudgwick."

Her agreeableness surprised him.

"He somehow had the impression that you're going to marry Banquo's eldest son."

Her low chuckle roused him more. "And did the notion rattle him?"

"Is it true?"

"Ye're rattled as well, Major Lord Rudgwick." She pushed away and he loosened his hold. "If I were betrothed, I wouldn't be standing this close to someone other than the person I'm pledged to."

As his vision adjusted to the dimness of the moonlight, her face came into focus. The softness he saw there belied her implied rebuke.

"Is it true, Lucie?"

"Don't be daft. Fleance and I are friends. I've just barely forgiven the nodcock for helping his father abduct me and tie me up."

He pushed a stray curl from her cheek. "And so why did you tell Dankworth you were going to marry him?"

"I didn't. Though I may have led him along the path to thinking it. When the villain—Dankworth is a villain isn't he? —told me himself that he spent a great deal of time in Norfolk, I thought, why not poke around a bit? Ye recall that Banquo's boys grew up in Norfolk?"

"Lucie Macbeth, you clever girl. You wanted to see if Dankworth would admit to an acquaintance with Banquo."

"He puts me in mind of Banquo. Not in appearance but..."

She looked away, biting her lower lip, afraid to reveal something she'd seen with that inner sight.

"Your intuition is good. You must have a care where Dankworth is concerned."

"What did he say to you tonight?"

"He somehow managed several insults all in one breath. I won't share the details." Sooner or later, he'd have to challenge Dankworth. "I was surprised to see him tonight."

"Aye. The dastard wasn't invited."

And he'd had the gall to ask Lucie to dance without a proper introduction, and the reckless girl had said yes. "He sulked away after his dance with you."

"And after his talk with ye." She rubbed at her temple.

"What did the Sight show you about him?"

Her chin came up and she studied him a long moment, and then sighed. "Nothing tonight. Only... a cloud around him."

"I had thought to question Bridgehampton about him, but I'll wait until we return from Norfolk."

"Lady Fiona will bring some of her grooms with us. There's no need for you to come with me—"

His lips on hers stopped the scold. When she didn't slap him or shove him away, he drew her closer, leaned in and traced his tongue along the seam of her lips.

She dipped back away from him. "You mustn't... Oh."

He kissed a path over her soft cheek and along her firm jaw, down to the pulse at her neck. She let out a long sigh and melted against him, lifting her chin, and matching her lips to his.

Wanting to touch her everywhere, to kiss every part of her body, he tugged her to him and lifted his hand to begin and then remembered...

The dead, cold work of metal and wood wouldn't feel anything. Not her softness, or her warmth, or the smoothness of her skin over lithe muscles and curves. Dammit.

Switching arms, he let his fingers drift up over her waist, linger under her breasts, and stroke upwards to the hard pucker just under her bodice.

"No." She poked him, and he eased her back, resting his forehead against hers. Her tight breaths matched his. Her nose was cold against his cheek, and he felt the sweep of her eyelashes.

"It's all right," she whispered, soothing herself or him, he couldn't say. "I know why ye kissed me that night in Brussels. Ye were going into battle. Ye thought ye would die. And I was... so grateful. And when I found ye that day in the hospital.... So relieved was I that ye could talk and laugh even. And now, look at ye: ye're very much alive." She pulled away and looked up at him. "Oh, ye lost a hand, but what is that for a true warrior? Why, 'tis said there was an ancient Roman General who lost a hand and went on to fight many more battles."

He'd have no pity from Lucie Macbeth. It was one of the things he loved about her. "You've given this some thought."

Her gaze searched his, daring him to rebuke her. And he remembered: she'd seen the battlefield. She'd helped tend to her father's wounds. She'd visited most of the hospitals looking for Hyde and seen the broken bodies.

She hadn't seen his ugly stump, though he didn't think she'd do much more than blink at the sight of it. When it came down to it, he didn't think she'd balk at him stripping off the straps that held the bloody prosthesis in place.

They would get there. Yes, they would. He leaned in, and the tip of her finger pressed him back again.

"Tell me, Major Lord Rudgwick, is it true that ye rescued Lady Harmonia from Dankworth?"

What the devil was she talking about? His mind was muddled by the warm woman in his arms. And dammit, now that he finally had Lucie alone, he didn't want to think about Harmonia.

"Lady Harmonia told me her father was angling to sell her in a marriage to Dankworth until the duke intervened."

That shameful story was one he'd only told to the closest of friends, for Harmonia's sake. And for his own. It made his betrothal look noble, when he'd primarily been operating from the same motivation as Dankworth and Grey; his financial interests.

Lucie didn't know about the mortgages held by the duke. "Saving her is not the word I'd use. But it's true that Grey was negotiating his daughter's betrothal."

"To Dankworth."

"Yes."

"Lady Harmonia made her feelings toward him clear on the street yesterday. Neither it seems does she want to marry ye, or so she told me."

He shook his head. "She makes her disinterest clear."

"And can ye blame her when she sees ye making eyes at me?"

"Making eyes?" He suspected Harmonia's unhappiness with the match ran deeper than jealousy or even vanity. But, oh hell, Lucie might be right. Not that he'd admit it. "I never make eyes at ladies."

"I was grateful for your help with Stephenson's men, and I enjoy your kisses, it's true. But I know, despite what ye said on the street yesterday, I'm but a passing fancy to ye, Major Lord Rudgwick."

She declared that belief forthrightly... but he heard the question in her voice.

"No, Lucie. You're not. I meant what I said about marrying you. And I think, if you are honest, I'm not a passing fancy to you either."

He held his breath waiting for the proud girl to deny that she returned his interest. It would make the challenge greater, but it wouldn't stop him.

"My home is in Scotland."

Your home is with me.

Perhaps his home could be in Scotland, at least part of the time. "I'd like to see this castle of yours. Hyde tells me there are a great number of stairs in it."

"Ach, I see. Besides setting Hyde to investigate Dankworth, ye've been questioning him about me. Are ye bribing him to bring ye gossip?"

"Does ale and kidney pie at the Star and Garter count as a bribe?"

Her lips quivered with the threat of a smile. "For Hyde? From a braw, brave man like yourself, it might be enough. I shall have to have another talk with him."

Braw and brave. He wasn't a slave to his vanity, but the words made his heart dance, and she saw it. When he leaned in, she pushed him away again, blinking away the shininess in her eyes.

"What am I to do? Ye're not taking me seriously. I would that ye'd not be so casual about my warning."

Lucie, dear Lucie. He couldn't have her worrying about him. "I *am* taking it seriously. I helped fish your mother out of the river, remember?" On that hellish March night, when Banquo had pushed Greer Macbeth into the Thames.

In the dim light, he could see her color rising, and her anger with it. *Thank God.*

He'd seen her valiant, helping to rescue her mother, and later, in the sloop where he and Macbeth had freed her and her mother from Banquo, he'd seen her ordering people about. Since then, the sights of the Waterloo battlefield, her own close call with death, the visions plaguing her, all those experiences had muted her spirits. He longed to lift away those troubles, to free her to be that valiant girl brimming with life again, and sometimes righteous anger, her soul glowing like a bright light. She'd be a fierce countess and, someday, duchess, a partner he could rely on. She was already on her way to being a strong, sensible woman. Her father knew that. It was why he'd entrusted her with the business.

She lifted an eyebrow. "Father wrote to me to say that this matter would give me a chance to see what a tiresome thing it is when someone muddled the legal business."

The blasted girl had read his mind. Proof that they were well-suited.

A rustling noise made them both turn to the open French doors. He stepped back.

"What is this place?" a woman asked with a giggle.

Shaking the leaves of a large fern as they passed, Harmonia and Jeremy appeared, Jeremy clasping the hand tucked over his arm, their shoulders brushing in a cozy *tête-à-tête*.

"The conservatory," Jeremy said. "And, ah, here they are. You've been missed, Miss Macbeth, Rudgwick."

"They'll be starting the supper dance soon," Harmonia said.

While Harmonia went straight to Lucie and linked arms, Rudgwick exchanged a long look with Jeremy. The younger man's disapproving shake of the head made him chuckle.

They let the ladies precede them and Jeremy whispered. "You were seen. The duke is livid."

Livid was the duke's perpetual state.

"And Harmonia?"

"Gleeful."

Rudgwick's heart soared. She'd have an excuse to throw him over.

He would come out of the scandal unscathed— an earl, a duke's presumptive heir, a hero of Waterloo. Harmonia, high-born, beautiful, and very rich, would fare well also. The one who might suffer society's wrath was Lucie, at least until he made an honest woman of her.

Not that she'd done anything truly scandalous, nothing more than allowing a kiss—two kisses. Three, if one included Brussels.

No, there'd been nothing truly scandalous. Not yet.

***

The Duke of Bridgehampton would never leave.

So it seemed to Lucie, for they'd said their farewells and closed the door on all the other guests.

Now, the first hint of dawn lightened the fog-blanketed sky, and the market carts were already clacking along the avenue toward town. Yet there sat the duke, erect and charged with energy like her own self when she was fair on her way to a sulk.

She chuckled and then stifled a yawn. Did dukes have girlish sulks? This one looked like he'd been doing so all his life. And when he snapped his fingers, everyone jumped. Even Rudgwick.

No... that wasn't fair. Rudgwick had responsibilities. He was an earl and expected to marry properly. He wasn't being a toady, just practical in his marriage plans. Which plans he was making a muck of by openly chasing another woman.

"I am not ready to depart yet." The duke's reply to something Lady Rudgwick said sounded very cross indeed. The other members of his party, along with Lord Jeremy who, come to think of it, was also lingering, looked as weary as she herself felt.

Lady Rudgwick exchanged a look with Lady Fiona, who ushered the duke, his granddaughter, the Rudgwicks, and Lord Jeremy to the morning room.

Lucie fell in line behind them and paused before closing the door. "Shall I send someone to rouse Cook to prepare breakfast?"

Lady Fiona's eyes showed neither humor, nor concern. "I've ordered coffee. But perhaps... Duke, shall we hold this discussion around the breakfast table?"

"No." He dropped into a winged chair near the cold hearth, and sat silently while the footman, Paul, made a fire. He didn't deign to look at Paul, or anyone else for that matter, until the door closed on the servant.

Then he turned his burning gaze in a circuit: Harmonia, to Bolton, to Rudgwick, and then finally, herself.

Her blood spiked, all her weariness departing. This hateful old man thought to come to her ball, to her kinswoman's home and pick an ill-mannered fight? The man was a bully, and a body must stand up to bullies.

"Ye're unhappy, duke," Lucie said. "Might as well have it out, then. Tell us what ails ye."

His skin paled to a glacial hue and the heated gaze turned a frigid blue. She fought a rebellious smile. Hot and now cold. He thought to freeze her like an insect caught in a frozen pond. He'd go to whichever approach worked, she supposed.

She felt movement next to her—Rudgwick perhaps moving to stand with her—and heard the rustling of gowns from where Lady Harmonia squirmed next to Lady Rudgwick, yet she wouldn't look away from the old man's challenge. She didn't fear him. What would be the point of it?

"She's right, duke." Rudgwick's warm baritone cheered her. He was, indeed standing with her. "Our hostess has been gracious, but I fear we are pushing the boundaries of courtesy and overstaying our welcome."

She glanced at him. Rudgwick had just called the duke rude, the scold so politely stated it put her in awe.

The old man harrumphed, and his gaze shifted away from her. "You were seen, Rudgwick. You, with this..." He flung out a hand at her.

This vulgar Scottish strumpet. Lucie pressed her lips on another defiant smile and looked at Lady Harmonia. The girl's eyes had widened, and her lips trembled.

She couldn't help being Scottish, and vulgar; well, all women who spoke their minds were deemed the latter. But perhaps she was also fair on her way to being a strumpet. She couldn't deny what she felt for Rudgwick. Sooner or later the attraction would snare her, which was why she'd as soon be leaving for Norfolk without him.

'Twas outside of enough. No matter what Rudgwick said, she...they...were hurting this young girl. "Lady Harmonia," she said, keeping her tone as matter of fact as possible, "Major Lord Rudgwick is your betrothed. He's a soldier as well as a lord, and a man of honor, and he knows his duty." *As I know mine.* "Mayhap men like that are rare in your noble circles, but Rudgwick is one of them. Nothing happened between us, nothing of any import." She swallowed the lie, telling herself it wasn't entirely a fabrication. They'd done no more than kiss. "Ye'll see the back of me very soon when I return home to Scotland."

"You're not returning to Scotland just yet," the duke said. "You were seen shamefully kissing a man with dark hair in the conservatory. It will be whispered that it was Rudgwick. But I'll not have a scandal that will taint my granddaughter. We will say that it wasn't Rudgwick, it was Bolton. You," he pointed at Lord Jeremy, and then turned his finger on Lucie, "and you. You two will marry."

Lady Harmonia gasped.

CHAPTER FOURTEEN

Vanished

"Wait just a moment, Bridgehampton," Lord Jeremy said.

Heart clanging with shock, she managed a breath and forced a defiant scoff. "I'm to marry Lord Jeremy?" *Are you daft?* The question marched to the tip of her tongue, and she held it back. Her gaze focused and her breath quickened as the rest of the room rippled and dimmed. The duke's lips had thinned to a pale grey, and white gleamed from his knuckles as he strangled the chair arms.

'Twas more than anger gripping him. 'Twas something like fear. A man trapped in a net he couldn't fight his way out of. 'Twas a terrible feeling, one she'd had a taste of.

A mist formed around the old man and the room started to shimmer.

"Seen by whom?" Rudgwick growled near her right ear. The anger she heard made her turn.

She'd seen a glimpse of this Rudgwick in the solicitor's rooms, but the duke was an altogether different sort of opponent. Rudgwick glared at

Bridgehampton, determined and valiant, a man who could impose his will by a word or by the sword if need be. Would he use that sword on the old man tonight?

***

Rudgwick faced the full force of the duke's anger. Oh, he'd experienced it before when the man tried to prevent him from rejoining his unit in Brussels. But he'd had enough of Bridgehampton's managing. It was time to set Harmonia free to choose her own husband. And Lucie...

He'd seen the haze coming over her and knew he had to intervene. He'd no longer allow the duke to hurt a young girl under his protection and the woman he loved.

With his glare locked on the duke's, he silently dared him to say who'd seen him kissing Lucie. No one, he'd guess, unless someone had been lurking outside. And who would that be? A servant? A servant wouldn't know to run to the duke.

Another guest? Possibly, but no one in that sedate crowd had been the sort to run off to the garden and peer into windows.

Except for Dankworth. He'd left after speaking with Rudgwick. Had he returned to talk to the duke? Or had he sent a note?

Lady Harmonia stood. "Yes, Grandfather. Who claims to have seen kissing?" Her voice shook with nervous emotion. "Lord Jeremy and I were there. We saw only a conversation. Like Miss Macbeth said, nothing happened."

"I heard no gossip," Mother said.

The duke's cold gaze swept over both ladies.

Color flooded Harmonia's usually serene cheeks. "You can't possibly think you can make Lord Jeremy—"

"Sit down, girl, and hold your tongue."

Harmonia spluttered, her cheeks flaming higher, her eyes bulging.

"Really, Bridgehampton," Mother said.

"You may be silent also, Sarah."

Mother gasped.

"Duke," Rudgwick said. "You do not command my mother."

Bridgehampton ignored him and went on, the dolt. "This is what comes from associating with the likes of..." he flapped a hand at Lucie.

Lucie stiffened next to him. Harmonia gave a little cry and ran from the room, and Mother rushed after her. Shaking her head, Lady Fiona followed them.

Eyes blazing, Jeremy headed for the door.

"Wait, Lord Jeremy," Lucie said. Rudgwick stood close enough to feel the tension radiating from her and stoking his own anger. How she managed the cool tone, he didn't know. "Let us turn from all this," she flapped *her* hand at the duke, "*girlish, inflamed sensibility.*"

He tore his gaze from the duke's sudden blush and looked at her. A cool mask had settled over her, a quiet hauteur, as dignified as the duchess she would someday be if he could convince her to marry him. If he could survive whatever threat she was seeing.

If *she* could survive the duke's ferocious glare.

"We shall discuss this calmly," she said.

A calm discussion. Ha! The duke wanted to kill her. He wanted to kill the duke. And Jeremy wanted nothing more than to go after Harmonia. He almost laughed. "Mother will see to Harmonia,

Jeremy," he said channeling some of Lucie's dignity.

He offered Lucie the seat Harmonia had abandoned then took the sofa, Jeremy sitting down next to him.

Lucie drew herself up. She tilted her head, studying Jeremy. "This is my first offer of marriage from a noble gentleman."

He bit the inside of his cheek to keep from smiling and watched as Jeremy shifted on the seat. "Miss Macbeth, I haven't—"

"I know, Lord Jeremy. Ye haven't offered. But the demand has been made in your behalf. 'Tis the English way, is it?"

Lady Fiona entered then, and Rudgwick stood and brought over a chair for her.

"Your mother will be right along," Lady Fiona said. "We've settled Lady Harmonia in your bedchamber, Lucie. Now what have I missed?"

"We're discussing the duke's proposal of marriage," Lucie said, her eyes glinting wickedly. "Since my father is not present, I must presume to make the necessary inquiries, Lord Jeremy. Can ye afford a wife and children on your income alone?"

The duke spluttered. "You unnatural girl."

She raised an eyebrow, and Rudgwick suppressed another grin.

"If Lucie didn't ask, I certainly would," Lady Fiona said. "Not just about your income, young man, but your character as well. Bridgehampton, you won't deny me this." She turned her gaze on Jeremy. "Can you afford to marry, young man?"

"I hadn't thought to...at present, I..."

Mother breezed in, glared at the duke, and squeezed between Rudgwick and Jeremy on the sofa, and the farce continued.

Lady Fiona's eyes twinkled. "We're discussing settlements, Lady Rudgwick. Since you've issued the proposal, your grace, were you planning to facilitate the match with financial assistance?"

"*No*," he thundered, quite out of character. Bridgehampton preferred cold menacing, not the explosive sort. Perhaps he was overwrought by Lucie's and Lady Fiona's pragmatism. "Northam may find you a post or give you an income, or you may go and live in your dilapidated cottage or her crumbling castle." The hand flew again at Lucie. "And be glad for her pitiful dowry, for you shan't have Harmonia's."

Jeremy stood. "I have not pursued Harmonia. There have been no improprieties between us."

Not yet.

But Bridgehampton had seen what anyone else with eyes could see, that the friendship between Jeremy and Harmonia might easily become something more. Jeremy was a strapping, handsome son and brother of a duke, with two strong legs and both hands. He was a good man, as well, and Harmonia was a diamond of the first water.

"Do sit ye down, Lord Jeremy," Lucie said. "I acquit ye of any dishonor toward Major Lord Rudgwick's fiancée."

"Yes, do sit, dear boy," Lady Fiona said. "And do not worry, whoever weds our dear Lucie will have found himself a great heiress, as I intend to leave her almost all of my worldly goods." She laughed at Lucie's look of shock. "Yes, darling girl, it's true. And I know that you have too much backbone and good sense to let yourself be bullied into a marriage, or at least to enter matrimony without writing a proper settlement agreement."

Lucie gazed at the older lady, eyes shining, throat moving as she swallowed. A drop of moisture spilled out and traced a path through the freckles on her cheek, washing away the impudence.

Lucie crying. He never thought he'd see it.

"Ye're so very good to me, my lady," she said.

"And you to me. Mind you, I hope to be in this world long enough to hold a bairn or two of yours, if you find a man worthy of such a prize as yourself."

Lucie blinked, and her gaze met his. His heart lifted at what he saw there. Lucie wanted him.

Just as quickly, she sent Jeremy an assessing look, and then turned a bland stare on the duke.

"I believe I must decline your offer of marriage, duke. Not that ye had the standing to make it. If there are rumors, then Rudgwick and I will simply deny them, and ye may do so, as well. No one will contest the word of a duke. As for Rudgwick, a hero of Waterloo will weather a scandal if there is one. Nor will Lady Harmonia be cut by the *ton*, not with her dowry. Any scandal will fall on me, and it's not likely to follow me to Calder."

Well done, Lucie.

"And you've yet to tell us the name of your witness," Rudgwick said. "Was it, perchance, Lionel Dankworth?"

That arrow struck its mark. The duke pounded the arms of his chair. "Had I known you'd invited him, I wouldn't have allowed Harmonia to attend."

Lady Fiona tilted her head, studying him. "Is he speaking of the stranger you danced with, Lucie? Was that his name? He's not known to me, nor did I invite him. When I saw him dancing with you, I thought he might be an acquaintance of one of the other guests. Is there something we should know about him, duke?"

The coffee arrived and the duke rose, ignoring the question. "Have a servant fetch my granddaughter. We are leaving."

"Oh, do sit down," Mother said. "Lady Harmonia is resting, and Lady Fiona has gone to the trouble of arranging coffee for us, and I intend to drink some. And if you will not wait, then you may depart without us. I shall beg Lady Fiona's footman to summon a hack for us."

"No, no," Lady Fiona said, "I won't send you off in a hackney. You must take my carriage. Or, in fact, I can arrange guest rooms for you and Lady Harmonia. You and Lord Jeremy as well, Rudgwick."

She looked his way and winked, and he swallowed another laugh that he knew would likely make Bridgehampton explode.

"I would dearly like that cup of coffee first, my lady," Rudgwick said.

***

As the others gathered around the coffee, Lucie slipped out into the hallway. She caught Paul leaning against the wall with his eyes closed, tiptoed quietly past, and moved up the stairs to her bedchamber.

Perhaps she was going mad. Rudgwick's kisses; Lady Fiona's news about making Lucie her heir; the notion of Lady Fiona holding a bairn—or two!—of hers... It was all too much.

She'd find a way to help Lady Harmonia, to free her of Rudgwick. So she could have him for herself.

And then what? He might run off and leave her as Father had Mother.

She tapped on the door of her bedchamber, and when there was no answer, entered.

Lady Harmonia wasn't there. But the lass's ball gown lay tossed on the floor, along with her petticoat and stays, and her dancing slippers. The clothes press stood open, garments strewn about. And a note lay atop the writing table under a pile of coins.

Lucie pushed aside the money and picked up the missive. "I've borrowed your trousers and some coins. I shall pay you back fully when I am able. Please don't tell until I've had time to get away."

She dropped onto the chair, then stood, and began contorting her body to grasp the blasted fastenings on her gown. Her only pair of trousers was missing. Not that she could begrudge Lady Harmonia the use of them. The poor lass had never had the freedom of wearing them before. Harmonia had probably taken her rough boots as well, and... ah, no, she'd left the *sgian dubhs*, her daggers. One of those treasured blades she'd carried the year before, the other she'd acquired in Edinburgh during her recuperation. Mayhap... mayhap she must bring them along tonight. She prayed she wouldn't need to use them.

More than one pair of half-boots sat in the cupboard, thanks to Lady Fiona's generosity. They would do, along with an old gown. She cast off her ballgown, her headpiece, and her jewels, and donned her plainest frock, a modest old thing that hid her bosom quite well and her old half-boots, and found a shawl and a generous mantle.

Then she shoved a sheathed dagger into each of her boots and made her way down the servants' stairs to the quiet conservatory at the back of the house where all the trouble had started. Most of the servants had retired, having worked like the devil the day before and late into the night. Not even the ever-present Hyde was around.

Saddling a horse was out of the question, and it was likely that Harmonia was traveling on foot, being not much of a rider. And no hack would pick her up dressed in Lucie's trousers and coats, which, sadly had seen a great deal of hard duty.

Lucie was down the drive and onto the road before anyone could notice her. She pulled the hood of her cloak over her hair and walked into the morning mist heading toward Cheyne Walk.

That was Lady Harmonia's most likely objective, to go to the home of her mother's old governess. Where else would the girl seek help? Though the woman was likely to send her back to the duke, if only to protect herself and her family from retribution, because there was something quite ruthless about the old man.

Lady Harmonia ought to have stayed with Lady Fiona. They would have hidden her somewhere in the house—the attic perhaps. Or Lady Harmonia might have traveled with Lucie to Norfolk and then on to Scotland. They might have found a way. Rudgwick would have helped them, and likely Lord Jeremy as well. He and Lady Harmonia could be married in Scotland.

With each wagon lumbering by, she moved to the verge, fighting unsettling memories. Rattling wheels triggered the dark recollections of the previous year. She ought to have put one of the blades into her pocket.

As the smell of the river grew stronger, and the fog lifted in patches, she spotted a boy ahead of her. The trousers had been rolled up at the bottom, and the coats stretched tight over the shoulders. She lifted her skirts and ran to catch up.

Frightened eyes turned on her.

"Shhh, boy." Lucie linked arms with Lady Harmonia. "I'll walk with ye. Is it far now?"

The girl stalled, freezing in place. "I don't... I don't remember."

Ach. Lady Harmonia's nerve was failing her. She shoved down a spark of irritation. 'Twas to be expected, Lucie supposed, from one more surely locked away in a tower then she herself was in her old castle. She remembered how timid her mother had been for so many years whilst living with their cousins. It had taken months—nay years—for her mother to shake out of her meekness.

Not that this proud lass was meek. Under the haughty air was a chit as headstrong as herself.

The wind shifted, bringing a stronger odor of the river and the night waste that fed the market gardens, and unease set her nerves to firing.

"Come along." Their arms locked, Lucie stepped out, dragging the girl with her. "There'll be tradesmen and servants about. We'll ask the first person we come across."

"There's no need to drag me."

Lady Harmonia tried pulling away, but Lucie clamped down harder. The chit's temper was flaring. Not a bad thing; if she was gearing herself up to fight, the fear wouldn't freeze her as it was threatening to do to Lucie.

Aye, the anger would help Lucie through her own fear as well. "I'm tryin'..." She cleared her throat of the fog seeping into her chest. "I'm tryin' to help ye, lass."

The girl's resistance eased, but her silence simmered with discontent. Outside that discontent, the world had quietened. The sky had lightened; if servants *were* about, the fog shrouded them. Even the market carts had moved on. Lucie craned her neck around both ways, searching, and the hood of her cloak slipped back. The chill air slicked her cheeks and curled around her neck.

She shoved down a clashing of nerves. She ought to have roused Hyde. Or a groom. She ought to have risked the duke chasing after the girl. She ought to have told someone.

Hoofbeats crept into her awareness, muffled by the fog and damp. She quickened her pace until they were running, Harmonia gasping to keep up, the galloping growing louder and faster.

Harmonia's blue eyes widened. Her arm slipped away, and she grasped Lucie's hand, gripping tightly as a dark cloud invaded the fog. A black-clad figure emerged and snaked around Harmonia's waist, and her hand was ripped from Lucie's grip.

'Twas the vision. Come to life.

Lady Harmonia's feet left the cobblestones. Her trousered legs kicked out and her arms windmilled to the sound of cloth ripping. Her cry was a breathless peep. She'd been too long a lady.

A shriek pierced this nightmare, Lucie's own battle-cry, and she launched herself into the fray. Her ungloved fingers found purchase, and then slipped, tugging hair, and scraping bristly skin. Hands came from behind her, grasping her, even while she lunged and snatched at the girl's clothing.

'Twas no good, no good at all. Lady Harmonia ripped away and disappeared into the fog to the shuffling horse, as she herself was carted off as well.

When she twisted, her shoulder jerked painfully. A fist struck her head, pain shattering through her, and the street faded to black and then cleared to a misty gray again.

"Got the red-haired one. What you want with her?"

A deep voice issued instructions that she couldn't quite grasp. And then she was flying, and her belly hit something solid, and she teetered, smelling horseflesh and leather. She tried to jerk herself down, but a hard hand planted itself on her bottom and squeezed, and lingered, and when she kicked out, another fist punched her again.

Harmonia's screams filled her ears. The lass had finally broken out of her lady-like shell.

***

Rudgwick accepted the cup of coffee and turned to offer it to Lucie, when he noticed she'd left the room.

Gone to check on Lady Harmonia? To warn her? To settle her down in her own bed and have her pretend to be sleeping when the duke demanded her departure?

It would be just like Lucie to attempt such a stunt. But really, Lady Fiona's offer of shelter wasn't such a wild idea, at least not for Lady Harmonia, given that the ladies were tired, and this was Chelsea where the early morning roads might be clogged with market wagons.

For his part, it wasn't a long journey to Knightsbridge. Oh no, he'd stay for other reasons. Hopefully in a guest chamber near Lucie's.

He shook off the thought, looked back at the sullen gathering, and worked his way through two more cups of coffee. The duke stewed in his anger, fortunately keeping mum. Jeremy frowned into his cup, a man trapped by civility and the rules of hospitality. A man who'd just dodged one of Bridgehampton's schemes. Mother had ceased her usual chattering and was engaged in a desultory conversation with Lady Fiona, reviewing the evening. Both ladies were deciding that it was time for a full breakfast.

Lady Fiona pulled the bell and the blond-haired footman who'd kindled the fire appeared, his eyes heavy from fatigue. He took his instructions and left.

A little while later, Hyde appeared in the doorway. His gaze lit on Rudgwick. He dipped his head and beckoned. Setting aside the cup, Rudgwick hurried out, and heard skirts rustling behind him.

"What is it, Hyde?" Lady Fiona asked.

"Begging your pardon, milord, milady. Happened to talk to one of the grooms. He was awaiting orders for the carriage, expecting the duke would want to leave. Saw a figure on the drive. Thought it was one of the extra girls called in for the party. Didn't think nothing of it. But then he mentioned he'd seen a boy leave a while earlier. And then Paul said... well, might have told the cook that the duke was riled earlier, and the young lady ran out in a huff, and then he just noticed that both Lucie and her young ladyship weren't in the morning room, and..."

Rudgwick turned on Lady Fiona. "Which bedchamber is Lucie's?"

"Take him, Hyde. It's the same room Macbeth and Greer shared last year."

CHAPTER FIFTEEN

In Pursuit

They hurried up the stairs and down the corridor. Hyde stepped aside, and Rudgwick didn't bother to knock.

The air in the room held hints of the perfume Lucie had been wearing, but she wasn't here. Nor was Harmonia. Two gowns had been tossed about. One was the gold-trimmed ivory that had revealed so much of Lucie's bosom. The other... he had no recollection of Harmonia's gown, but this must be hers.

"Are horses missing?" he asked.

Hyde shook his head. "None were taken. Too many grooms about for that."

"Have the stable saddle ours."

"Aye, sir." Hyde hurried to the door.

"Three of them," he called. "We'll meet you outside."

Then he went to fetch Jeremy.

***

"Scarpered," Jeremy said, adding a coarse oath as he hurried out with Rudgwick. "On foot. To where?"

"I don't know."

Hyde had three horses waiting. One of them was Athena, equipped with a man's saddle. She swished her tail and dipped her head to him.

"Dammit," Jeremy said, "this will be Lucie Macbeth's doing."

"Don't think so, milord." Hyde said tightly. "They didn't leave together. Lessin' they planned to set off one after the other, but I know Miss Lucie wouldn't send a girl off on her own in Chelsea."

Hyde might sometimes want to thrash his red-haired charge, but he was loyal.

"Don't be an ass, Jeremy. Likely she noticed Harmonia missing and went after her on her own."

"Without seeking our help?" Jeremy cursed again. "Reckless chit."

Lucie didn't trust him to help. Or... in fairness, maybe she didn't want to alert the duke. He, as well, would have found a way to put the blame on Lucie.

"Spirited chit," Rudgwick said. He'd save the scold to deliver in person.

Hyde sent him an appreciative look as they all mounted and moved down the drive. When they reached the road, he pulled up and looked both ways.

Blast it. Where the devil should they search?

"Groom didn't see which way they turned," Hyde said. "Might've hopped on a market cart and gone toward town."

It made as much sense as anything else. Yet... "Did they have money? The Rose and Crown is a coaching inn." He remembered Lucie and Greer's abduction the previous year. "Or there are boats for hire at Cheyne Walk."

The ladies could get to the other side of the river and travel to the coast and from there go on to France where Lucie's cousin and his new wife would shelter them. It was far-fetched but nothing was an impossibility, especially if Harmonia was trying to escape from her grandfather's tight control. And Lucie was just brave enough to help her.

"Cheyne Walk," Jeremy said. "Harmonia mentioned an acquaintance near Cheyne Walk. Someone her mother knew." He spurred his horse.

"Hyde, ride to the inn and inquire there. If they haven't been seen, meet us at the wherries."

He turned Athena towards the river and caught up with Jeremy. They picked their way through the fog, listening. Chelsea wasn't silent. Tradesmen were up and about, moving carts around, wheels clacking, and they dodged the occasional laborer, heading off to his workday, or kitchen boys carrying crates of produce.

No one would admit having seen a boy and a red-haired girl, and they didn't stop long enough to question them more. They rode on, the smell of the river growing stronger.

Call it the Sight, but Rudgwick's neck prickled with the same feeling he'd got before battle. And then a woman's screams split the morning air.

"There," he said pointing, and they turned their horses toward the noise.

"Which way?" Rudgwick said.

They'd spent precious minutes scouring the streets, speaking to carters and laborers, finally finding a kitchen boy who said one of the maids in the house had seen two horses fly by, one carrying a screaming lad and the other a lady.

The lad had left the house first. That wouldn't be Lucie; she'd have no reason to flee. Which meant that Harmonia had donned Lucie's trousers.

They rode in widening circles, searching before turning their horses toward the Rose and Crown. Hyde met them halfway, reporting that Dankworth had hired a carriage and horses the night before, claiming to have his own coachman.

"Paid in good coin," Hyde said. "And if he's pockets to let, where's the blunt coming from?"

"Borrowed in advance of a dowry." Jeremy clipped out the words. "He's headed for the Great North Road. He's forcing a marriage."

"Ostler said he's taken the rig for a week," Hyde said. "That won't get him to Scotland and back."

Rudgwick's heart thudded. "He could go to Norfolk and back in that time."

"To the bank." Jeremy let out a breath.

"The banker's holding something. If not money, then something worth money to someone." Or something that might force a marriage with Lady Harmonia if the scandal would not already do so.

The duke had to be told, and the others needed better mounts than those Lady Fiona could provide. "Jeremy, ride to Knightsbridge and have my groom ready fresh horses. Also have someone fetch my boots and my pistols down to the mews. Hyde and I will join you there shortly."

"The ladies—"

"Will be in a lumbering carriage." He hoped. The fog was still in. The roads near London would be crowded with carts. "Let's make haste and catch up with them properly armed."

He turned his mount toward Lady Fiona's, and Hyde fell into place without argument.

While Hyde went off to gather weapons and rouse grooms, Rudgwick found the duke and the ladies in the breakfast room. They'd been gone long enough for hot trays to line the side table. A fresh pot of coffee filled the room with its fragrance as the footman poured cups.

The duke stood up from his untouched plate, eyes burning in a face as white as the table linens. What flashed on his face looked almost like guilt.

What the devil was the old man up to? That business of Lucie marrying Jeremy had been beyond the pale. And now this... Had he had a hand in this? There was no way he'd have allowed Dankworth to take Harmonia. But Lucie...

Damn the man. He was as big a villain as Dankworth.

"Harmonia and Lucie have been taken."

Mother gasped. Lady Fiona uttered a small cry. The duke pressed his hands to the tabletop looking ready to topple.

"It appears, duke, that Lady Harmonia left this house of her own accord, and upon finding her missing, Lucie went after her. We heard screams near Cheyne Walk, and a witness saw two people being carried away on horseback. Dankworth took a carriage at the Rose and Crown last night and has his own man driving it. We've searched but must assume he's already put Harmonia in the carriage and set out."

"And Lucie?" Lady Fiona asked.

"I don't know. But Jeremy and I are going after them. Lady Fiona, I need as many of your men as you can spare."

"Of course." Lady Fiona hurried out of the room, tugging the footman along with her.

"Harmonia taken." The duke straightened.

"He's been after her dowry, after all," Rudgwick said.

"It's your fault, Rudgwick. Your n-negligence."

He fixed the older man with a hard glare. "*Is* it mine?"

Mother cast a look of concern at the duke. "Laying blame won't get them back sooner. Go, Rudgwick. Find them. Bring them home."

As he turned on his heel, he heard Mother's concerned voice and Bridgehampton's answering bellow. "Let go, Sarah. Think you a man with one hand is a match for Dankworth? Must go. My men will reach Gretna before them."

Bridgehampton had taken the bait. The last thing he wanted was for the old dastard to get his hands on Lucie. If he was right, Dankworth would keep both ladies in his clutches, at least until he'd got what he wanted in Norfolk. After that, Lucie would be of no use to him.

He caught up with Lady Fiona and begged paper and pen, and a messenger to carry a note. Hand shaking, he paused over the paper, took in a breath, and dashed out a quick message. There was no telling how soon Sir Thomas would see it or what he would do with it.

By the time he, Hyde, and Lady Fiona's men reached his own stable, dawn had broken, though the mist still layered the streets. His valet was there with his riding attire and boots, and he hurriedly changed and mounted.

***

A hammer pounded inside Lucie's head, and she heard a moan. The muffled sound came on her exhale after a particularly hard whack against something solid. She took in a breath and caught it sharply. The smell was like death, a smell she remembered from Waterloo.

"*Ayg ub.*"

The quiet plea—it was a plea, that much she knew from the tone, though she couldn't understand the words—came from near her nose. She became aware of a hard object—a rock?—under her jaw. She forced one heavy eyelid open a slit.

Panic spiked in her, and a shiver went through her, not just from the cold. She'd had a cloak earlier, hadn't she? That had vanished. Her seat—for she was seated—rattled, and thin streams of gray light lined the sides of the window curtains, and... she shifted. Her feet moved only as one. Her hands were pulled tautly behind her back. And they were tied.

She wriggled around until she was sitting mostly erect and managed to lift the other eyelid.

Panic flared again, turning her blood to ice. She was confined, in a coach, one moving at high speed. She turned her head.

They were in a coach. Lady Harmonia was seated next to her, equally bound, her wide eyes flashing fear. She squirmed and babbled something against a white linen gag while the coach dipped and rocked, and the angry hammer in Lucie's head struck again.

A curse escaped her. Muffled. Because of course, she was gagged as well, and it seemed that they might have robbed a coffin for the handkerchief stopping her speech.

Merciful heavens.

She'd blacked out again. The physician in Edinburgh told her to beware other head injuries. She blinked and the light increased—she hadn't been out long. The sun was coming up. And the injury to her head was the least of her worries. This sorry excuse for a coach wasn't the property of a nobleman. It was hired and, thank heavens, empty except for the two of them.

"*Ayn wer*," Lady Harmonia said.

"*Aa?*" *What?*

Oh God. They had to do better than this.

"*Aynwer.*" Lady Harmonia dipped her head toward the coach door.

Lucie heard the clapping of hooves. A rider accompanied them. *Aynwer... aynwer...* She squinted, trying to see through the slits in the flapping curtain, while her mind tried to fill in the missing consonants. *Aynwer...* She glimpsed a fine boot, a gentleman's boot. *Aynwer... aynwer...*

Dankworth.

Good God. He'd kidnapped Harmonia and taken her as well.

Anger flared in her belly and spread to her hands and her stiff toes and... she wriggled one foot and then the other. Both blades were still there.

Scooting around on the seat, she turned her back to Harmonia, flapping her hands.

"*Aa?*" Harmonia asked. Then her eyes widened, and she turned toward the door.

Lucie's fingers found the girl's and worked their way up her hands to the ropes tying her.

As she searched for the rope ends, they pulled to a stop. The carriage jerked, and horses stomped, and the door jostled. She quickly put her back to the squab and let her head flop onto Lady Harmonia's shoulder again.

The door creaked. Lucie opened her eyes a slit. "Still out, Miss Macbeth?"

Lady Harmonia squawked through her gag. Lucie let her eyes flutter and emitted a groan.

It *was* Dankworth. Another man, roughly dressed in dusty coats, looked over his shoulder.

"Should I fetch them something to eat?" the man asked. "Be a long way to Scotland."

"We'll stop on the way anon, but not yet. Watch them."

Beady eyes peered in at them.

"Here now, Jem, shut that door."

Lucie recognized the third voice as that of the man who had taken her.

"Two prime ladies. He can't marry both of them."

"Not ours to worry about. We're paid well enough."

"Which one of you does he favor?" Jem asked in a wheedling tone. "Reckon I'll take care of t'other." With a laugh, he shut the carriage door.

Lucie had seen naught but a timber wall over stucco and a mullioned window. No one in the inn could have spotted the two bound women inside. As the carriage pulled out, she angled her body and went back to work on the cords binding Lady Harmonia.

No one would know they were taken, or where to begin looking. Not Rudgwick, not Lord Jeremy, not Hyde, not the duke. They would have to save themselves. Once they were loose, they could attempt an escape at the next inn stop.

Finally. Lucie shook loose the ropes binding her wrists and pulled one hand free. Her arms and shoulders burned; she shook until the blood chased away numbness and then ripped the gag from her mouth.

"Let me get the last binding off of you," Lady Harmonia said.

"Shhh," The carriage was slowing, and no wonder; it was full dark. Surely, they couldn't go on over rough country roads, or at least not at the breakneck pace of the earlier hours.

With her free hand, she fetched a blade from her boot and freed their feet.

They'd been working at the ropes for hours, it seemed, feigning confinement at every stop, and counting their blessings that Dankworth had remained on his horse. She eased the curtain aside. The narrowness of the road meant he was either in front or behind. Either way, if it was dark enough, if the carriage slowed enough, he might not notice his captives slip away.

Lucie bent her head close to Lady Harmonia's and whispered instructions.

The rumble of men's voices outside interrupted them. Lucie lifted the curtain again. The carriage shook and jerked sideways, wobbling, and then righting itself. A pistol cracked, and a body flew over the side past the coach door.

Her heart lurched, adrenalin rushing. Rescuers or highwaymen?

"Come." She pushed at the door. It flew open, and before she could move, she'd toppled into the arms of a man.

"Don't think to shoot," he shouted. He yanked her close, her backside to him, his hand around her throat. The voice and smell assaulted her. This was the brute who'd bashed her in Chelsea.

"Let her go."

Her heart leapt. *Rudgwick was here.*

Oaths and fists crunching signaled a melee she couldn't see. Behind her, the carriage swayed. "Let her go," Lady Harmonia said. Lucie's captor jerked her around, swore and raised his free hand. The dim light of the carriage lamp reflected off metal, aimed at Lady Harmonia.

Lucie's own haziness cleared, and she remembered her blade hidden in her skirts. She slashed, the brute roared and fired, just as Lord Jeremy darted out of the darkness and knocked Lady Harmonia aside. Gunpowder filled the night air and choked her. She slashed again and twisted away, collapsing into a bush. Another shot blasted the night. The man grabbed at his stomach and fell.

Rudgwick staggered from the darkness and knelt by her, his breath coming in tight gasps.

"Lucie." Still gripping a smoking pistol, he wrapped his arm around her.

She put a hand to the muddy road and steadied herself—and him. "Ye're hurt."

"'S no-nothing."

She got to her knees and pulled him close, gulping air.

"Dankworth's breathin', milord. Tied 'em up." The whispered words came from Hyde. Other men shuffled around them in the dark. The brute who'd held her was being pulled to the verge.

"Let us help you." Lady Harmonia reached for her, and Lord Jeremy helped Rudgwick up. The coach rolled to the side of the road, door flapping, and stopped.

"We're cutting the team loose." Jeremy took the pistol from Rudgwick's hand, tested the heat of it, and shoved it into his coat pocket. "It will buy us time. Not many will be traveling on Sunday but there'll be coaches along tomorrow. Someone will stop and investigate, but we'll be —he glanced back at the brute lying there—at our destination by then."

Rudgwick staggered. Lucie wiped her blade on her skirt and stowed it into her boot, then slid under his arm.

And then saw the problem. His hand—his false hand—dangled. The stump must have been bashed around in the fight. The old injury pained him.

"I have ye, Major Lord Rudgwick. Did he stab ye?"

"No."

"Shoot ye?"

"No."

"Coshed your thick head?"

He managed a pained laugh.

"Can you ride?" Lord Jeremy asked.

She felt Rudgwick's pride stirring, his spine firming as he rallied his valiant self, and tears threatened to spill.

How she loved him. What were they to do?

"Of course, I can ride. Are you well, Lucie? How is your head?"

"Still as hard as yours," she said.

"Harmonia?" he asked.

"I'm fine."

Lord Jeremy set his arm about the girl. "Are you sure?"

"Yes."

"And the rest of the men?" Rudgwick asked. "Any injuries?"

Rudgwick had mustered men to come after her and Lady Harmonia. They'd somehow guessed the route. She would have to ask him about it later.

Hyde appeared and reported no wounds but a few scrapes for their men.

"The coachman?" Rudgwick asked.

"Dead," Hyde said. "The shot winged him, but he cracked his neck fallin'. That other man is gut-shot. Dankworth's knocked out or pretending. Boys are tying him up."

"Take his clothing and boots," Rudgwick said. "His purse, as well."

Hyde chuckled.

"The same for the gut-shot one. Make sure we leave them both tied securely."

Lady Harmonia gasped.

Rudgwick's voice had hardened along with the rest of him. Whatever pain he was still feeling, it was bolstering his resolve. "We'll show them as much mercy as they did you two ladies. Finish up and let's mount."

She wondered if Rudgwick had used his false hand as a club and thought better of asking, at least for now.

Lord Jeremy led Lady Harmonia off and Rudgwick stepped out. She heard his sharp intake of breath.

Forget waiting to ask. "I take it the hand didn't make a good club?"

His laugh was pained. "I landed badly dismounting."

"I see." In her mind's eye, she did see. He'd had a pistol in his good hand. He'd steadied himself with the other.

While the other saw to his orders, they reached his mount, and she let out a long breath. Athena glanced back at her and snorted. The valiant girl had carried him to her rescue and now would take them—somewhere. Best get on their way.

Lucie cupped her hands.

"No," he said.

"Yes."

"I'm too heavy—"

"Swallow that lordly pride and get up, Major Lord Rudgwick."

He *was* heavy. And she was, truth to tell, going on sheer determination. Now the fight was over, her head hurt like the devil. Although not nearly as bad as after the bashing she'd had last year, though, and that gave her hope.

She took the hand he stretched out to her, put her foot on his boot and hopped behind him, rucking up her skirts, circling him with her arms, and resting her cheek on his strong back and the fine wool covering it. Her eyes filled with moisture again. She would go with Rudgwick, no matter *what* the future held, no matter if it was to be good or ill, for who could know that?

Except... she'd seen glimpses of the future, hadn't she? Harmonia's abduction had come true. Rudgwick had been injured dismounting, though that wasn't quite the same as going over a balcony ledge. She prayed that was the end of the bad. The other vision...

She melded herself against him and let his heat seep into her. Best to keep her wits about her and think about that later.

They moved down the road out of sight of the others, and Rudgwick stopped. His hand settled over hers, pressing the reins into hers, and he let out a long breath.

"Lucie, thank God. Thank God, we found you. Why the devil did you go after Harmonia on your own?"

Her cursed anger flared. A scold was a perfect cure for visions of intimacy.

And he was right. "It *was* one foolish thing on top of another. I'll grant ye that." The words, once spoken, spiked more tears. She was more shaken than she realized. "All I could think of was the poor lass, with a villain of a grandfather back at Lady Fiona's. I'd no idea there was a more determined villain lurking outside. I th-thank ye for coming after us."

He stilled and she felt the shift of his shoulders as he looked back at her. "Don't you dare cry, Lucie Macbeth."

She laughed. 'Twas true, she was blubbering. "Aye, sir, Major Lord Rudgwick."

He lifted her hands and pressed his lips to them. Their mount shifted, and she squeezed Rudgwick tighter.

Before she could speak, Lord Jeremy rode up with Lady Harmonia. He held out the pistol he'd taken from Rudgwick. "Reloaded," he said.

Rudgwick sighed, took the weapon, and stowed it under his coats. Three more horses joined them. She recognized Hyde from his greeting, but in the dark, she couldn't identify the two other men.

"Who—"

"Two of Lady Fiona's grooms," Rudgwick said.

"It's too dark to ride cross country," Lord Jeremy said without preamble. "There are too many marshes and bogs we might stumble into."

"Bogs?" Lucie said. "Are we not on the road to Scotland?"

CHAPTER SIXTEEN

Norwich

"We're in Norfolk, Lucie," Lady Harmonia said. "Are we going to Thornview Farm?" She leaned closer. "Thornview Farm is Jeremy's estate."

"We thought of that, as well as Rudgwick Abbey," Lord Jeremy said, "And discarded both destinations. After Gretna, they're the first places your grandfather will look for you, my dear."

Lucie's mind had stuttered over the notion of being in Norfolk. She was supposed to be traveling to Norwich the next day. She'd studied a highway map and knew that Norfolk was not on the Great North Road.

"Not Gretna." She huffed out a breath. "He was taking us to Norwich."

I've got the redhaired one, Dankworth's henchman had said. 'Twas herself he'd been after, not Lady Harmonia.

"We could go back to the Angel Inn in Larling," Lord Jeremy said. "Dankworth didn't change horses there. If he's rescued, he may push on to Norwich."

"Or to his cousin's home in Mundford," Rudgwick said. "It's not far."

"Should we not be taking him to the magistrate?" Lucie asked.

The moment the question left her lips, she remembered the discussion on the road. "No, never mind," she said. The magistrate might well be Dankworth's relation, and they'd be delayed. The duke would find Lady Harmonia, and push for Rudgwick to marry her immediately.

"What *is* your plan for avoiding the duke?" she asked.

"We just passed a narrow road leading east," Rudgwick said. "Do you recall our exploring last month, Jeremy? Perhaps we can find our way to an inn on the Ipswich Road."

"I still have my map." Lord Jeremy dismounted and after a worrisome interlude while one of the grooms fetched and lit a small lantern, he studied it.

Lucie had sensed that Rudgwick was flagging, but she knew it was so when he waved away the map and told Lord Jeremy to lead the way. He took the reins from her, and they turned south.

"And after the Ipswich Road, then what?" she whispered.

He reined up and growled at the grooms to move on. Hyde grumbled something and moved on more slowly.

"You don't trust them," she said.

"Hyde, I trust."

"Of course."

He peered over his shoulder. "I wish you were seated in front of me."

"Ye're in pain. I'm holding ye up. Now answer my question and then let's catch up with the others."

"A friend lives near Yarmouth. A few hours ride. He'll help us."

"How? To do what?"

"I'm going to take you to Scotland and marry you." He picked up her hand and kissed it. "If you'll have me." Then he nudged the horse and they moved on.

Scotland. Oh, how she wanted to go home. She'd take Lady Harmonia with her—the lass might as well hide in Scotland for a while, given her ruination. She could, if she wished it, and he wished it, marry Lord Jeremy there. If she didn't wish it, she could come to Menteith, and Father would protect her from the duke for as long as possible.

Ach, but it would be hard for Father, making an enemy of a powerful duke. And he wasn't always in the north, what with wrestling with the court in Edinburgh over Banquo's estate.

Banquo's estate.

She had business to see to in Norwich.

"We can't be more than an hour's ride from Norwich," she said.

"Perhaps two."

The horse stumbled and she felt Rudgwick's sharp intake of breath. Mayhap the stump had been injured and the wound opened, though she hadn't seen any blood. He needed tending and time to rest.

Lady Harmonia was the one who had to flee England. She herself must visit the bank in Norwich, and she was certain, Rudgwick wouldn't let her go with just Hyde as a nursemaid.

And she didn't have the letter Father sent her.

She'd written to him the evening after they'd purloined the letters and included the name of the bank in her report. 'Twas certain the mail hadn't reached him yet. She'd somehow have to brazen it out and persuade the bank manager to tell her about Banquo's holdings. Bankers had ways of conveying funds. She didn't have to carry coins to Scotland herself.

Rudgwick would have to help her.

***

Rudgwick settled onto a chair in their inn room and groaned. The landlord of The Old Ram in Tivesthall St. Mary remembered the two noble lords from their visit the month before. They'd spent two rainy nights drinking his good ale and hearing stories about Roman artifacts found in nearby Caistor St. Edmund.

Whether their notoriety was good or bad remained to be seen, but they couldn't have gone on. Jeremy pressed extra coins upon the man, who'd found rooms for all their party. Lucie and Harmonia shared the best chamber; he and Jeremy a lesser one. The grooms were in the sort of small room normally allotted to traveling servants.

Hyde, who'd set a much-needed bottle of brandy next to him, had pledged to sleep on the floor. He was here now, rousing the embers to take the chill away, helping Jeremy out of his coat, and badgering Rudgwick about fetching a local sawbones.

A knock at the door diverted Hyde, and he went to answer it.

"Ye can't be here," Hyde said.

"Aye, we can. We've come to help." Lucie's determined voice cheered him.

"Let her in, Hyde," he said.

Jeremy looked at his coat, threw up his hands, and went to usher in Lucie and Harmonia. "I suppose we couldn't damage your reputation any further," he said.

Harmonia grinned back at him.

Both ladies were bedraggled and dirty, as if they'd been dragged through mud. Even in the dim light, Harmonia's tightfitting trousers and coats revealed a womanly figure, and Lucie's bodice and skirts had rips in them. It was a wonder they hadn't been further molested.

"Aye," Lucie said. "Ye could accompany Lady Harmonia back to our room, Lord Jeremy, and stay there with her while I tend to Major Lord Rudgwick's injury."

Rudgwick sat up. As far as he knew, there wasn't, in fact, an injury needing tending. Merely the stump inflamed and angry and paining him like the devil.

"I fear I'm not a very good nurse," Harmonia said.

"I'll tend to the Major," Hyde said. "Get ye gone, Miss Lucie."

Lucie leveled a long look at the servant. "Ye used to carry laudanum in your pack."

Hyde reached for the saddle bag he'd brought in with him.

"No laudanum," Rudgwick said, starting to rise.

Lucie nudged him back and dropped to her knees in front of him. "A wee drop for the pain?"

Curls that had escaped from a messy bun framed her face. A bright red spot on her cheekbone was fading to purple. "You've a bruise on your face," he said, fighting a surge of anger that made blood pulse into his phantom hand, bringing pain with it.

"Oh, aye. And ye've a cut here." Her palm cradled his jaw, spiking his blood again. "And Lady Harmonia has burns from the ropes binding her."

"Jeremy will look after Harmonia."

She looked back over her shoulder.

Lady Harmonia reached for Lord Jeremy's cast aside coat. "Come, Jeremy."

His friend's eyes glimmered with indecision. He held his breath watching, holding his tongue as well. Jeremy knew they were going to Scotland, but he had scruples about pressuring Harmonia to marry him—he was just that honorable. And it was a decision for him to work out with Rudgwick's erstwhile fiancée.

"Hyde will fetch some salve for your wrists, my lady." Lucie bent over the dangling prosthesis, studying it, and then topped off his glass of brandy and held it for him. "For the pain," she said.

"I'm stayin' with the Major." Hyde pressed a tin into Lord Jeremy's hand, and the couple slipped out of the room, closing the door behind them.

"Lady Harmonia needs a chaperon more than I do," Lucie said.

Hyde's answering grunt made Rudgwick laugh. "Perhaps I'll kick you out, Hyde."

"Only try, Major, and ye'll see what's what. I have my orders from Colonel Macbeth."

"Mouthy, isn't he?" Lucie murmured. "'Tis what Father says about Hyde. Now, if ye'll drink up and stand, Major Lord Rudgwick, Hyde and I will help ye out of this coat."

With the brandy warming him, her fingers roaming under his coat, and Hyde's surprisingly gentle assistance, they slipped the sleeve off his good arm and eased the other carefully over the stump. He made to sit again, but Lucie stopped him.

"The waistcoat and shirt as well."

Hyde furrowed his brow.

"Hyde, do ye see that spot of blood on his shirt? We must have a look at him. He's not likely to ravage me with ye lurking about, and I'm not leaving the room."

She went to work unbuttoning the waistcoat, helped him slip it off, and then studied the shirt before undoing one cuff and frowning over the other.

"My valet packed an extra shirt."

She raised her gaze to his.

"Cut this one off if you wish," he said.

"That may be better. Not for the world would I hurt ye any more than I must."

Desire sparked through him, and he clasped her hand. "Then say that you'll marry me. Promise me."

Hyde cleared his throat, and at Rudgwick's answering glare, went off to his saddlebag muttering.

Her lips curved into a smile. "Mayhap I will," she whispered, "when all is settled and ye're free, that is. Now, let me see to this neckcloth."

***

Her fingers trembled as she fumbled with the stained linen cloth. 'Twas a simple enough knot which perhaps made it all the worse. She suspected some of the fancy knots effected by gentleman were only held fast with their jeweled stickpins.

Rudgwick's hot gaze didn't ease her discomposure. The pain in his eyes was fast being supplanted by hunger. He was plotting to rid them of her nursemaid, Hyde.

But she was glad Hyde was here because she'd likely need *his* help for the bank as well.

She'd convince them both to help her. They would get to it.

Hyde appeared with scissors. The knot finally loosened, and she pulled away the dirty neckcloth. His shirt opened to the sight of tanned skin and dark chest hair that had her gulping for air. She stepped back and waved Hyde forward.

"Coward," Rudgwick said.

Lucie shrugged and shook out the neckcloth, studying it. The fine cloth might wash and dry before morning if they kept the fire hot.

Hyde was peeling the shirt away, revealing a braw left arm and a broad muscled chest dusted with more dark hair that her fingers itched to touch. The strap of a harness crossing shoulder and chest reminded her of his injury and the pain that came with it.

She'd been curious about Rudgwick's amputation when he'd resided with them in Brussels, but she hadn't dared to intrude on him then. The surgeon she'd seen in Edinburgh for her head injury had served for a spell in the army. The genial, talkative fellow had sawed off bones aplenty, and was happy to oblige her curiosity on the subject.

"Lean forward now, Major Lord Rudgwick." She knelt again and began easing the right sleeve down, avoiding the sight of his chest and flat belly and the interesting placket of his tight pantaloons. Hyde swept the white linen from his back and began feeding the top of the sleeve to her.

A strap somewhere had broken, and the cloth was bunching around it, causing Rudgwick to flinch with even the slightest of tugs.

"Hyde, pour his lordship another glass of the brandy, will ye?"

When Hyde turned away, she placed the flat of her hand on his chest. With his dark hair in disarray and a shadow of beard, and the missing hand, he looked like a pirate. A spurt of pure animal desire shot through her—his or hers, it didn't matter. His galloping heartbeat matched her own. He set his hand over hers.

She wasn't sure whether the pain would keep Rudgwick off her. Which was more powerful—pain or desire? Desire, she hoped. Because if there was too much pain, 'twould only be Hyde with her at the bank tomorrow.

And thank heavens she had Hyde nearby muttering. He'd keep her off Rudgwick.

She smiled at the thought and found her breath. "It's a braw man, ye are, Major Lord Rudgwick. Drink up, then."

"I'll soon be a bosky one." He took the glass and gulped. "Get on with it, my lovely."

She chuckled and went back to easing the shirt sleeve down, finally tugging it off.

A system of straps and buckles attached the prosthesis to Rudgwick's upper arm and shoulders. One of the arm straps had broken completely.

"I've heard of this," she said. "A German inventor came up with a contraption that allows ye to use other muscles to open and close the hand. Is this the same?"

"Yes, I imagine."

Did the petulance in his voice signal pain, or his irritation with the ineffective device which produced only a weak grasp with its spring-actioned fingers.

"May we remove it, my lord?"

"Yes." He hissed out the word with a tight grimace. A bruise was blooming on his cheek, and dark circles under his eyes. He'd missed a night's sleep chasing after her.

"Hyde, I'll steady the hand while you work on the straps."

Between them they quickly slipped off the prosthesis and she sat back on her heels. There were bloody spots on the sheath covering the stump.

Rudgwick's hand came down over the sheath. "Hyde will tend to it. Or I will. I don't need either of you."

"Ye've asked me to marry ye. Do ye think I'm so faint hearted I can't look at the raw skin of your stump? I am a Highlander, Major Lord Rudgwick."

He blinked and let her pry his hand away, and she quickly ripped off the sheath, making him gasp.

She had to hide her own dismay. The strong forearm dotted with dark hair ended in an angry pink mass. The cloth had adhered in some places and left raw patches of skin.

"We'll need that salve." Hyde headed for the door.

"Wait." Lucie lifted the forearm to study the other side. "See if the landlord has some pure honey. 'Tis good for healing wounds. And we'll need to fashion a new sheath with some clean cloth. And a clean stocking, a brand new one if we can find one."

Hyde paused at the door and went out.

The moment the door closed, Lucie gave into impulse and fell against Rudgwick, setting her head to his chest and slipping her arms around him. The threatening tears that had plagued her sprouted again, and she shook with the fight to hold them back.

"Lucie." Rudgwick's hand touched her back, tentatively at first. Then his hand fisted in her hair, and he lifted her head.

"Ow," she said.

"I've only one hand to raise you and... you're crying. Come here." He set his hand under her arm and nudged her to her feet, then tugged her onto his lap.

"Thank you," he said, and then she felt the press of his lips on hers. She opened her mouth and welcomed him, and for long moments they kissed. His right forearm steadied her shoulder, while his other hand roamed free, his fingers scooping the back of her head, loosening the few hasty pins she'd shoved in.

He froze, his lips hovering above hers. "A lump."

The press of his finger made her wince and sit up.

"He hit me. The fellow you left gut-shot."

"You lost consciousness."

"For a time. Long enough for them to tie me up."

He pressed his forehead to hers. "Oh, my Lucie. What else happened to you?"

"Naught that I know of."

"And Lady Harmonia? Did they hurt her?"

"We'd just freed ourselves from the gags when ye appeared. We didn't have time to discuss it. But I don't think so. She would have fought, and her clothing isn't ripped."

"But yours is."

"Those tears happened when we escaped. They didn't rape us, but the one fellow, the coachman it must have been, was talking about when we reached Scotland, Dankworth could only marry one of us. But we weren't going to Scotland, were we?"

Rudgworth frowned. "Was he taking you to the bank in Norwich or to his cousin's estate?" he mused.

"He couldn't very well take a kidnapped heiress, a duke's granddaughter, to the cousin, unless the man is as rum a fellow as himself. I fear we were headed for the bank. What was that banker holding for Banquo? Surely not more money than he'd gain by forcing Harmonia to marry him in Scotland."

He lifted a lock of her hair and rubbed it against his cheek. "You're going to say that we need to visit the bank."

Her heart swelled with love, and she laughed. "We must, Major Lord Rudgwick."

"Dankworth might make his way there by then."

"We'll bring along Hyde."

"Who'll return to us tonight sooner than I'd like." He traced a finger down the side of her head, over her jaw and neck and bosom, over her belly and around to her hip. "Is your father in Edinburgh or has he gone home to Menteith?"

"He last wrote that he was planning to be in Edinburgh until June."

"We'll go to Norwich and see if we can bully the banker. And then we'll go to Edinburgh. I want your father's blessing before we marry."

"Oh." She squeezed her brimming eyes closed on a memory of her father's smiling face. The air grew heavy, and the room swirled, and she remembered the vision. This room with its tester bed and its heavy window curtains was not the room in her vision.

"No tears," he said.

"It must be the coshing." She'd rarely cried as a child and young girl, and she'd never had visions then.

She put a hand to his jaw and kissed him, and only stopped when footsteps in the corridor drew closer and Hyde entered. The sight of her in Rudgwick's lap made him blink and turn away, but not before she saw the start of a grin.

Reluctantly she got to her feet and took the dish of honey from Hyde.

***

This was a very bad idea.

He didn't need the Sight to tell him that—his jangly nerves, like at the advent of battle, spoke volumes.

He'd been drunk with brandy and kisses and pain when he'd fallen in with this plan. He'd recovered from the first two, more or less, and only a bit of the pain remained, but he felt odd and annoyed preparing to go out in public with his sleeve pinned up. He wasn't the hero of Trafalgar after all, merely a cavalry officer who'd played a small part at Waterloo.

The false hand rested in his saddlebag until repairs could be made. He had no idea who would do them since he had no plans to return to James Potts' workshop in Chelsea anytime soon. Surely, with an esteemed medical college, Edinburgh had someone who could mend the bloody thing.

Lucie came through the door of her bedchamber into their shared parlor. "Ye're fashing, Major Lord Rudgwick. I can see it in your eyes."

A cavalry officer didn't show fear to the troops. "Nonsense. It's only..." He held up the covered stump. "It had some use juggling the reins or steadying a pistol."

"Ye have me for that." She swept a hand over her person. "Will this do for a visit to a banker?"

The brown cloth would look dowdy on anyone else, but the hint of russet in the tone made her hair shimmer and her eyes sparkle. "You know you look lovely."

Early that morning, he'd rented a chaise at the Old Ram to convey Lucie and Harmonia, and the postilion delivered them to the Bell where he and Lucie had taken rooms as Mr. and Mrs. Thorne. They'd sent Jeremy, Harmonia, and the other two servants on to Musbury, praying the duke's men wouldn't be looking for her on the road to Yarmouth.

Harmonia was happy to retain the trousers, but Lucie couldn't appear at the bank in a tattered gown. Norwich was a grand town with a grand cathedral and bustling market. They'd sent a maid from the Bell off to fetch a gown from the market while Lucie bathed in her bedchamber, and he nursed a tankard in the taproom and eavesdropped. There were plenty of strangers at a busy city inn, but none of them appeared to have anything to do with Dankworth or the duke. Where Lucie was concerned, he didn't think he needed to worry about the duke's men. He couldn't believe the old man would stoop to physically harming her to get her out of the way, not even to keep her away from Rudgwick.

It was afternoon before Lucie was dried and dressed and they were ready to visit May, Falton, and May, Bankers of Norwich and Swaffham.

Hyde walked out from the suite's other bedchamber carrying both saddlebags.

"Shall we go?" Rudgwick reached for the new shawl the maid had purchased for Lucie. "I'd like to be on the road soon." He wanted to reach their destination before dark.

A rap at the door made his blood spike. Lucie had sent the maid away, and there was no reason for another servant to visit. He put his hand on the pistol tucked under his coat and waved Lucie back into her bedchamber.

CHAPTER SEVENTEEN

A Visit to the Bank

The daft girl came to stand beside him. "What if it's Dankworth," she whispered.

Hyde set aside the bags and went to the door. "Yes?" he asked.

"It's Sir Thomas," the muffled voice said.

Rudgwick let out a breath. Hyde opened the door a crack, then wider, and then welcomed Sir Thomas Abernathy and another man Rudgwick recognized from Whitehall into their private parlor.

"There you are, Rudgwick." Sir Thomas removed his dusty hat, revealing his shiny pate. "Miss Macbeth, I'm glad to see you looking so well. You remember Halladay?"

Rudgwick nodded to the man.

"Are you going out?" Sir Thomas asked.

He glanced at Lucie. She nodded.

"Yes, actually," he said. "We were on our way to the bank."

"Excellent. Shall we sit?" He pointed to one of the wooden chairs tucked under the table.

"Of course. Hyde, fetch tankards for—"

"No time for that," Sir Thomas said, pulling a chair out for Lucie. "This won't take more than a few moments, and then I'll accompany you, if I may, Miss Macbeth." He reached under his coats and removed a paper, handing it to Lucie."

She read it in silence and passed it to Rudgwick. It was a letter from her father to the bank in Norwich.

"It's a hastily prepared counterfeit," Sir Thomas said. "Quicker than retrieving the original from Chelsea."

"The original was addressed to Mr. Stephenson," Lucie said. "Father didn't know which bank to write to. But the signature is well done."

"Thank you. And Lady Harmonia, is she here?"

"No," Rudgwick said. "We have sent her to safety."

"There's a powerful duke hounding Sidmouth about his granddaughter's abduction."

Sidmouth, the Home Secretary, was Sir Thomas's superior, and would be well equipped to complicate their flight, if he so chose. Rudgwick couldn't recall whether Sidmouth and Bridgehampton were close political allies. "He will have his granddaughter back anon," he said.

"I hope so. The duke has sent Runners to find both of you and throw you into Newgate on charges of kidnapping, and if he can't find Lady Harmonia, murder."

"He's mad," Lucie said. "Dankworth took us. Surely the duke knows that. And what of Dankworth?" Lucie asked. "Where is he?"

"Lord Jeremy and I rescued the ladies from Dankworth," Rudgwick said.

"He's not dead?" Sir Thomas asked.

Lucie shook her head. "In truth, 'twould be a blessing if he were."

"Dankworth took the road through Thetford. We caught up with him there. He wasn't dead when we left him. He should have been found by a passing coach by now, or he may have slunk off to his cousin's estate at South Hall."

"I'll send men to look." Sir Thomas nodded to Halladay, and the other man soundlessly slipped away. "We've uncovered your man, Stephenson, by the way, at the Star Inn here. I have men speaking to him now." He tapped the table. "Shall we go, then? I'm anxious to hear what Elizabeth Garvey May has to say."

"Who?" Lucie asked.

Sir Thomas rose and helped Lucie up. "The banker."

"A woman?"

"Indeed. A widow, in fact. She's been a partner in the bank for years, but her husband and son recently died—under suspicious circumstances. Her husband, Bartlett May, was very nearly brought up on charges of sedition. The patriotic societies of Norwich have been a thorn in the government's side for twenty years. The prosperous businesses suffered when they could no longer trade with France—legally, that is. We've heard whispers the last decade of supplies disappearing from naval stores and finding their way to the French."

Lucie rubbed at her forehead. "I see."

So did Rudgwick. His pulse quickened. They'd heard those rumors about supplies for Wellington's men in the Peninsula being diverted as well.

Had Dankworth and Grey been involved? Was the duke being blackmailed? By whom? On what evidence? He hadn't told Sir Thomas about the ledger sheets they'd found with Bridgehampton's name.

His mind raced going over the facts. Perhaps Banquo had been a blackmailer. Was the bank holding something besides money? It would be to Dankworth's benefit to obtain any incriminating documents against him.

And if he had evidence against Grey, he could bleed the duke.

"Rudgwick," Sir Thomas said, interrupting his thoughts, "I propose we give Miss Macbeth the chance to conduct business with Mrs. May woman to woman, while we sit, quietly available to grab clerks by the throat or toss them about if needed."

Lucie's mouth opened but no words came out. She sent Rudgwick an inquiring look.

"Lucie, I may have told Sir Thomas about our visit to Stephenson's office."

She smiled. "Father did want me to learn from this. I thank ye, gentlemen, for your confidence in me."

***

Lucie rested her fingertips on Rudgwick's forearm above the turned-up sleeve as they crossed the threshold of May, Falton, and May. Inside, a well-polished counter lined the lobby, with two clerks seated behind it, speaking with customers. A porter greeted them and asked their business.

Sir Thomas appeared at her other side.

"We're here to see about the estate of a recently deceased relative," Lucie said. "We believe your bank is holding funds for him."

"The relative's name?"

"Will be shared with the bank officer with whom we speak," she said sweetly.

The porter cleared his throat. "Excuse me, but I will need to know—"

"You heard the lady," Rudgwick said, in his frostiest aristocratic tone. She gave his muscular forearm a gentle press and squashed a smile.

The porter raised his eyebrows and then sighed, as if he received this sort of brush-off all the time. He walked to the counter.

"Well done, my lord," Lucie murmured. Her gaze swept the room, and she noticed a middle-aged woman in black standing in the open doorway of what must be a private office. Her dark hair, streaked with white, was simply styled and her steady scrutiny was accompanied by a growing frown.

Lucie's breath tightened and an ache started near the new lump in her head. Elizabeth May—this must be her. The woman's dark eyes narrowed as a mist rose about her, iron gray fading to burnt brown, the shade of Lucie's new gown.

"Lucie." A hand squeezed hers. "You are well."

She tore her gaze from the woman and looked up at Rudgwick. Lady Fiona had pulled her up with those exact same words.

"Come along," Sir Thomas murmured. "She's beckoning us."

Furniture crammed the room—worktables, chairs, and shelves filled with boxes. Documents, newspapers, and correspondence sat neatly stacked next to ledgers. Two young men studied their arrival with interest while pulling on their coats and departing.

The woman led them to the corner and took her place behind a massive desk, from which she could watch the room and its occupants. Behind her was the door of the bank's vault.

She took her seat on a leather-upholstered chair, her back as rigid as the sturdy door behind her, and watched as Sir Thomas pulled over a wooden chair. Rudgwick handed Lucie into the seat and then both men stepped back.

"I am Mrs. May, the bank's director," she said. "Where is Mr. Stephenson? I was expecting him to accompany you, Miss Macbeth."

Lucie let out a breath, her head buzzing in the dark mist swirling around them. The smell of rising brimstone wouldn't surprise her.

Rudgwick and Sir Thomas remained silent, as they'd promised.

"Did ye indeed, madam?" Lucie extracted the forged letter from her reticule. "My father and I found Mr. Stephenson's services unsatisfactory." She handed over the missive prepared by Sir Thomas. "My father is attempting to settle the estate of his late cousin, Giles Banquo."

Mrs. May scanned it and raised an eyebrow. "I don't know you, Miss Macbeth, and I can't just hand over money based on a letter like this. Mr. Stephenson was handling this account."

"Did ye not tell him he must bring this letter? Or did ye plan to put him off yet again when ye saw it? We are both practical women, Mrs. May, with responsibilities, yours to the bank, mine to my father and our people, including the children of Giles Banquo. He left two minor sons, Fleance and Giles. My father, Colonel Finnley Macbeth, Baron of Calder, and my cousin, Malcolm Comyn, Earl of Menteith, are their guardians. I own I'd be surprised to have ye hand over coin to me today, but I'd like an accounting of any property ye're holding for him, and cash or other valuables."

"With only this letter, that won't be possible."

"The death was witnessed by Lord Menteith and properly recorded in Sussex. 'Tis a fact that Giles Banquo left behind a humble jumble for Father to unsnarl. If ye don't have the authority to help me, is there a Mr. May or a Mr. Falton I can speak with?"

"Mr. Falton is long dead, and my husband is deceased. *I'm* the bank's director."

"Ach. Ye're wearing black so the loss is recent. My condolences, Mrs. May." She leaned forward and lowered her voice. "Are ye aware that the Crown has an interest in what ye're holding for Banquo?"

The russet mist faded to the same grey pallor of Mrs. May's taut lips.

"Someone else had an interest, as well. Someone who wanted it so strongly he plucked me off a Chelsea street, bound me, and gagged me, and carried me off to Norfolk. I ken that he'd planned dragging me here with him, and then what? Would ye have entertained Lionel Dankworth, Mrs. May?"

One finger moved, tapping the desk blotter soundlessly, while the blood drained from the woman's face. Her shoulders dropped in a long exhale, and she bent to open a drawer.

Rudgwick and Sir Thomas stepped forward.

Mrs. May held up her hands and glared at Lucie. "Who are these men?"

"These are my father's good friends, the Earl of Rudgwick, and Sir Thomas Abernathy."

Mrs. May's eyes flared at that last name and moisture sheened her forehead. "I'm retrieving something from my drawer," she said. "Not a weapon."

"Ye may proceed."

The thick packet Mrs. May pulled out opened to a collection of documents. The banker slid them over to Lucie. She gazed at them, bewildered.

"I haven't known what to do with them," Mrs. May said. "I found them after my husband and son died a few weeks ago."

Lucie scanned each item, listening to the banker and pausing over one letter before moving on to the next. 'Twas as if a dam had broken as the confession poured out. News of Banquo's death had reached the bank in August. Before that, money had poured into his account, some of it funneled through Mr. Stephenson's office, but there was a lull in the autumn, and then the deposits resumed. Her husband had explained that Banquo's investments were continuing to pay.

She drew a ledger from another drawer. "This is Banquo's account." She opened it to the last page.

Banquo was quite wealthy. Except...

"What was the large withdrawal in late April of last year?" Lucie asked. Ten thousand pounds had been taken, a fabulous amount of money. "Sir Thomas, have a look." She slid the ledger to him. "Banquo died before that date."

The older lady's jaw tightened. "I don't know. My husband and son kept these records."

Lucie's mind raced through the facts she knew. She could almost feel sorry for Mrs. May—though she didn't entirely believe her. The documents were a mix of letters and shipping records, and she'd warrant that each one of them contained a scandalous secret. The lady's bank had stored these records, taken the deposits of a criminal, and sent money where? Did that large amount go to fund Bonaparte's last campaign? Or was it embezzled by the banker's late husband?

"Sir Thomas is with the Home Office," Lucie explained. She took the documents onto her lap and shoved them back into their wrapping. "We must take these. As for the ledger..."

"My man will copy it," Sir Thomas said, "while another one chats with you, Mrs. May." He slipped out and returned moments later with Halladay and another one of his men.

***

Rudgwick had wanted to carry the documents. Lucie, however, insisted the spoils were hers to guard.

"Doona worry," she said, clutching the packet. "I have it." Those three words had been charged with meaning but with Sir Thomas lingering, he couldn't ask what it was she meant.

They left Sir Thomas's men busy copying and interrogating Mrs. May, who deserved every bit of pain she was suffering for her bank's enablement of what he and Sir Thomas concluded was a blackmailer. The banker had been taking a cut, as had Mr. Stephenson. Dankworth likely had been one of the victims, along with Bridgehampton. Dankworth wanted to get his hands on the documents and have the money continue to flow his way.

Back at the Bell, they discovered that the landlord had given their abandoned suite to another party. The best room available was a cramped upper floor room at the back with two narrow beds, a small table next to the hearth, and a closet-sized chamber with a cot for a servant. Upon entering, Lucie claimed the privacy of the servant's cot, avowed that her head was aching, and went off for a rest, returning moments later with the collection of documents she'd forgotten to leave with them.

Then she'd lingered, and now sat with Sir Thomas studying the papers.

Rudgwick stood at the window watching the light fade. He'd desperately wanted to whisk her away to the safety he prayed Harmonia and Jeremy had reached. If all was well with the pair, if Musbury had agreed to the plan, they would have thrown off the ropes, raised sail, and be on their way to Scotland by now.

He'd rather not travel the Yarmouth Road at night though. Dankworth still hadn't been found. They'd beaten the villain to the documents, but he was capable of attempting revenge.

He himself hadn't done more than watch Sir Thomas and Lucie work—and it was amazing the man let her participate. He didn't wish to know the names of the traitors or adulterers or anyone else worthy of blackmail, other than Dankworth, Grey and Bridgehampton, and he hadn't heard any cries of *aha* from Lucie stumbling across those names.

Once Rudgwick had involved Sir Thomas, it was too late to save the duke from his folly—or rather, his son's folly. Not that Sir Thomas hadn't been investigating Grey all along. The thought of the old man's dishonor saddened him. How had Grey fallen so low as to drag his father and daughter along with him?

With luck, there was no evidence in the packet of papers to implicate Bridgehampton's son. But if Grey had been implicated, perhaps Prinny would take pity upon one of his close advisers, given that his own brother, the Duke of York, had caused scandal through the actions of his mistress.

When it was dark enough to light the lamp, he sent Hyde down to fetch dinner and then seated himself at the cramped table. Lucie rubbed at that spot on her temple, and he remembered the glaze coming over her that afternoon.

"Are you well, Lucie?" He'd ask her about the afternoon episode later.

"I am fine. Will these documents be useful to ye, Sir Thomas? Nothing seems very clear to me."

"We shall see." Sir Thomas removed a pair of spectacles and squeezed the bridge of his nose. "I shall write to your father and let him know how well you did today. Should you ever consider offering your services to the Crown, from time to time a capable woman is needed."

Lucie blinked and then smiled. It was a weak smile, hiding something: fatigue maybe, or hunger. She'd kept watch at the Ram for part of the night, and they'd not eaten since breaking their fast after arriving at the Bell.

And he'd never allow his wife to run off after traitors with any of Sir Thomas's men.

He knew better than to say *that* out loud. "You'll be a formidable opponent for any swindling factor or merchant in Calder or Cambridgeshire, Lucie," he said.

Lucie blinked and then bit her lip.

"Well." Sir Thomas gathered papers. "I think I'd best remain with you until Hyde returns. Meanwhile, will you surrender these spoils to the Crown, Lucie?"

She sighed. "When I think of the suffering of Father, and Major Lord Rudgwick, and..." The door opened, and Hyde entered, carrying a platter, and ushering in a maid equally laden. "And Hyde... Would that they'd not have had to endure that last battle. Traitors ought to be punished. I'd see no one drawn and quartered though."

Halladay poked his head in, and Sir Thomas stood. "The Crown's justice can be harsh."

"Before you go..." Rudgwick gestured to the maid setting out the platter and dishes.

Eyes averted, she finished and hurried out.

"What of Dankworth, Halladay?" Rudgwick asked.

"The bodies of two men were found on the road near an abandoned carriage. Neither met the description of Dankworth. We've checked all the inns and other likely spots in Norwich to no avail."

"We're transporting Stephenson to London for more questioning," Sir Thomas said. "Perhaps Dankworth will follow him."

"Are you returning to town, now, Sir Thomas?" Rudgwick asked.

"Soon enough."

"Will you carry a note to my mother?"

Sir Thomas nodded. "Quickly, though."

Rudgwick fetched paper and pencil from his bag, and scribbled a hurried note, telling his mother that they were all well, and would write soon.

Lucie bent over his shoulder. "Will you add a quick message for Lady Fiona?"

He glanced from her to Sir Thomas and back again. Sir Thomas was sure to read whatever they wrote. "Shall I tell her you send your regards?"

"Yes. And tell her to have the drapers hurry and finish the gold bedchamber for me."

Mischief lurked in her golden eyes. That was a code if ever he'd heard one.

Sir Thomas must have thought so too because his lip quirked as he tucked the note away. "You must keep my offer in mind, Lucie. Enjoy your dinner. Safe travels."

The door closed and Rudgwick lifted the lid on the platter. "Did you have dinner below, Hyde?"

"No, milord."

"Come and join us."

Hyde stood chewing his lower lip. The hair on Rudgwick's neck rippled.

"I'm not the only one having spells," Lucie said. "What is it, Hyde?"

"Only that the maid carrying the food was asking too many questions. I'd best go see what's what."

"Eat first, and we'll both go," Rudgwick said.

"Mayhap it's Dankworth setting her to it," Lucie said, staring at the food he'd scooped onto her plate. "Ye must let me be the one to put a knife in him."

"Or mayhap," Hyde said, "he'll follow Sir Thomas to go after whatever was at the bank."

She set down her fork and looked up at Rudgwick through her eyelashes. She reached deep into her bodice, wriggled a bit, and drew out a paper.

CHAPTER EIGHTEEN

Dankworth Returns

"I think this was the only one about Grey."

Rudgwick's heart lifted, and a laugh bubbled up. *I have it,* she'd said. Then she'd gone off to the tiny adjoining room and returned moments later. Had Sir Thomas been hoodwinked? Surely not.

"How... Oh, never mind." He spread out the paper and read.

Grey, desperate for money, had written to Dankworth about joining in a new scheme to siphon boots from a shipment paid for by the Crown and sell them at a premium to the French.

"A duke's son wouldn't engage in trade," Lucie said, "but I suppose if Dankworth ran his relative's slave plantation he wasn't above nefarious practices."

"What was he selling?" Hyde asked.

"Did your boots ever wear out when you were trudging through Spain?" Rudgwick asked.

Hyde chewed and swallowed. "More'n one pair. We wondered why the ones we took off dead Frenchies looked the same as ours."

The food, slices of fragrant roast beef, peas, potatoes, and crusty bread, looked suddenly unappealing. Rudgwick pushed back his chair.

Hyde came around the table with his knife and reached for his fork.

Color rising, he spluttered for words. "I'm not..."

"Reckon until the hand's mended I can help ye with this," Hyde said.

"Or ye can eat with ye're fingers, we won't mind, will we, Hyde?" With her fork, Lucie folded a thin slice of beef and then speared it. "Though I'm not verra hungry either."

"Been that sort of a day," Hyde said, finishing and returning to his plate. "But in Spain, I was hungry aplenty. Happened rations were slim even for the Major from time to time. Eat now, the both of ye. If we're going to have Dankworth to wrestle with, ye'd both best have all your strength and some sleep too."

Lucie flashed Rudgwick a smile. "Mouthy servants," she whispered.

He shared a long look with her, his heart lifting. Needs must; he'd eaten with his fingers a few times in the field, inelegantly, hurriedly, one hand on his sword, with hardy comrades who didn't care. This wasn't so different.

***

Sleeping was out of the question, at least until Rudgwick and Hyde returned to the inn room. Lucie went to the window, pushed back the curtains that Rudgwick had closed, and fought the sticky dormer window open, taking in a deep draught of coal-scented air.

The long drop into the quiet close below sent a chill through her, and she stepped back. The windows in the backside of the building across were open but dark. It was quiet as well, the only noise the clopping of horses and creaks of carriage wheels on the street. The murmur of voices traveling up the narrow stairs from the busy taproom below signaled that she wasn't wholly alone.

She'd turned her own lamp as low as possible while she waited, wanting to be invisible until Rudgwick returned.

He and Hyde had followed the maid who came to fetch dishes, planning to question her. That had seemed more than an hour ago, though she had no way of knowing; the room had no clock, and she had no timepiece.

She did, however, have her blade, only one since she'd given the other to Lady Harmonia before they sent her off with Lord Jeremy. Tonight, Rudgwick had wanted to give her the pistol, but she'd convinced him he might need it more.

The room's key rested on the plain deal table, waiting for the signal they'd agreed on. At Rudgwick's insistence, the letter was back on her person until he returned. 'Twas a fierce responsibility, holding the duke's reputation in a piece of oilcloth tied under her gown at her waist. He was a dragon, for sure, yet she didn't know the man well enough to hate him. What Rudgwick meant to do with the letter, she wasn't sure, but it no doubt had something to do with unshackling himself from Lady Harmonia. Perhaps allowing the lass more freedom as well.

A loud boom resonated through the alleyway from the street beyond, and she went to peer out, ducking in as a wave of dizziness overtook her and leaning her forehead against the sash. Distant alarmed cries reached her ears and grew louder.

The ache overtook her so, she almost missed the rattle behind her.

Heart pounding, she listened for the prearranged knock. Another rattle followed. In the dim light she saw the door latch move and groped for her blade sitting next to the key, moving in slow motion through the sudden dark fog creeping under the door.

Her nerves rattled, too, like the iron latch. Dankworth was here, or someone just as vile.

Metal scraped in the door lock, and, with a sharp click, the latch moved.

She launched herself at the door, pressing her weight against it, fighting the lever to stay still.

"There's been an accident, miss," a woman said.

The boom she'd heard... no. She didn't believe it. Both Rudgwick and Hyde were soldiers. The building hadn't shaken. Nor had the men planned to leave the inn. Even if matters arose, even if they'd had to go out, they could take care of themselves, and she must do the same. This was a trap. She remained silent, deciding her next move.

"Your man and your servant were hurt in that blast."

The latch moved again, and she held it steady, waiting, her hearing growing more acute. Outside on the street, the voices had settled. 'Twas likely naught more than fireworks. If anyone had been hurt, there'd be a greater commotion both outside and in.

"I'm Sally, as brought ye the dinner tonight." There was a pause, and then a whispered, "Mebbe she's not here?"

"Enough," a man bellowed. The latch wrenched violently, and the door crashed open, sending Lucie fleeing. She braced herself on the wall near the window, gulping in great breaths of air and watching a black cloud enter and shift.

Blood rushed to her arms and legs. Her hand froze around the hilt of the knife she was somehow still holding. A gust of air from the window pushed some of the cloud back, revealing a tattered man looking worse for his sins.

Dankworth's coats were stretched too tight to button, and his trousers skimmed his calves and pulled obscenely over his privates. His scuffed and worn boots must have come from a laborer. He looked like a rogue in one of Rowlandson's caricatures. Seeing the murderous look in his eyes, she knew better than to laugh.

A head popped up behind him. 'Twas the maid who'd carried up their meal and carried away their dishes.

"I've got rid of the others and brought ye here," the woman said. "I'll have that coin now."

Lucie's heart did a flip. *Got rid of?* "Good Sally," she began, willing her voice not to shake. She'd run the lass through herself if Rudgwick or Hyde had been harmed. "As it stands, ye're an accomplice, lass. This man's a traitor to England. That baldheaded man who was here with us today is from the Home Office and he has the proof."

Dankworth's expression flashed fury. She swallowed and went on. "This fellow here will hang for treason, and if he hurts me or my men, 'twill be for murder. And ye'll hang alongside him for your part in it unless..." The darkening of Dankworth's features made her stop. Whether Sally would help or not was uncertain, but her eyes had widened with what seemed to be fear. Perhaps she wasn't as mercenary as she seemed.

"Enough," Dankworth bellowed again. He flung a coin into the corridor and slammed the door shut on the girl.

He hadn't seen the look on Sally's face. Lucie prayed she'd repent and send help.

Meanwhile, shaking in her half-boots or not, she must help herself. She had her tongue and her blade.

Dankworth stood near the door with the table between them.

"'Tis true, ye know." It wasn't, but it was a worthy lie. "Sir Thomas Abernathy has *everything*. 'Tis him ye need to go after, not me. I'm of no use to ye."

"What have you done with Lady Harmonia?"

Ach, he was still after the poor lass's dowry. How to answer? If she said Lady Harmonia was back with the duke, he might decide he wanted her own small dowry and insignificant title. On the other hand, he might bite at the chance to snare a true heiress...

"Mayhap her granddad has caught up with her by now, but I doubt it." How much would he know? Dankworth had seen Lord Jeremy when they were rescued. "Lord Jeremy was seeing to her safety."

"He's taking her to Scotland?"

"*Eloping?* Are ye daft? Lord Jeremy's too much of a gentleman to steal an heiress, even if he's rescuing her first from a dastard like yourself. Nay, he has an estate hereabouts he said, and an old lady cousin there in residence who can serve as chaperone if the duke hasn't yet arrived there. I suppose though, 'twill take some time for the old duke to puzzle that out and find them."

"Where in Norfolk?"

She had no idea.

What had she seen on the map she'd studied that would throw Dankworth in the wrong direction? There'd been an old Roman road with a funny name running north and west... She'd start there.

"He said there's a Roman road that ends near his manor." The guidebook she'd consulted talked about the west part of Norfolk jutting out with the sea all around. "And he said he can sit on his terrace of an evening and watch the sun set over the water."

The bushy blond brows drew together. "You're lying."

"No." She shook her head. "I was rattled about what ye did to us, yet I know what I heard. Besides, why should I lie? Go on after her. Lady Harmonia is nothing to me."

He swiped a hand through his scraggly hair, and leaned closer, his eyes glowing. Not with tears nor admiration. More like the bosky, glazed look of a drunk.

"How fast will the duke's men travel?" He shook his head, the glaze transforming into a mean glare. "And so... I shouldn't bother with *her*. I should settle for a scrawny redhaired witch and become a Scots baron, like the duke suggested."

Her temper flared. Would that she really was a witch and could turn him into a bug and stomp him and...

What? He'd talked to the duke about *her*?

He was trying to rattle her that was all. The duke would happily foist her on anyone, he wanted her that much out of Rudgwick's sights.

"'Tis a poor plan. 'Twill be years before I inherit."

"Oh, I can make that happen sooner."

Rage spiked in her. Threaten her father, would he? She willed her anger to cool, tamed her tongue, and steeled herself.

"Did you visit the bank, Lucie?"

There was no use denying it. "I did. With Sir Thomas Abernathy."

Dankworth's chapped lips moved in an ugly grimace and settled into a sneer. "His Grace will be disappointed. He wanted me to get there first. With you."

The duke again. As if Bridgehampton would be conspiring with the likes of him.

She remembered the old man's flash of palpable fear. It might be true, at least where Lucie was concerned.

And what if it were? Dankworth was trying to muddle her. She'd deal with the duke later.

"You look shocked. He was fine with me escorting you to Norwich, you know."

If true, the duke would regret it. She had the means to make him very sorry. She'd give the letter straight to Sir Thomas. She opened her mouth to say so and remembered that flash of fear on the old man's face again.

Lucie, you fool. Shut your mouth.

"'Tis neither here nor there what the duke was fine with. He'll be busy answering how much he knew about his son's treason. And yours."

The sneer grew bolder. "It was bad of you to invade Stephenson's office. I'd just reached an understanding with his clerk." Dankworth circled the table, and the wild anger she'd inherited from the Macbeths flamed.

"Would that my father *was* here."

"A broken-down soldier?" Dankworth scoffed.

"Oh, aye. A broken-down soldier against a scraggy princock like yourself." She forced a laugh and gripped her blade. "My odds are on Colonel Finnley Macbeth."

"Oh, I'm a cock all right." His hand went to his fall. "I'll take you to Scotland, and your father will thank me for marrying you."

"He'll rip out your guts while ye're still drawing breath. And Rudgwick—"

"Won't come for you; he's unavoidably detained. And noblemen don't want soiled goods."

He was too close now, and too big, bigger than her and stronger, and she'd been fighting for two days now.

She'd fight longer. She'd fought off Jamey Paisley. She'd never submit.

Pity, the Sight wouldn't tell her how to stomp on this insect.

"Why not make a run for France?" she said.

"Maybe I'll go there, after Scotland."

"Ye won't make it to Scotland."

"I told you, Rudgwick won't protect you, nor your servant."

"Think ye they're the only men who'll protect my honor? I promise ye, Dankworth, on my mother's life, if ye harm me, ye'll die a terrible death. 'Tis no matter if Rudgwick won't help. In Scotland, 'twill be at the hands of my father; in France, 'twill be my cousin who rips out your heart. Stand down. Go. Now. While ye still can."

He inched closer, his hand still undoing his buttons. His leer sent her blood spiking. It was too late for talking.

She heard distant voices outside on the street, a crowd of men on their way to or from the inn's tavern. She leaned her head toward the window and screamed.

"There's a crowd in the taproom. No one will hear you."

"*Murder*," she shouted. "*Help. Help, help, help, help.*"

Dankworth flew at her. She feinted sideways but not soon enough. He clutched her throat, with first one hand and then both. His eyes bulged, dark with fury, yet his lips still pulled back in a semblance of a smile. A hard object poked her belly.

Dear Lord. Her vision blurred, and she struggled for air... and remembered her dagger.

Heart racing, lungs tightening, she swung the knife around and up as she'd been taught seeking the soft part of his back. The blade bit through coarse cloth and soft tissue and met something hard. He yelped and slapped at her hand. The dagger went flying.

With his grip eased she gulped air and brought her knee up sharp—and hit the hard length of his thigh as he shifted.

Her head bumped the wall, his weight pressed against her, and cool air touched her leg. When he leaned in, she lurched away from his lips and shouted "No," bringing her hands up to claw his face.

"Bitch," he roared scrabbling at her hands. "I'll..."

Dankworth flew backward.

Rudgwick was here. She sank back, caught her breath, and watched in horror as the vision she'd seen that night at the theater came to life.

***

Moments earlier

Rudgwick raced up the stairs, pistol in hand, and heard the screams at the first landing. By the time he reached the chamber door, the screams had stopped.

Not too late. He couldn't be too late.

The blasted latch rattled but didn't give. A metal pick lay on the floor, and the face plate bore deep scratches.

He backed up and kicked, and kicked again, and harder.

"No," Lucie cried.

The wood trim gave way and the door crashed open.

The bastard had her up against the wall. He had no clear shot. A shot might pass through Dankworth and hit Lucie, and... he needed his hand.

He stowed his pistol and charged in, yanking Dankworth back, and landing a quick kick. Startled, Dankworth staggered and blocked the next blow, and the next one.

And then Dankworth launched at him, raining blow after blow. More than one landed on his stump, sending a fiery pain that nearly doubled him up. And then he was flying toward the open window.

He braced his hand on the wooden frame, his useless arm flailing, kicking backwards as Dankworth snatched at his legs. Behind him, Lucie shouted, metal cracked on bone, and Dankworth cursed.

The daft girl was rescuing him. He turned around, and Dankworth, head bleeding, charged him.

He cartwheeled backward and grabbed for the ledge, swinging sideways, legs scrabbling, while inside Lucie had picked up the fight. He had to get back to her.

The toe of one boot found the fascia board trimming the roof and wedged there.

Dankworth appeared at the window. "Let's dispose of your remaining hand, Rudgwick, shall we." He yanked on the window to slam it down, but it stuck.

While Dankworth struggled with the window and swore, Rudgwick scanned the dormer for another hand hold.

"Curse you," Dankworth shouted. He spun around suddenly, just as Lucie shrieked.

That was a battle cry, not fear. But brave as she was, she was no match for Dankworth.

He set a boot to the tile and scrabbled, sliding back and almost losing his grip.

Where the devil was Hyde? The maid who'd locked him up had promised to fetch Hyde.

Arm muscles burning, he searched with his dangling foot for another toehold. He'd pull himself up and in. He could do it. He had to do it.

Dankworth appeared once more, blood running down the side of his head. He reached for the window sash again, but his hands froze on the wood. His eyes went wide, his mouth opened in shock, and he clutched his middle. With a loud *oof*, he flew out of the window past Rudgwick, grabbing at Rudgwick's leg as he went. But losing his grip, he slid down the short stretch of roof to the board, where he clung, swinging wildly.

Lucie leaned out, gripping the window ledge with bloody hands. Her hair was in disarray, her face blotchy with anger.

"I've got ye," she said, grasping Rudgwick's good arm.

"Help me," Dankworth cried.

"Hold on, Rudgwick," Lucie said, straining and adding her strength to his own. "Ye great heavy lummox. Have ye a toe hold?"

He laughed. He would make it. He wouldn't fail now.

He scrabbled up, hit a slippery spot, and slid back again to the board.

"Again," she said.

With a mighty effort he pushed against the fascia board, and she tugged him chest high to the window ledge, his shoulders and arms dangling into the room.

Wood cracked. Dankworth's scream pierced the night air and ended in a loud crunch below.

Lucie's breasts pressed against Rudgwick's back as she leaned out over him. He heard her sharp intake of breath, and then felt the yank on his trousers as she levered him in. His thighs scraped the ledge, and, with her last powerful tug, she pulled him all the way in, so that he landed atop her on the plank flooring.

Her chest rose and fell with desperate breaths. "The board broke," she said in a shaky voice.

Blood trailed along her cheek, mingling with her wild curls. He'd never seen anyone more beautiful. Bracing himself on one arm, he reached to brush back her hair, swallowed an oath, and mopped at her face with his stump. "Did he hurt you?"

"No." She lifted her head and pressed her lips to his. He sank down upon her, savoring the feel of her and the touch of her lips and the knowledge they'd both survived.

Lucie nudged him. "I hear Hyde's voice outside," she whispered.

The door opened. "Get the guests back to their rooms. Go along then."

That was the innkeeper's voice. Rudgwick stifled a groan. The man would surely call for a justice of the peace. There'd be an inquest to find out how Dankworth had died. They'd be stuck here in Norwich.

CHAPTER NINETEEN

Bound for Scotland

Two pairs of stout boots shuffled in. "Nothing to see here," the innkeeper said. "Just a man and his woman having an argument. There's never trouble at the Bell. And close that door."

They just might make it to Scotland. "Lucie." He kissed her forehead. "Lucie."

He'd almost been too late.

She lifted her head and kissed him fiercely again. The boots moved closer, and he lifted his head.

"Gone over." The innkeeper peered out the window, making rumbling noises deep in his throat. "Not going to be a pretty sight. In the alleyway though." He paused. "Damage to the building. That'll cost some to repair."

"What's that?" Hyde asked. The innkeeper stepped out of the way and Hyde looked out. "Had too much to drink," Hyde said. "Mayhap he came up against footpads in the alley. Mr., er, Thorne, are you and the missus all right?"

Rudgwick rolled off Lucie and struggled up on his shaking arm. "A few scrapes," he said. "And my pockets are deep enough to pay for repairs. Not that I had anything to do with the damage. I seem to have been locked in a storeroom by Sally."

"Aye," Hyde said. "Your niece, ain't she? Sent me off on a wild goose chase she did when I ought to have been here sorting these two out."

At the mention of Sally, the innkeeper's eyes flashed, and he rubbed at his stubble. "There's a gambling den around the corner," he said, falling into the plot. He crossed to the door and opened it a crack. "Get a lantern and some of the boys."

"How badly are you hurt?" Rudgwick whispered.

She sat up next to him and shook her head. "Oh, Rudgwick," she whispered. "'Twas the vision. Do ye remember?"

"From the theater. But—"

"Lady Fiona said they're not always exactly true, but there's always some truth to them."

A throat cleared near them. Hyde was watching them, eyes glowing. "Don't know about that Sally," he said in his usual bellow. "If she were my niece, I'd take a strop to her."

Rudgwick dropped another kiss on Lucie's forehead. They were alive. If Jeremy and Harmonia had arrived safely, if they could keep the duke away, they could still find their way to Scotland.

They couldn't afford to be stuck in Norwich attending an inquest. Hyde had found a fortunate weakness to exploit.

Rudgwick staggered up and reached a hand to Lucie. She stood, revealing a bloody knife that had been hidden under her skirts. He kicked it under the bed.

"Begging your pardon, but what happened here, Mr. Thorne?" the innkeeper asked.

He set a hand to Lucie's cheek. "Go and rest, my dear. I'm so very sorry." He held his breath wondering if she would snap at him.

She sniffed, and tears—real tears rolled down her cheeks. He pulled her into a hug and kissed the top of her head.

"I'll fetch some hot water," Hyde said.

Lucie stepped into the servant's room, and Hyde left. Then Rudgwick spun a tale about the maid's unaccountable actions, after which he'd returned to his room and heard a fight in the alley while he was arguing with his wife. He'd lost his grip when he looked out to see what was afoot, being worse for wear after visiting a local gin shop earlier.

***

It was after midnight before all had quietened. Hyde had gained confirmation from the inn staff that Dankworth was dead, all their scratches and bruises had been tended to, and enough money had changed hands to smooth matters with the innkeeper. They made their way down to the stables, saddled their horses, and rode out with as little fanfare as possible.

It was a surprisingly clear night, and once out of Norwich, they followed the River Yare, traveling slowly and resting the two horses frequently.

Lucie could the see the pain in Rudgwick's eyes, though he didn't complain. He'd taken a thrashing from Dankworth, a great deal of it on his arm. She'd offered to walk alongside, but he insisted she ride with him and this time in front. In truth, it was chilly, and she welcomed his body warming hers. They'd had the road to themselves for the journey, not even a highwayman about, nor any of the duke's men.

The duke. She must tell Rudgwick what Dankworth had said. But not now. They were all bone-weary and tired.

"I pray there's a bed at our destination," she said.

"I'd like that also." He nuzzled her ear, sending a shiver of awareness through her. "Not long now. Dawn will break soon, and then we'll travel more quickly."

They rounded a bend and saw two riders approaching. Lucie accepted the reins while Rudgwick reached into his coat.

"Don't shoot me in the back, Major Lord Rudgwick," she whispered.

She felt his answering chuckle rumble through them.

The other horses slowed. "My lord," a man called.

It was the two grooms who'd accompanied Lord Jeremy and Lady Harmonia.

"What's happened?" Rudgwick called.

"We've been sent to look for you."

"We were delayed. How are the others?"

"Had some trouble finding the place, my lord, but we all arrived safely. We'll take you to them."

Rudgwick eased the pistol back into his coat. "Lead the way."

'Twas morning, a foggy one, when they reached their destination, a snug riverside cottage. The smell of the sea and the scent of coal filled the air. With its brick chimney spitting out smoke and four dormers perched across the thatched roof, the cottage looked like the home of a modest farmer.

"Whose home is this?" Lucie asked.

"A friend's," he said, and she heard the fatigue in his voice.

"Rudgwick." Lord Jeremy came around the side of the dwelling, his bootsteps soft in the wet grass. "We were worried."

"All's well," he said, "Is everything readied here?"

"Yes."

"Good. We must leave quickly." He leaned forward and his breath tickled her ear. "No rest for the wicked," he whispered, "at least not yet. I hope to leave immediately."

Lord Jeremy came and plucked her off the horse. He looked fatigued also, but he'd had a chance to shave.

"How is Lady Harmonia?" she asked. "How was your journey? Have you heard anything of the duke or his men?"

"She is well, thank God. Our journey was uneventful, and neither the duke's men nor Dankworth have appeared." Jeremy patted her hand. "And I'm grateful you were with her when she was abducted... You're injured, Miss Macbeth. What's happened?"

"Dankworth won't be troubling us again," she said.

Rudgwick dismounted and handed his reins to the groom. In the light of morning, she could see the pain and exhaustion etched into his face.

Lord Jeremy's frown deepened. "Those are fresh bruises, Rudgwick. What happened?"

The cottage door opened, and Lady Harmonia appeared, still wearing Lucie's trousers. The girl waved, and Lucie waved back.

"We'll tell you all," Lucie said, taking Rudgwick's whole arm, and setting it about her waist. As shaky as she herself was, she worried he'd tumble right here on the muddy drive. "Help me in then, Major Lord Rudgwick."

She took a step and wobbled, and Rudgwick's arm tightened around her.

"Steady," he said, swaying against her.

She chuckled. "Like two bosky old soldiers, we are."

Before Rudgwick could answer, Lady Harmonia came down the short walk and took Lucie's free arm.

"You're hurt." She pulled back and looked at Rudgwick. "You're both hurt. Come along through to the kitchen. There's a fire and we'll toast some bread. I'll warm some of Musbury's cook's fortifying stew for you, too, before we leave."

"Musbury?" Lucie asked, allowing herself to be ushered up the walk to the door.

"Lord Jeremy's friend. This is his cottage. I quite like him, though I do think he could do with a more regular housekeeper, and—" she leaned in close, "—a proper water closet."

Lucie laughed, realizing she was meant to. Lady Harmonia had come through the fire and the frosty hauteur had thawed.

"Not that I'm ungrateful," Lady Harmonia added. "Musbury is saving us."

Lord Jeremy cleared his throat. "Only Musbury?"

Lady Harmonia flashed Lord Jeremy a smile that showed how matters lay between them. "And you and Lord Rudgwick as well."

The short hall led to a kitchen in the back. An older woman in a plain gown and smock bobbed a curtsy and bustled about heating more water.

"I'm afraid Musbury only has coffee," Lady Harmonia said.

"That will do." Lucie spotted a bench and went to it, seating herself and bringing Rudgwick down with her.

Lord Jeremy dropped to his haunches in front of them. "Shall I fetch a doctor?" he murmured.

Rudgwick waved his stump. "No." He gritted his teeth.

Lady Harmonia arrived bearing two steaming cups. Lucie watched as Rudgwick's hand shook around the earthenware mug. The girl frowned, her gaze flitting over Rudgwick, who was far worse for wear than Lucie.

"How did this happen?" she asked.

"Major Lord Rudgwick rescued me," Lucie said. "From the proverbial fate worse than death at the hands of a monster. He'd been locked in a storeroom by Dankworth's accomplice, who also led Hyde astray. He barely made it to me in time. Dankworth, I fear, landed more punches than Rudgwick," Lucie bit her lip and decided Dankworth's other victim had a right to know the villain's fate. "Dankworth landed more punches, that is, before falling out of the attic window onto the pavement below."

Lord Jeremy's eyes widened. "You pushed him out of a window, Rudgwick?"

Rudgwick shook his head and chuckled, tiredly. "No. He pushed *me* out. And then Lucie evened the score by shoving him after me."

Lord Jeremy stood. "*You fell out of an attic window*? We must certainly fetch a doctor."

"I didn't fall. I was able to hold onto the windowsill." Rudgwick handed the shaking cup to Lord Jeremy. "While Lucie dealt with Dankworth."

A tremble went through her. She'd recovered her knife, finally. She'd driven it into Dankworth's kidney. She'd killed a man.

Oh, but it had been just, and necessary, and never, never, never did she *ever* want to fight like that again, knowing the man she loved might fall to his death if she didn't succeed. Closing her eyes against the memory, she roused her courage. "All's well that ends well. I'm only ashamed that it took me so long, Major Lord Rudgwick."

He gave her a wan smile. "She pulled me back in as well. You're stronger than you look, my love."

His love. She felt heat rising into her cheeks and tried to cover it by gulping a mouthful of the hot drink. Technically, he was still tied to Lady Harmonia. He oughtn't to be whispering words of love to another woman in front of the lass.

"I'd like to leave soon," Rudgwick said. "Where is Musbury? Is everything ready?"

"He's organizing supplies." Lord Jeremy said. "He'll be along soon."

"And where exactly are we going?" Lucie asked. "No one has told me."

Despite his fatigue, Rudgwick raised an eyebrow at her.

"Why, Scotland, of course," Lady Harmonia leaned close. "Before Grandpapa catches up with me. That's why Jeremy sent men to find you. We didn't want to leave without you, and Musbury says we must catch the tide."

The duke. Dankworth had said the duke was fine with him kidnapping Lucie. She must tell Rudgwick. But not now, not while he was so weak and hurting.

"You're here." A man had entered through the kitchen door. Fair haired under a billed cap, he sported a full beard a shade darker than the hair on his head. He accepted a cup from the older woman then came to greet the men and Lady Harmonia and be introduced to Lucie.

Musbury was shorter than Rudgwick and Lord Jeremy, and with his broad frame, round cheeks, and heavy jumper he looked like a sturdy barrel.

"You're done in, Rudgwick," he said. "Would you rather wait until the next tide to leave?"

"I'll do." Rudgwick said. "The sooner we go, the better." He took Lucie's hand and swept a gaze over her. "It's cold on the water. Are there extra coats? Jumpers?"

"I have blankets and some quilts here we can bring. Mrs. Carruthers might be able to run home and find something warm for the lady in exchange for good coin."

Rudgwick dropped her hand and dipped into his pocket. "I do have a few shillings left."

"Clean stockings and some honey as well, if she has them," Lucie said, squeezing Rudgwick's hand.

Musbury picked out a coin and went to speak with the servant, who hurried away.

"It's good we're leaving," Musbury said. "My man just came back from Belton with the cable I was needing and says there were men in Yarmouth looking for two ladies, one comely and dark haired, the other a red-haired Scotswoman. Offering a reward."

Lucie glanced at Rudgwick. "How much?"

"Not enough to tempt me or my crew, miss. I know Rudgwick and Bolton here would have my guts for garters if I betrayed them." His smile revealed a row of beautiful white teeth, only one of them chipped. "And I hear your father would as well."

"If you can convey us safely to Scotland," Lady Harmonia smiled up at Lord Jeremy, "as soon as I get my hands on my inheritance, I'll double the duke's reward."

Had Lord Jeremy proposed. Or was it the lass asking for *his* hand? She was showing herself to be as determined as her grandfather. Or as Rudgwick.

"According to Sir Thomas Abernathy, Sidmouth has been drawn in," Rudgwick said. "Yes, Sir Thomas helped us in Norwich, and that is another story. I don't believe he has any interest in turning Harmonia over to the duke, but nevertheless, we should be on our way."

"Does this boat have a cabin?" Lucie asked. "Tell me we won't be sleeping amongst the day's catch."

"It's a two-master, Miss Macbeth," Musbury said, with another grin and some pride. "Two cabins and five berths. You ladies will have your privacy, and the men may take shifts sleeping."

'Twould be better than rattling up the Great North Road in a chaise, she hoped. "I'll keep myself and my red hair below deck until we reach the open sea."

"I'll go find those quilts for you," Musbury said.

"You should eat while we wait for Mrs. Carruthers." Lady Harmonia went to fetch bowls.

Lord Jeremy's troubled gaze followed her. "Are we doing the right thing?" he mused. "The duke will be furious with her."

"He'll forgive her and blame me," Lucie said. "Major Lord Rudgwick, let me tend your wounds."

Before he could answer, Hyde entered with the two grooms, and Jeremy turned to give instructions while the new arrivals ate. Hyde would travel with them; the two grooms would enjoy a fishing holiday on the Yare and eventually return to London with the horses.

She was happy to see Rudgwick eat with some appetite. The stew was tasty and fortifying, and yet it lay heavy on her stomach. Before they could finish, Mrs. Carruthers arrived with both a heavy jumper that she herself had knitted, an old coat, and a pair of darned but clean stockings, and then fetched a honey jar from Musbury's stores.

Rudgwick refused again to be nursed just yet, so they made their way to the river where Musbury's small yacht and two crewmen were waiting.

As she'd promised, Lucie went below to the small cabin. Two narrow berths piled with the quilts from Musbury's cottage flanked each bulkhead. She felt the sway of the boat and thumping of boots as the small crew arranged rigging and sails and cast away from the mooring.

The berth beckoned, but she couldn't sleep yet. Her back against the bulkhead, she watched through the small porthole as they slipped down the river and into the estuary.

"Miss Lucie." Hyde's voice woke her.

"Oh drat." She rubbed her eyes and sat up straight just as Rudgwick bent and came through into the cabin.

"We woke you," he said. "Go back to sleep. My arm will wait."

She poked at his chest. "Sit ye down."

After a short battle, Rudgwick submitted to having his wounds tended, with Hyde watching and a bottle of gin at the ready. Rudgwick took a healthy swig and told her to proceed.

He bore the unwrapping stoically, but when she saw the fresh bruising and broken patches of skin, she wanted to weep. Oh Hades, by the time she finished treating and wrapping, she *was* weeping.

He set his hand to her jaw, his calloused thumb sweeping her cheek.

Hyde cleared his throat. "I can see the docks through this wee porthole. Ye'll want to go up, milord, and have a look."

Rudgwick chuckled and pressed his forehead to hers. "Get some rest, my love."

A rap on the door brought Lady Harmonia, clutching Mrs. Carruthers' warm garments. "They sent me below," she grumbled. "As if Grandfather's spies could recognize me. But if you're going to be here, Rudgwick—"

"No. We can't squeeze another body in here. I'll go up." His lips were warm against her forehead and then he stood, stooping under the low ceiling.

Hyde gathered the discarded bandage and capped the gin bottle.

"The two of ye need rest as well, Hyde," Lucie said.

"We'll rest later," Rudgwick said. "After we clear Yarmouth and the nearby coastal patrols."

He left her stewing and feeling suddenly waspish.

"Well, ye're in trousers—my trousers," she told Lady Harmonia. "Why not go up on deck with them?"

"Musbury said I must wait below." She dropped the jumper and coat on the bed with a grimace of distaste.

The haughty hoyden. "'Twas kind of the old woman to sell us her warm clothing," Lucie chided.

"What? Oh, yes. I'm just thinking about what lies ahead. Will I get seasick and cast up my accounts over Mrs. Carruthers's things?"

"Ye've never traveled by boat?"

"I've only ever been on a punt on Grandfather's lake."

Despite all her privilege, the lass hadn't done much of anything. "Ye may get sick; probably will if the sea is rough. It likely won't last the whole journey."

"That's what Musbury said. And he couldn't tell me how many days we'll be at sea. It depends on the wind and the weather. We might even have to stop on the way. Musbury assured me I'd be safe if we do."

Musbury, Musbury, Musbury. "Have you set your cap for Musbury now?"

Lady Harmonia's eyes widened, and she frowned. "Of course not." She plopped down onto the narrow berth where Rudgwick had sat.

Lucie stifled a laugh. Donning trousers, running off to sea, and plopping down; Lady Harmonia was not the same girl she'd met in Rudgwick's drawing room.

"I don't think Jeremy wants to marry. I've dropped many hints, and though he smiles and acts agreeable, he hasn't asked me."

The lulling motion of the ship sent a new wave of fatigue swamping Lucie. She yawned and began taking her hair down and plaiting it. "Why do ye not ask him?"

"Is that what you did? Did you propose to Rudgwick?"

"Me?" She scoffed. "Propose to Rudgwick? I did not."

Her predicament came back to her. All the kisses and whispered words of love and visions of intimacy... She knew herself. Wherever this led, it must be on her terms or not at all. "And I won't marry him as long as he's your fiancé."

Lady Harmonia stiffened, shocked.

"Nor will I be any man's mistress," Lucie added, for good measure. The silly chit must know where things stood.

"But... I release him, Lucie."

"Ye can't," she went on, her stubborn anger rising, "since it's not ye who made the promise. It's your grandfather." She yanked off one boot and then the other, stretched out on the hard bunk, and pulled a blanket over her. "But don't ye fash, lass. Rudgwick may be able to persuade the old codger." She'd given him the means. He could decide when and how to use it. "If ye go up on deck, tell your daft fiancé he must get some rest."

***

Rudgwick sat on the deck, leaning against the cabin's bulkhead, and letting the cold air and salt spray hasten the dulling effects of the gin from the second bottle they'd passed around. They'd left Yarmouth more than an hour ago. They were closer to Ostend than to Edinburgh; they could flee to the Continent and surrender Lady Harmonia into the care of Menteith and his wife. He'd had a whispered discussion with Jeremy about it, and then gone back to his gin.

They'd turned north and were running into weather. A blast of cold wind ripped across the ship. The day was advancing into a chilled late afternoon.

Father had kept a yacht near his small holding in Kent. Before the army, before he'd inherited the title, he'd gone out on the water as often as possible, for as long as possible. It brought a feeling of freedom, an anticipation of adventure.

He'd had his adventures on land, though. And after, sailing home from the war, then back to Flanders, and home again, he'd been too weighed down by grief and duty to savor the sea.

Today was different entirely. He wasn't enjoying freedom, anticipating adventure, or wearily returning to one duty or another; he was fleeing the duke's power, as certainly as Harmonia was.

It was a tactical retreat only. When he next saw the duke, he and Harmonia would prevail. Poor Jeremy and Lucie were caught up in the intrigue.

Lucie. She hadn't agreed to marry him yet. And what if she didn't? He couldn't face that future.

If she didn't, he'd go back into the army—even one-armed, the army would need him at some obscure outpost. Unless he'd disgraced himself too much by this adventure.

"Rudgwick." Jeremy eased down next to him. His overlong hair was windblown, he needed a shave, and his eyes still bore the worried look he'd had since... Well, since they'd left Thornview Farm and returned to London mere days ago.

"Are we doing the right thing, Rudgwick?"

He laughed and shook his head. "You asked that before. I've been feeling guilty about involving you in this. Of all of us, you don't have to be here."

"I wouldn't leave you to this madness alone."

"You did your part in rescuing the ladies from Dankworth. And in getting Harmonia safely away from Norwich. I'm not sure Sir Thomas would have let her slip through his fingers, not with the duke leaning on Sidmouth."

"And that is another story you owe me. What else happened in Norwich?"

"Sir Thomas appeared just as we were leaving for the bank. He went with us, however, it was Lucie who spoke for us and brought the manager, Mrs. May, to the point." His heart filled, thinking about her strength and determination. He told Jeremy about the trove of documents the lady delivered.

But he didn't tell Jeremy about the one he was carrying inside his coats. He prayed his friend wouldn't ask. He didn't want to lie to him.

"You ought to go below and rest, Rudgwick." Harmonia's voice startled him.

She'd appeared from nowhere, shivering in the icy wind, her hat pulled low.

"You're cold." Jeremy jumped to his feet. "Let me get you a blanket. And Harmonia is right, Rudgwick. Sleep, and you can keep watch tonight and give your bed to Musbury."

"I suppose I should." He unwound his creaky limbs and stood. He wasn't sure sleep would come. The fresh air helped him ignore the pain.

"I'm not going to marry you, Rudgwick," Harmonia said. "I release you from your promise to me. Nor will I sue you for breach of promise."

A shudder went through him. The contract, the financial obligations to the people he was responsible for, his father's loans and legacy and honor, had been nagging at him for too long.

Harmonia wouldn't sue him, and the duke would be in a poor position to do so, not with the letter he had pressed to his heart. Lucie had given him the key to his freedom. Blast Bridgehampton's arrogance and pride.

And his own. The duke was his kinsman, and the crime had been his son's. Was he any better than Stephenson, blackmailing Bridgehampton to be released from a marriage agreement?

"You are speechless," Harmonia said, "and very cold."

He roused himself. He'd been unfair to this girl. None of this was her doing. "Lady Harmonia, thank you, and... I'm sorry. I've been a dreadful fiancé. You deserve better."

She drew herself up. "We were a mésalliance. Let us leave it at that. Now, it's warmer below, but I came up because I couldn't sleep, what with Lucie shivering and crying out with nightmares."

Lucie was having nightmares? Rudgwick turned toward the ladder.

"And I need to speak to you, Jeremy," Harmonia said in a stiff and haughty voice.

Rudgwick looked back. Jeremy gazed down, befuddled at his hand in Harmonia's. "Lord Jeremy. I've come to care for you deeply. Will you marry me?"

Rudgwick smiled and hurried down the short ladder.

The small cabin was warmer, but not by much. The dim light from the portholes showed Lucie curled on the thin, narrow mattress, her red plait spilling across the ticking. She rolled to the bulkhead with a shivering moan, and he made his decision.

He sat on the opposite berth and fought first with one boot and then the other, prising them off. Hyde was asleep, and Jeremy was too busy to help him.

That thought made him smile through the straining and contortions. The bunk was narrow—all the better for sharing the heat of his body. He lifted the quilt, and stretched on his left side, fumbling the cover back with his stump, and then tugging her close.

Her hair smelled of lavender, and her body and legs spooned up perfectly with his. It was his last thought before slipping, finally, into blessed sleep.

***

Her breast tingled with a butterfly touch and warmth flowed through her body. They were back in the inn room, not the one at the Ram, nor either of the rooms at the Bell. This room was plainer and cleaner, the curtains a light dimity cloth that fluttered in a breeze. The Axminster carpet had seen many years, yet the colors were still beautiful. A bedside table bore an oil lamp, still lit, but turned down low. Flowering vines trailed up the wallpaper.

The Sight was providing more details.

She lay curled on her side, and... she was naked, and a large hand framed her breast, the thumb sweeping lazily, inciting hot warmth.

"Lucie, my love." She rolled onto her back, and he moved over her, his body long, muscled, and hard, pressing against hers.

"Rudgwick," she whispered.

A snuffling snore in her ear made her giggle, and...

She opened her eyes. Her forehead was all but pressed to a dark plank wall. And she wasn't alone. Warmth surged along her back and her legs, and an arm rested atop her waist, the sleeve folded up.

She was fully dressed, and so was he. Their bed rocked to and fro in a lazy, rhythmic rolling that had nothing to do with them, and she remembered... They were on Musbury's boat headed for Scotland. And home.

All visions had some truth, Lady Fiona had said, and this was the truth of that one plaguing her. Nothing intimate would happen here.

Another adorable snuffle followed with a twitch of his arm and the slightest of moans.

"Rudgwick," she whispered.

A sigh tickled her ear, but she knew he was sleeping—finally. If they weren't stopped by the coastal patrol, if they didn't get shipwrecked, they'd be in Scotland soon enough, and then what? She sent up a prayer, snuggled deeper into the bunk, and joined him in slumber.

CHAPTER TWENTY

The House on India Street

No one had been watching the back door at the house on India Street. Lucie went through, her companions creeping in behind her.

The kitchen maid was stirring gravy, the cook was putting the finishing flourish on roasted fowl, and one of the footmen was lugging a tray of dishes to the scullery.

Several dishes. Hope rose in her. Perhaps Father was still here, and Mother with him. And they had guests... that last would be unusual.

Or perhaps Lady Fiona had traveled north. She might have completed the long journey in the many days it had taken them to sail from Norfolk, delayed as they were by storms and unreliable winds.

"Mrs. Mac," Lucie called. Her fellow travelers, Rudgwick, Lady Harmonia, Lord Jeremy, and of course Hyde, stood behind her.

All eyes looked up filled with astonishment, and then annoyance, and then recognition. "Miss Lucie." The cook, Mrs. MacGillicutty, dropped her spoon. Bertha, the kitchen maid, flashed a grin.

Thomas, the handsome young footman, knew better than to smile, but his eyes brimmed with pleasure at seeing her.

"I'll fetch Mrs. Brodie," Thomas said. "Mr. Brodie will be too busy with the dinner guests." He hurried off.

Mrs. Brodie served as housekeeper and her husband as butler in Lady Fiona's Edinburgh home.

"Oh, lass, we were that worried," Mrs. Mac cried. "Your da and ma will be that happy to see ye. I've got to get this fowl plated and then I'll see to ye and yer company. Bertha, hurry with that. Ye look done in, miss. We'll get ye fed in but a moment."

Lucie let out a long breath though what she wanted to do was toss her smashed bonnet into the air and yell *huzzah*. They'd somehow arrived safely in Leith, and then traveled the streets from the port to this newer part of Edinburgh and Lady Fiona's home without incident.

And her mother and father were here. Mayhap that was why her neck had been prickling the whole way here.

Next to her, Rudgwick chuckled. Was he at all nervous, facing Colonel Macbeth, Baron of Calder, over his daughter's honor?

Mrs. Brodie hurried into the kitchen, swept her gaze over the four of them, and curtsied.

Lucie smiled. Despite their tired coats, despite the scruff of their beards and their overlong locks, the housekeeper, a woman of middling age and an experienced domestic, had surmised that Rudgwick and Lord Jeremy were Persons of Consequence. Lady Harmonia as well, even dressed as she was in the gown Lucie had purchased in Norwich, ill-fitting on her voluptuous shape.

Lucie herself wore the stained and hastily mended gown she'd worn the night they were taken by Dankworth. The lass, after all, was younger and higher ranked, and needed the better dress. Not to mention that if she presented Lady Harmonia in trousers, her parents would know Lucie had taken the trews with her to London.

She made introductions, not stinting on names and rank. She trusted Lady Fiona's staff, and wasn't afraid of the duke, not now that they'd reached sanctuary. They followed the housekeeper to the breakfast room, took seats at the small table there, and Mrs. Brodie set out a bottle of whisky and four glasses. Hyde had stayed below in the kitchen.

"The gentlemen will like a drink, I expect," Mrs. Brodie said, "and the ladies might like one as well. I'll fetch some tea and then some dinner for ye. Lady Fiona has guests—"

"She's here?" Lucie cried. Tears threatened, and she beat them back.

"Aye. She of all of them wasn't fashing about ye. She said his lordship," she dipped her head to Rudgwick, "would see to ye."

He'd seen to her all right. Rescued her; escorted her to the bank; eased her nightmares. Though he hadn't come back to her narrow berth after that first night, more was the pity.

"My parents are here, aren't they?"

"Aye."

"And who else is here for dinner?"

"Lady Fiona's guest." Another bow to Rudgwick. "His lordship's mother, Lady Rudgwick. And at table is Mr. McCormack and Laird Paisley."

Mr. McCormack was Father's Scottish solicitor, but... "Paisley? He was well enough to travel south?"

Mrs. Brodie blinked. "Ye've not heard. The old laird passed on weeks ago. This is Jamey Paisley."

Blood drained from her battered head, and she held onto the edge of the table. Blast it all. She didn't need another encounter with Jamey Paisley, who somehow believed she liked his slobbering kisses and grabbing hands.

She'd run from him once when she was all on her own, and he'd meant to force her acceptance. That had ended with her tumble and the loss of a valiant horse. This time she'd stand her ground. 'Twould be easy with Rudgwick beside her, and Mother and Father knowing what was what. In the immediate aftermath of the accident, she hadn't been in a right enough mind to tell them what he'd tried, and then later, she'd thought not to trouble them with it until she returned from her visit with Lady Fiona.

"Why is Paisley here?"

The housekeeper glanced at Rudgwick. "I expect your mother or father can tell ye that, miss."

Which meant that she knew. The whole household knew. Laird Paisley was here to badger Father for her hand.

"I'd thank ye to not reveal our presence to the guests."

"No indeed. I'll wait until the ladies withdraw and then I'll tell your mothers and Lady Fiona. Rest here, and we'll bring ye up dinner."

***

Laird Paisley. Who the devil was he? Lucie had flinched when the name was mentioned. Her back had gone up, and her freckles had popped as she'd paled and then they'd drowned in the rising flush that he knew to be anger.

When the housekeeper left, Rudgwick cleared his throat.

"Laird Paisley?" he asked.

Her mouth primmed and her face looked pinched. She sighed. "A neighbor in the Highlands."

"Ah." Hyde had mentioned a neighbor's son was courting her.

Harmonia watched with interest, and Jeremy, ever the diplomat, diverted her, urging her to try the whisky.

"Jamey has taken the notion that we're to marry." She spoke through clenched teeth. "And we most assuredly will not."

Another man wanted Lucie. Many men would, of course, but why would this one provoke such anger in her? "Why would he have that notion?"

Another sigh. "I might have not said no directly. But when he kissed me..." She shuddered.

Another man had kissed her. Rudgwick wanted to dash into the dining room and thrash the fellow. Lucie was his.

She was silent so long, he asked "And?"

Jeremy had tugged Harmonia over to a window and was pointing at features outside. The days being longer this far north, there was still plenty of light for whatever they were observing.

"I ought to have known better. My parents were in Edinburgh. He wanted to see my cousin Malcolm's distillery, so we rode there, just the two of us. On the way, it started to rain. I would have plowed on, but he wanted to shelter at a bothy we came across. He kissed me." She grimaced. "I fear I had to cosh him. And then I rode off. I'd taken one of my cousin's mounts, Pegasus. Such a valiant fellow, he was."

He reached for her hand. "That was the accident."

"Aye."

"Shall I cosh him again for you?"

She raised shining eyes to him. "He doesn't deserve the honor of being coshed by a man like yerself."

He would have kissed her again, but the door opened and the merry-eyed footman who'd fetched the housekeeper carried in a tray. "Mrs. Mac says it's the best she can do on short notice," he said, uncovering platters of sliced ham, vegetables, and potatoes, and fragrant bread rolls with butter.

"Have we taken your dinner?" Rudgwick asked.

The lad smiled. "Not at all milord. We ate earlier, we did."

"No stale biscuits," Harmonia said. "No potted meat. I shall embarrass myself and all of you tonight."

Before they'd finished their lemon custard and cakes, the door opened, and three ladies hurried in.

Lucie leaped from her seat and threw herself into her mother's arms.

Harmonia was only a bit more sedate greeting Lady Rudgwick. Jeremy joined in that greeting.

Since both mothers were busy, Rudgwick swept Lady Fiona into an embrace. He was, in fact, genuinely glad to see her.

Lady Fiona beamed up at him. "It does my heart good to see you here. Thank you for bringing Lucie home to us." Mother and Harmonia were disentangled by then, and Lucie introduced her mother to Jeremy and Harmonia. In truth, Greer Macbeth might have been Harmonia's mother, so alike were they with their dark hair and blue eyes.

"Tell us everything," Greer said.

The housekeeper brought more tea, and Lady Fiona poured more whisky, and they settled in while Lucie and Harmonia described almost everything that happened since the night of her birthday ball.

Harmonia, he was certain, left out bits and pieces of her interactions with Jeremy. Lucie didn't mention the letter she'd taken or their various kisses, and when she came to the point of Dankworth's death, she shook her head and went silent.

Taking a life, even that of a scoundrel, was clearly weighing on her conscience. For his part, it was the story they'd told the innkeeper that troubled him. He prayed the bribe was enough, and Sally's involvement enough of a mitigating factor, that an innocent man wouldn't be picked up for the death. The innkeeper had hinted that since Norwich was a market town filled with visitors, and Dankworth had been dressed as if he'd stolen his clothing off some good wife's drying line, no one would pursue the matter with vigor. Their escape wasn't precisely honorable, but then nothing to do with Dankworth was.

Harmonia was describing the storm they'd encountered off the coast of Durham when the door opened and a redhaired giant of a man entered, sweeping the room with a gaze that landed on Lucie. She was up and out of her seat again before he could take another step.

She stopped in front of him and curtsied. Macbeth was having none of that. He pulled her into his arms. "Lucie, Lucie," he murmured into her hair. He nodded to Rudgwick then set her back and studied her.

"You've a healing bruise, and..." He sniffed. "Ye need a bath, lass." He raised an eyebrow at the rest of them. His scars from Waterloo had healed well, yet they etched a deep trail over his head and face.

Harmonia's mouth had dropped open, and Jeremy eyed the old Scots warrior with a respectful frown.

Rudgwick was used to the scars, having watched them healing in Brussels. He laughed. "It's been a long journey, Colonel Macbeth. We are all a bit ripe." He extended his hand, and Macbeth clasped it in both his big paws.

Lucie cleared her throat and introduced Harmonia and Jeremy.

"Where is Hyde?" Macbeth asked.

"He's well, Father," Lucie said. "In the kitchen, regaling the servants with his adventures."

"He always has much to say, does Hyde." Macbeth frowned. "I've had a letter from Sir Thomas Abernathy and another from the banker in Norwich. Ye did well, Lucie. 'Struth I'm glad ye had Rudgwick to help ye. I thank ye, Major Lord Rudgwick."

Rudgwick sensed a dismissal coming and opened his mouth to ask for a private audience, but Macbeth spoke first. "I've left MacCormack and Paisley with a bottle of her ladyship's whisky. I'd best get back soon before they send for Brodie to open a second one. My lady, do ye have a bedchamber for these two lasses and a tub of hot water? Mayhap, Lucie, yer mother can find the both of ye fresh gowns."

Lady Fiona put an arm around Lucie, beckoned Harmonia, and nudged both girls toward the corridor. "I fear we haven't finished the renovations yet, but I have chambers that will do for both the ladies and the gentlemen."

"I'll have a word with both of the gentlemen first," Macbeth said. "I'll send them along later. Greer, my love, will ye help get the lasses settled?"

"I would like to stay, Father," Lucie said, returning to him.

He cupped his big paw around her cheek and his eyes twinkled, and Rudgwick felt a sense of relief. Not that he'd worried Macbeth would skewer him. It was true, he'd compromised Lucie. Indeed, he and Jeremy had compromised both young ladies. But they'd also saved their lives.

"I know ye'd like to stay, lass. But I must talk to Rudgwick and Lord Jeremy, and..." He sniffed and waved a hand in front of his nose. "I'll expect ye back here in an hour."

"Come, Lucie," Greer said. "Lady Fiona has brought your trunk with her. Sarah, will ye come as well? Ye can help me pick out a gown for Lady Harmonia."

Mother dropped a kiss on Rudgwick's cheek, winked at him, and followed the ladies out.

When the door closed, Macbeth filled their glasses, poured one for himself, and toasted them. "I thank ye, Rudgwick, Bolton, for your gallantry. I regret enlisting Lucie's help. Putting her in the path of Dankworth... 'Twas a lucky thing he was set upon by footpads." He raised an eyebrow.

He knew. How could he possibly—

"Sir Thomas wrote to me about it."

Rudgwick shook his head. "He was still in Norwich?"

"His men were. What really happened?"

Rudgwick took a fortifying drink and set down his glass.

"It was a near thing. Lucie stabbed him and shoved him out through the window. And then she pulled me back in through the same window. Your lass is a valiant lady, Colonel."

Macbeth squeezed his eyes shut a moment and then motioned them to the chairs. "There'll be time to hear the whole story. For now, we must talk about what to do for the lasses." He sat down heavily. "There must be two weddings."

Rudgwick stood. "Colonel, I would like the honor—"

"There's a young laird in Lady Fiona's parlor who'd marry Lucie." Macbeth went on as if Rudgwick hadn't spoken. "Though Lucie has turned him down more than once."

"I'll marry Lucie," Rudgwick said. "If she'll have me."

"Ah" Macbeth pinned him with eyes the same golden color as Lucie's. "But ye're engaged to the young lass, the duke's granddaughter."

"Lady Harmonia has given me my congé," he said. "She doesn't wish to marry me. Bridgehampton will come around to accepting the matter."

"Mayhap, but he still expects ye and the lass to marry. When I spoke with him today—"

"*Today*?"

"He's in Edinburgh." Macbeth's eyes twinkled. "Convinced we have his granddaughter squirreled away in the attic or cellars. He'll be back on the morrow, he said, with Runners, and since we won't hide the lass in the attic or cellars, he'll expect her to marry *tout suite*. He'll expect you to honor the marriage contract, Rudgwick. Ranted on about breach of contract and lawsuits. I've Paisley here willing to save Lucie's honor and add the Calder lands to his own, but for the duke's granddaughter—"

"You have me," Jeremy said. "Lady Harmonia and I will marry. Mine is a mere courtesy title, but my brother is the Duke of Northam, so she is not marrying below her rank. We shall marry first, and the duke will have no suit against Rudgwick."

"The lady is willing to marry ye?" Macbeth asked.

Jeremy's lips quivered. "In fact, Colonel, she suggested the notion first. I was... I am reluctant to cause a rift between her and her grandfather. He is her only living relative."

The letter Lucie took from the bank might just be the leverage to do something about that. Rudgwick would never ask the duke for money; civility toward his granddaughter and her husband would do.

"Commendable," Macbeth said. "Do ye care for her?"

"I do."

"And Rudgwick, have ye spoken with Lucie?"

"More than once. She's pointed out to me that Harmonia is an impediment. She's said no, and more recently, maybe." She'd also fiercely declared she wouldn't be his mistress, but he didn't want to broach that subject with her father because in fact he'd never openly asked her to fill the role. "I care for her. I'll take care of her. I simply must keep her out of the way of villains, though, or train myself to fight better one-handed."

"A fierce metal hook might be just the thing," Macbeth said.

He laughed. "Do I have your blessing, sir?"

"If ye can obtain Lucie's blessing, ye have mine. Now, MacCormack is a solicitor. I'll pack Paisley off to his gambling den, and then ye'll tell MacCormack what ye have in mind for a dower for each of the ladies, and then ye may go off and wash. We'll send one of the lads up to brush out your coats and shave ye, and by the time ye come back, there'll be some marriage agreements waiting along with your brides.

"I'll meet MacCormack," Rudgwick said, "But I won't pinch pennies. You decide what's fair for Lucie."

"I'd never expected to marry at all, much less an heiress," Jeremy said. "Rudgwick, what was in that agreement of yours?"

"Mother will know. She paid much closer attention than I did. Colonel, can you ask the housekeeper to fetch her down here?"

Macbeth went off to his errands and left them.

Jeremy filled their glasses again and raised his. "To wedded bliss."

They clinked glasses and drank.

"Will it be tonight?" Jeremy grinned. "I hope so. I'd rather not have to run out looking for a blacksmith though."

"This isn't Gretna Green, lad," Macbeth said.

They hadn't heard the door open. Macbeth ushered in a diminutive fellow and made introductions. Ian MacCormack offered felicitations and asked for their full names and those of their brides. When the butler carried in paper, quills, and ink, the solicitor sat down and began writing.

Mother hurried in and MacCormack rose, waiting patiently through her gushing congratulations, and then took his seat again and began listing her demands for Lady Harmonia.

Macbeth's eyes gleamed as he led both men out and turned them over to the butler. "Doona worry, Rudgwick, ye haven't completely put yourself in the hands of a Scotsman. I'll warrant yer mother will argue for ye if she feels I'm asking too much."

He laughed. It was true. Mother had excellent business sense. He gripped the older man's shoulder. "Thank you, Macbeth. Or shall I call you Father?"

Macbeth's eyes misted. "Aye, ye may. As long as my girl allows it."

***

An hour wasn't quite long enough for Lucie and Lady Harmonia, but it wasn't yet midnight when Lady Fiona and Mother came to escort them to the parlor. They'd washed, had their hair tidied and styled, and donned fresh gowns. Lady Harmonia wore one of Mother's best, being of a similar size and shape. Since Lady Fiona had packed all of Lucie's things and brought them north with her, 'twas her ivory ball gown the maid carried into her tonight. For Father's sake, Mother fixed a fichu over her bosom.

She'd have liked to lie down on her half of the bed in the cozy chamber with its dark curtains and tartan rugs, but she sensed there'd be more to this night, and she was far too excited to sleep anyway. Father had wanted to speak to Rudgwick and Lord Jeremy. She was anxious to hear what had transpired.

They fell in behind the older ladies in the corridor. "It feels wonderful to be clean," Lady Harmonia whispered in Lucie's ear. "Will we marry tonight?"

She shook her head. "I don't know." Would Father countenance a hasty wedding for herself? Would he interfere in the duke's business by seeing the lass married?

Lady Harmonia squeezed her hand. "If your father won't arrange it, Jeremy and I will find a way, and then Rudgwick will be free."

She swallowed a lump in her throat and found herself chuckling. "Is it truly what ye want?"

"Yes." Lady Harmonia smiled. "It's what we both want."

In the parlor, Father and his solicitor, Mr. MacCormack rose to greet them.

Lady Rudgwick was also there, a pair of spectacles perched on her nose as she sat at a table reviewing a document under the light of an Argand lamp. She waved a greeting and went back to her reading.

Footsteps in the hall made her turn. Rudgwick stood in the doorway, Lord Jeremy behind him. Rudgwick came straight to her and sniffed the air near her cheek.

Lucie laughed. "Better?"

"I wasn't complaining before."

Lord Jeremy had made straight for Lady Harmonia, pulling her aside and speaking with her. She looked up at him in rapt attention, her face softening, her smile growing brighter. Then she went up on her toes and kissed him, a featherlight kiss that made Jeremy smile.

"Well," Lucie said.

"Yes. Shall I ask you now, Lucie, or wait until Lady Harmonia is well and truly unavailable?"

"Rudgwick, ye daft man."

Father called everyone to attention.

"Let's hear what he says," Lucie whispered.

Lord Jeremy announced his and Lady Harmonia's wish to marry immediately; Mr. MacCormack proffered a marriage agreement, which, as it happened was the document Lady Rudgwick had been reviewing. Both the young people signed and proceeded to declare their vows in the presence of more than one Scottish citizen, as Father had called in the butler, Mr. Brodie, and two footmen as well.

Hyde carried over glasses of spirits. He'd been there all along, but she'd just noticed him.

"No toasting just yet," Rudgwick announced to the room. He went down on one knee, sending her heart leaping.

"Lucie Macbeth, will you do me the honor of making me the happiest man on earth. Will you marry me?"

Finally, he was free, and so was she. "Aye," she said, trying to breathe. "I'll marry ye, Tristan Hamilton Howton."

He leaped to his feet and his lips met hers in a kiss that promised forever.

"That's enough for now," Father said. "Let us proceed."

As if in a dream Lucie listened to Rudgwick's promises and repeated the words back to him, scarcely hearing the congratulations of the family that followed.

Family. Hyde had felt like family since the first night they met. Even Harmonia and Jeremy seemed like family now. Jeremy was like a brother to Rudgwick. And Harmonia... well, there was nothing like being kidnapped together to forge a special bond. Lady Rudgwick hugged Lucie and requested she call her mother, providing her own mother wouldn't mind. Mother did the same with Rudgwick.

She hugged her father. "Ye truly don't object?"

"I own, I once did. But your mother, and his mother, and Lady Fiona told me I mustn't fight the claims of the heart."

"Did ye... did ye *see* the trouble too? Is that why ye sent him to me?"

He drew back and studied her. "Ye have the Sight, Lady Fiona said."

She shook her head and then slowly nodded. "I suppose that's what this is."

"I'm sorry, lass. Ye'll come and talk to me when ye're troubled, won't ye?"

"I will."

She thought of that persistent vision of passion and a warm glow filled her. The desire had glimmered within her even before her fall, and then bloomed steadily until she was almost mad with it. Perhaps the night together on the boat hadn't been the truth of that vision.

"Attention, everyone," Father said, "MacCormack has something to say."

"Thank ye, Colonel. My lords and ladies, I've a record of your vows and the names of the witnesses. Both important elements of the nuptials. But ye're not truly wedded until the marriage has been consummated. Without the consummation, a marriage challenge might succeed."

"The duke claims he will be here tomorrow before breakfast," Lady Fiona said. "I should be mortified to have to bar him from entering."

Insides quaking, Lucie fought for composure, else she would melt right here into a puddle in

Lady Fiona's parlor. She felt a tug on her hand and looked up into Rudgwick's dark eyes.

Jeremy and Harmonia were already walking toward the door where Mrs. Brodie waited, and they fell in behind them. The housekeeper led them up, chattering about the bedchambers, the refurbishing, the linens. Rudgwick clutched her hand, his touch charged with the same desire inflaming her nerves. They said goodnight to Lady Harmonia and Lord Jeremy at the door to the small room the ladies had shared earlier, and then followed the housekeeper up the stairs to another chamber tucked into the back of the house.

CHAPTER TWENTY-ONE

Bewitched

The cozy room might have once housed a governess. A low fire had been laid—not that Lucie would need it. A covered tray, wine, and two glasses set atop a small table. She glanced at Rudgwick and caught his smile, and knew the repast would be for later.

She heard the latch click as the door closed on the housekeeper and looked around the room—anywhere but at her... her *husband*.

Her heart leapt and moisture flooded her throat. Rudgwick was finally, *finally,* hers.

On the bed crisp white sheets had been turned back. Gauzy white curtains hung at the windows, and on the floor...

Her breath caught. The chamber's Axminster carpet had seen many years, yet the faded colors were still beautiful. She looked around, memories of a dream flooding her: a bedside table bore an oil lamp, still lit, but turned down low. Flowering vines trailed up the wallpaper.

Rudgwick nuzzled her neck. "What's wrong, my love?"

It wasn't an inn room in the vision, nor the cabin of Musbury's ship. It was one of Lady Fiona's third best bedchambers.

She laughed out loud. "Nothing, Rudgwick. Not a thing is wrong, except we're both wearing far too many clothes."

His hand moved to the back of her gown while he bent and studied her face. "You're not having a spell now. But...?"

How had he come to know her so well? She took in a deep breath. "But I did have a spell. Many spells, visions, and an incredibly detailed dream." She swept out a hand. "Us. Together. In this room. I thought it was an inn room. I thought ye had..." She waved her hand again.

"I would never force you, Lucie."

She looked at his dear face with its healing bruises and cuts, and the whiskers which just wouldn't stop sprouting. His dark eyes, his strong jaw, and his lips... She remembered the first time he'd kissed her. "Ye'd never have to, Rudgwick. Ye bewitched me with that kiss at the duchess's ball."

***

He'd bewitched her?

"Is that what this feeling is?" He pressed his lips to a spot on her neck. The tremor that went through her echoed in his privy counsellor. The gown was the one she'd worn at her birthday ball, only she'd mercifully covered her bosom, else he'd never have been able to keep his wits for their wedding. He slid a finger under the silk fichu at the back of her neck, tugged out the silky garment, and tossed it aside. "Bewitchment. Enchantment. Beguilement."

Now that he was free to study and stare, he spotted a constellation of freckles above her left breast and kissed them. "You captivated me the first night we met, Lucie. I wanted you then, and every day since."

He brought his hand around and searched for the gown's fastening, and quietly swore when he fumbled the hook.

"I've helped myself out of this gown before," she said, her hands moving down his chest, leaving streaks of fire where she touched until...

He choked out another curse. She'd reached his fall and begun to unbutton it.

"Lucie—"

"If ye cannot wait, doona worry. We've a consummation to accomplish. We have the rest of our lives to be naked and, well, I've seen the naughty drawings of men in coats with ladies whose gowns are rucked up—"

He pressed his lips to her mouth, silencing her. He could wait. He must wait. But, oh... she pressed against him, and he wanted her desperately.

But she was a virgin. He couldn't just take his own pleasure with no thought of easing the pain he would cause her. He clutched her close with his right arm and searched with his left and... there. One hook, and then another, and another came loose.

While he undressed her, and kissed her, he felt her hands traveling over his body, pulling his shirt up, sliding under his trousers and then up his back. He tugged at the tiny sleeve of her gown, broke the kiss, and stepped back.

Her dress fell away, revealing all but the tips of her breasts hidden under the edge of the chemise, resting atop the unnecessary stays. Her smile was dazed, her color high.

He moved behind her and pulled the tie of the stays, hurriedly loosening them and pushing them over the shapely hips and the bottom he'd seen outlined by trousers the first night they'd met. He pulled her close, held her, kissed her neck, and nudged the chemise down, down, down, freeing her breasts for fondling.

"If only I had two hands."

"Ye're doing quite well with one," she said.

Her gasp made him chuckle. With one tug he loosened the drawstring of the chemise, pushed the whole garment to the floor, and spun her around. A blush rose under the freckles of her creamy breasts, swept up her neck, and flooded her cheeks so they were as bright as her hair.

Her hair. "Lucie, Lucie." Embracing her again, he pulled out combs and pins and swept his fingers through the fragrant, abundant, still-damp strands. He nudged her backward, seating her on the bed and kneeling before her.

Her knees and elbows locked together, and her hands clutched his shoulders. "Let me undress ye."

"You're so beautiful, Lucie. Don't be shy."

"At l-least take off the coats?" Her palm moved to his chest.

She was having an attack of nerves, his virgin bride.

"All right." He stretched out his arms. She pushed at the lapels, stood, moved around him and pulled off the left sleeve, then eased the right one over his stump so gently that he felt only the barest flicker of pain.

"Now the waistcoat," she said, and helped him out of it. Her arms came around him from behind, her fingers untying his neckcloth while she blew hot breaths and dropped kisses on his neck until the cloth flew away and the shirt floated up and over his head.

Skin to skin, she pressed against his back. "Boots," she whispered. "Stockings." Her breath tickled his ear. "Trews."

Chuckling, Rudgwick stood, bringing her with him. He flipped her onto the bed and wedged himself between her knees. "All in good time," he said, looking his fill.

***

Lucie leaned back on her elbows, pleasure driving out shock. Rudgwick's touches... his kisses...

She gasped as his tongue explored and his breath heated her at her core. Her right breast rejoiced at the touch of his fingers as he tweaked and stroked, pleasure within her, waves of it, rising and building, more powerful with each sweep and nibble. Madness and pleasure melted together toward something she couldn't... she couldn't...

An explosion of bliss made her cry out, waves and waves of it rolling through her until she was almost senseless.

She came to with Rudgwick watching her, his chin resting atop her belly, a hot, hungry grin on his face.

"Tristan Hamilton Howton," she said, struggling up. Too lightheaded to say more, she scrambled down from the bed, shoved him back on his bottom, yanked at his boots and his stockings, and finally, finally, pushed him all the way to the Axminster carpet and undid the last button of his fall.

She fell back on her heels with another gasp. Pleasure moved in her again, and a wordless desire pulled her toward him.

He beckoned. "Come here."

She shook her head and began rolling his trousers over his hips. He tucked his hand under his head and watched her, that half-smile forming, his hot gaze melting her insides. She yanked the garment over his feet, tossed it aside, and knelt over him, sliding her hands up the sides of his legs.

His muscles twitched with the effort of what must be his restraint. He was a coiled spring ready to bounce. He *was* bouncing, *there*. She touched a finger to him, and he launched to his feet, pulling her with him. And then she was flat on her back and... there he was, raised above her, the dark hair of his chest brushing against her bare breasts, his lips dipping to meet her own. Her insides pooled and heated into a raging desire that gripped her beyond her means to resist, and she opened all of herself to meet him.

A small thrust, a pinch, another thrust. She lifted her hips and gasped as he filled her.

***

Lucie's breast tingled with a butterfly touch and warmth flowed through her. She heard a soft chuckle and opened her eyes.

Rudgwick lay watching her, sleepy eyed and smiling, his hand cupping her breast.

They'd both fallen asleep after their coupling. The fire had died down, the oil had burned low, yet it was still night outside.

She rolled toward him and ran the pad of her thumb over his bristly cheek. "Have we properly consummated our marriage?"

"Perhaps we should keep trying to make sure we've done a proper job of it."

"Ye're a rogue, Major Lord Rudgwick. I suppose it's Lord Jeremy and Lady Harmonia who must worry about a challenge from the duke."

The duke. She sat up and gathered the coverlet to her breasts. What had Lady Fiona said?

"The duke is here in Edinburgh?" she asked.

"So your father said. The duke accused him of concealing Harmonia." He reached for her. "What is it, Lucie? You're trembling."

Dankworth's words about Bridgehampton were coming back to her, bringing with them the terror she'd felt at that particular moment. She lay back and nestled against him.

"I didn't tell ye... I haven't had a chance, and then I forgot. That night at the inn, Dankworth said—he said quite directly—the duke wanted him to carry me off to Norwich, to take me to the bank. He said..."

She closed her eyes and saw the mad, mean face of Lionel Dankworth. "'*I should settle for a scrawny redhaired witch and become a Scots baron, like the duke suggested.*'"

Trembling overtook her. Rudgwick wrapped her in his warmth, dropping kisses. "You are slender and beautiful, not scrawny," he whispered. "Redhaired, that's true. And you *can* work magic. I'll testify to that." Her heart eased as he stroked her cheek. "Am I a Scots baron now? I don't know what the marriage contract said. I didn't read it. You, however, are an English countess and the chatelaine of Rudgwick Abbey."

"Oh, Tristan. 'Tis a frightening thought."

"It has something of a frightening history, and some say even a ghost or two. They will love you, those ghosts."

He spoke then, telling her about Rudgwick Abbey, its tenants and villagers, its rooms, and its history. And then he moved on to describe another of his estates until her eyes drifted shut and she fell asleep.

A rustling noise woke Lucie. She pulled up the covers and propped herself on her elbows. A maid knelt by the hearth. From the slant of the light pouring in the window, 'twas early morning. Last night was her wedding night and... She was alone. Rudgwick had left her.

The maid gasped. "Beg pardon, my lady." The round-faced girl studied the floor. "Mrs. Brodie said to make ye a fire and when ye're ready, a bath. But not ta wake ye. I'm ever so sorry."

Where was Rudgwick? Where was her husband? 'Twould be unseemly to ask the maid.

Oh, bugger that. "Is Lord Rudgwick at breakfast already?"

The girl blinked and color rose in her cheeks. "He's gone out with the Colonel this morning."

"With my father?"

"Yes, milady."

Milady. She'd carry a title forever now and perhaps never know who was toadying and who was true. Though Rudgwick was worth it.

She would dress and find Mother. She would know what the two men were up to.

"Somewhere in this house I have a robe and a day gown. Can ye ask Mrs. Brodie if someone can help me dress?"

The girl hurried off, and she slid from the bed, gathering the coverlet around her.

***

Lucie had dismissed the maid sent to help her dress and was slipping into her shoes when Rudgwick walked into the bedchamber.

She propped her hands on her hips. "And where did ye and my father run off to?"

He beamed her a smile. Whatever he'd been doing with Father must have been a stunning success.

"We paid a visit to the Duke of Bridgehampton this morning. Your father went along as my bodyguard. Which fortunately turned out to be unnecessary." He gathered her into his arms. "You're starting to tremble again."

"Did ye show him the letter?"

"No. But I told him I had it in safekeeping. It's in Lady Fiona's safe."

"Will he bother us? Will he bother Lady Harmonia and Lord Jeremy?"

"He will not. I told him that it was you who persuaded Mrs. May to turn over the letter, and you who stole it out from under Sir Thomas's nose. I might have also said you had the duke's reputation in mind. But of course, I told him, at that moment you didn't know he'd set Dankworth to kidnap you." He laughed. "I've never seen two older men leap to their feet so quickly. Bridgehampton to issue denials, and your father..."

Lucie gasped. "Did he issue a challenge? Oh, I hope not. I hope he thrashed him then and there."

"No. Neither of those. It *would* have been a sight to see. However, I intervened. I have no wish to inherit Bridgehampton's title anytime soon."

"Why did the duke do it? Does he hate me that much?"

"He denied telling Dankworth to take you. I believe he might have suggested you as a bride for him, though with your father glaring daggers, he wouldn't admit to it. Any husband would have done for you, as long as it wasn't me. But we foiled him, my gallant Highland lass."

His kiss was long and languid, and he tasted of coffee. She'd yet to break her fast, turning away the offer of a tray so she could make her way downstairs more quickly.

"I rang a peal over him, you'll be happy to know," he said. "After all, thoughts of him interrupted our lovemaking in the wee hours." He set her back from him. "We'll have a long lie-down this afternoon, shall we? For now, are you hungry?"

"I am. But I might be willing to forgo breakfast."

"Not with the duke below in the breakfast room."

"No, Rudgwick." She poked his chest. "I can't meet him here. I can't be responsible for what I might say. Ye're asking too much of me."

He gazed at her, love and faith shining in his eyes.

When she sighed, he cradled her face in his hand. "He doesn't want to lose his only grandchild, and he's promised to reconcile with Harmonia. She and Jeremy are coming down for breakfast. Whether or not they make peace will be up to Harmonia, though I know Jeremy desires the duke's blessing. And I believe Harmonia will be happier and her reputation more easily mended if they could come together as a family. You understand that."

Rudgwick knew her too well, and he was right. She'd been estranged from her father for most of her life. She didn't wish such loneliness on anyone, and if the duke were truly willing to make amends with Harmonia, she wouldn't ruin that.

She took his arm. "All right then, Major Lord Rudgwick."

"Who?"

"Tristan Hamilton Howton."

He rewarded her with a kiss, one she matched with her own, and it was a long moment before they put desire aside and went down to breakfast.

***

And there he was, the Duke of Bridgehampton, seated at Lady Fiona's breakfast table looking bilious and uncomfortable. Rudgwick nodded to him and raised an eyebrow. Across the table from the duke, Mother's gaze bounced between Rudgwick and the duke. She knew of the morning visit. She didn't know what had been said.

She would ask in due time and he'd refer her to the duke. Regarding the letter, he'd promised to keep the old man's confidence.

At the head of the table, Macbeth shifted a newssheet and called Lucie over for a fatherly kiss.

Rudgwick took a seat and accepted a cup of coffee from the smiley footman. The almost smirking footman, actually. Lady Fiona's staff found it vastly entertaining that they'd hosted two weddings and the wedding nights that followed.

Lucie returned, touching his shoulder, and taking the chair next to his, and then she patted his leg under the table. Lady Fiona and Greer breezed in.

"Your grace," Lady Fiona exclaimed. "We are honored. The children will be here shortly."

In fact, the children—Jeremy and Harmonia— had already appeared in the doorway, Jeremy looking like the starry-eyed happy groom that he was, and Harmonia looking like a well-pleased woman.

"Now what?" Lucie murmured.

The duke gave no sign of hearing her, but he rose from the table and went to greet the new arrivals.

If Jeremy had been equipped with a weapon, he would have drawn it by now. He edged in front of his bride. To her credit, Harmonia raised herself up an inch taller and held the old man's gaze.

"Harmonia," he said. "My dear. I was so worried."

She blinked.

"He's pulled a chink from her armor," Lucie whispered.

The duke glanced at the table, clearly uncomfortable. All eyes were fixed on him. Not even Mother would open her mouth to save him.

"You are married," the duke said.

"We are." Jeremy squeezed Harmonia's hand.

"I know your brother, Lord Jeremy. We do not always see eye to eye on politics, but he is a good man. Will you care for my granddaughter? She is the dearest thing in the world to me."

Harmonia's back stiffened even more, but her eyes grew shiny.

"I love her as well, and yes I will care for her."

"Jeremy rescued me from that dreadful man," Harmonia said in a strong voice.

Jeremy tugged her a bit closer. "I know it is after the fact, but we would like your blessing, your grace."

"You have it." The duke's head dipped. "And in return, I... I beg your... your forgiveness."

Harmonia's shoulders lifted and dropped with a great exhale of breath, and the tears were released as well. She reached for the old man's hands and then fell against him. He held his arms straight for a moment, and then wrapped her close.

That coat was Westin. The duke's valet would have a fit about the tear stains. Rudgwick chuckled and glanced at the plate that had appeared. Lucie was busy attacking his bacon and sausage, wielding the knife furiously, her cheeks flushed.

"I suppose I can accept your help until I get my hand fixed." He'd had some success with steadying his fork with the false hand. "The meat is a poor substitute for the duke though."

She finished and glared at him, and the glare turned to a smile, and then a laugh. And then, he kissed her, right there at the breakfast table, in front of her parents, his mother and Lady Fiona, and the duke.

A prolonged masculine throat-clearing got their attention. They looked up to find all eyes upon them. The duke was back at the table, and Harmonia and Jeremy were snickering behind their napkins. Macbeth wouldn't skewer him now that they'd married. And this was Scotland. Weren't the Scots less formal and more forthright?

"Duke," Lucie said, "When ye find yourself up to it, I should like an apology as well. Ye know for what."

Mother gasped and closed her mouth on an unspoken question, her brow furrowing. She would give the old codger a much-deserved interrogation later. For now...

"Lucie," Rudgwick said, standing, "I should like a word with you in private."

"But your breakfast... My coffee... I haven't—"

He latched on to her arm and waggled his eyebrows. Color rose in her cheeks, the mulish look faded, and she rose. "As you wish, Tristan."

Passing the footman, he whispered a request for a tray to be delivered to their bedchamber, then hurried her up the stairs.

Inside they found two maids changing the bedsheets. Both servants curtsied and looked at the floor, while Lucie colored deeply and fled to the window.

"Carry on," Rudgwick said. "Finish that task, and then, if you could remind the kitchen, we'd like a breakfast tray in our room. And coffee."

His bag had been delivered and he fetched it, removing the damaged prosthesis. "I thought to make inquiries at the medical college about repairing this," he said, beckoning his bride.

"The surgeon who treated me last winter might know of someone," she said, rallying from her embarrassment. "May I see it? If it's only the strap, we might find an upholstery shop to make repairs."

The maids finished, the door closed, and he tossed the hand aside and reached for her. "Lady Rudgwick. Angry and embarrassed all in the course of no more than a quarter hour."

"And hungry. Ye forgot that."

"What am I to do with you, my Highland lass?"

"Feed me," she teased.

He heard footsteps on the stairs. "In a minute. What else."

"Hide the knives?"

He laughed and drew her into a kiss. At the knock on the door, he released her.

The food was quickly set out, the coffee poured, and the servants slipped out. She looked at the repast and then at him, and then stepped into his arms.

"Love me, Tristan Hamilton Howton, Major Lord Rudgwick, as I love you."

"I do," he said. "And I will. Eat heartily. I intend to spend the rest of this day, and every day loving you."

EPILOGUE

Late August 1816
Calder Castle
The Scottish Highlands

"The steps again, lass?" Rudgwick said. "Are ye tryin' to do me in?"

Lucie gave a loud laugh. Her husband's mimicking of the Scots accent always tickled her.

"The night is clear, my lord," she said with the haughtiest English inflection she could manage. "You will kindly enjoy a nighttime picnic with me."

She'd dispensed with her stays and wore a wrapping-front dress. He could manage it with absolutely no fumbling.

"Besides," she said. "We have the castle almost entirely to ourselves."

They'd spent the late spring in Edinburgh, Rudgwick seeing to repairs to his prosthesis and treatment upon his stump. Lucie, as well, had seen the physician. There'd been endless letters dealing with the business of his estates—and the duke's. Bridgehampton had stayed in Edinburgh, taking a suite at the hotel, and spending time with Jeremy and Harmonia. In June, both sets of newlyweds boarded a yacht—a large one, luxurious compared with Musbury's, and properly staffed. They'd sailed north, and then west, stopping along the way, and then traveling overland from Skye to Menteith.

Two dukes waited there for them, both Bridgehampton and Northam, Jeremy's brother, along with the Macbeths, Lady Rudgwick, Lady Fiona, Banquo's boys, Hyde, and Rudgwick's very English valet Darby.

They married there in the kirk, a double wedding attended by parishioners and gentry far and wide.

Paisley had been there too, curse the man. Father somehow had placated him—or threatened him, Lucie wasn't sure which. Or maybe the threat had been issued by Rudgwick. In any case, Paisley had turned his attentions on another landowner's daughter, the poor lass.

A few days after the church wedding, the party had traveled to Calder for one night. When the others returned to Menteith, Lucie and Rudgwick stayed at Calder. She showed him around, introducing him to their few tenants, before going over the books with the factor, and later dining with the local gentry. It had rained much, but this day had been clear, and stars glittered in the night sky.

They reached the top of the stairs and came out upon the roof.

Rudgwick walked to the parapet.

She kept back a few feet. As much as she liked the view, being so high up still made her dizzy. "On some winter nights, we can watch the mirrie dancers in the sky, the Northern Lights. It's a sight to see, rare and special. And that way," she pointed, "Is south. Look hard and we might see Rudgwick Abbey."

They would travel there next week so Rudgwick would not miss the harvest and Michaelmas feasting.

His arm came around her, solid and strong, despite his injury. "I can't wait to show you the priest holes at the Abbey. We used to hide in them, my sister and I. Frightened Mother half to death."

"I wouldn't think she'd be frightened of anything. Look how she handles the duke."

Besides a harrumph, he was uncharacteristically silent. Rudgwick wasn't keen on the growing closeness between his mother and Bridgehampton.

"It's beautiful here," he said finally. "So quiet. Peaceful. Though I can envision a redhaired Macbeth lass dropping pitch upon marauding Douglasses."

She laughed and refrained from bringing up the Paisleys who she often thought deserved a drenching of hot pitch.

"Come," she said, leading him to a blanket spread out on the flat roof.

"Ye'll not be plying me with whisky and then shoving me over the balcony, lass, will ye?" he teased.

"Not if ye behave." She eased herself down and reached for a basket. "We've a bottle of claret, some bread and some cheese. If the mice haven't got to it yet."

"That's appetizing." He wedged the loaf under his arm, tore a hunk and handed it to her. She passed him a glass of claret and lifted her own.

"What is the occasion?" he asked. "Is it our four-month anniversary?"

"The occasion is us," she said, clinking his glass. "Our family, and the children we'll have." She watched him take a hardy swig. "Those priest-holes you mentioned—are they dangerous?"

"They could be. Some are hard to open from inside, especially for a child. Mother always found us before... Lucie?"

"I've missed my courses for three months now, my lord."

He set down the glass and took her hand. He was speechless again, a rare thing for Tristan Hamilton Howton.

"I believe, sir, that I'm carrying our child."

With a loud whoop, he pulled her down to the blanket for a tender kiss, and then they watched the stars glimmering, and whispered their dreams for their love and their life together.

The End

If you enjoyed this story please consider telling other readers by leaving a review at the bookseller of your choice, or at Goodreads.com or Bookbub.com.

A Note from the Author

As I mentioned in my afterword for *Fated Hearts*, the real Macbeth lived and ruled in a bloody time when kings seized power by force. In Celtic governance, the passing of leadership from one king to the next was called tanistry. Titles weren't automatically passed from father to son. Rather, the heir was chosen from kinsmen related through the male line.

It sounds like a recipe for conflict, and we see that in what we know of the real Macbeth's history.

As I planned this story, cherry-picking through the known details of the real Macbeth, I took heart in the knowledge that William Shakespeare did the same thing. The Bard presented his Scottish play in 1611 with one audience member in mind: King James I.

Macbeth was the last Celtic king of Scotland. Duncan's son allied with the English to defeat Macbeth. Ever after, the Celts would not be able to shake off the English yoke, culminating in the reign of James who ruled first in Scotland as James VI and then, upon the death of Elizabeth I in 1603, united both crowns, ruling England as James I.

The witches were a nice touch conjured by Shakespeare. The late 16th century was an era of witch hunts in Scotland and persecution of those believed to practice witchcraft. Shakespeare would have known of his new king's obsession with witchcraft, and James's 1597 book, *Daemonology*.

Regarding Macbeth's title, I was disappointed to find that Scottish barons are not part of the peerage and are not addressed as "Lord" and "Lady". This topic is covered in fascinating detail in a Wikimedia article.

I hope you've enjoyed this sequel to *Fated Hearts*. I'm grateful to my editor, Tessa Shapcott for catching my many Americanisms, but any historical errors are mine alone.

I'm grateful, as always, to my husband, for his support and encouragement during the writing of this story. Sadly, he passed away in October 2021. His strength, and honor, and loving kindness will always find a way into each of my heroes.

To find out more about my books, visit my website, https://alinakfield.com, and sign up for my monthly newsletter.

All the best,

Alina K. Field

Other books in the Tragic Characters in Classic Literature Project

The Monster Within, The Monster Without
by Lindsay Downs (Frankenstein)

I Shot the Sheriff
by Regina Jeffers (Robin Hood and the Sheriff of Nottingham)

The Colonel's Spinster
by Audrey Harrison (Pride and Prejudice)

The Redemption of Heathcliff
by Alanna Lucas (Wuthering Heights)

Captain Stanwick's Bride
by Regina Jeffers (The Courtship of Miles Standish)

Glorious Obsession
by Louisa Cornell (Orpheus and Eurydice)

Books by Alina K. Field

Sons of the Spy Lord Series

Marrying Mr. Gibson

Previously titled *The Bastard's Iberian Bride*

Paulette Heardwyn rushes to visit her dying guardian, set on learning the truth about her father. But the only man with answers takes his secrets to the grave, leaving her penniless— unless she marries his illegitimate son

The Viscount's Seduction

Lady Sirena Hollister has lost everything, even her fey abilities. But when the fairies hand her a chance at a London Season, her schemes for revenge stir up an unknown enemy, and spark danger of a different sort, in the person of a handsome Viscount.

The Rogue's Last Scandal

Falling—literally—into the arms of the *ton*'s most outrageous rogue seems a risky path of escape, but Maria Graciela Kingsley y Romero has no other choice. Only England's greatest spy lord can help her, and he is not to be found—so his son will have to do!

The Counterfeit Lady

Vowing she'll never submit to an arranged marriage, an earl's daughter bolts for the seaside cottage that will someday be hers. But she finds her quiet refuge occupied by the last man she ever wants to see—an American artist, who's also a thief. And, quite possibly one of her father's spies.

Avenging the Earl's Lady

The long war is over, but honor requires vanquishing one last enemy, and the Earl of Shaldon has no time for romance. But when the lady he longs for interferes in his plot, and his enemy strikes at her, nothing else matters but avenging his lady.

Novellas and Holiday Stories

The Marquess and the Midwife

A Christmas Novella
Finalist, 2016 National Reader's Choice Award

Uncovering a lie drives a new marquess back from a self-imposed exile at Christmas to find the only woman he's ever loved. Finding her turns out to be easy, uncovering her stunning secrets, a bit harder. But winning her back will be the greatest challenge of all.

A Leap Into Love

A Sweet Regence Romance Novella, a sequel to
The Marquess and the Midwife

Can a gentleman be too charming?
The ladies of Upper Upton think so.
When the single ladies of the village conspire to teach their charmer a lesson that might bankrupt him, the town's loveliest young widow—who's sworn off marriage forever—steps up to warn him.

Liliana's Letter
Finalist, 2015 National Reader's Choice Award

The Matchmaker Meets the Matchbreaker

Liliana Ashford's future as a professional chaperone depends on her wealthy charge's successful marriage, but her own close encounter with a scoundrel years ago makes her determined to save the girl from the same kind of rogue.

The Ghost of Depford Hall
A short, sweet Halloween story, a sequel to
Liliana's Letter

It's her mother's last All Hallows' Eve.
When family, friends, and tenants gather,
goblins, ghouls, and ghosts are banned from this
All Hallows' Eve party.
Only, no one told the Ghost of Depford Hall!

Courted by the Earl

Previously titled *Bella's Band*
A 2015 RONE Award Finalist

Saddled with his brother's title and debts,
nothing about this new life makes the Earl of
Hackwell want to stay—until he meets a lady
with a secret that can change everything.

Rosalyn's Ring

2014 Book Buyer's Best Winner, Novella
Category

Done with grieving her losses, a late nobleman's
daughter has fallen into a tidy spinster's life in
London. But when one snowy Christmas Eve, a
young woman needs rescue, she seizes the
chance to do good—and to recover a family heir-
loom that ought to be hers.

Haunting Miss Fenwick

Thrilled to finally have a permanent home, a
Squire's daughter won't let a supernatural
creature scare her away. While hunting the ghost
she doesn't believe in, she stumbles upon a
mysterious flesh and blood man who might be
the key to all of her problems.

The Upstart Christmas Brides

The Duke She Despised

Hiding her true identity, a young vicar's widow takes a position as housekeeper in a remote Scottish castle at Christmas for a new duke who years ago sabotaged her chance for happiness. She quickly falls for the duke's charming but not very competent factor, not knowing that he's hiding something also—he's the duke she despised!

Convincing the Countess

When a business-minded aristocrat encounters a fetching widow he knew years earlier as the bride of a ne'er-do-well earl, temptation steers him along a track that may derail all his plans. Can he convince her to set a course for her future that includes him?

The Impetuous Heiress

Before dashing Lord Loughton can make amends with his neglected fiancée, the lady's meddling cousin delivers her to his doorstep. He soon realizes more is amiss than his carelessness. Can he uncover her secrets and win her back before he loses her altogether?

Available in Spring 2022

The Macbeth Series

Fated Hearts,
A Love After All Retelling of the Scottish Play

A Scottish Baron returning from two decades at war meets the wife he divorced and the daughter he disavowed before she was born, only to learn that everything he'd believed was a lie. Determined to win back the only woman he's ever loved he must first face the viper who drove them apart.

The Comtesse of Midnight

A Scottish Earl on a quest for the elusive Comtesse de Fontenay, rescues a French lady smuggler during a devastating storm, taking shelter with her. As the stormy night drags on, he suspects she knows the lady he's seeking, the lady who holds the secret to his identity.

Claims of the Heart

Since a perilous fall, Lucie Macbeth has been seeing more than a settled future as the heiress to a Scottish barony. The visions plaguing her include a man—one far above her class and breeding, and English to boot. He's engaged to a duke's granddaughter as well, and thus wholly inappropriate. Though she can't marry him, and she won't become any man's leman, when the Sight warns her of danger to him her conscience, and her heart tell her she can't walk away.

Find out more at
https://AlinaKField.com
and sign up for my monthly emails
for news about upcoming books and
sales.

Fated Hearts

Friday, 3 March, 1815

A crush was what they called these suffocating occasions, and the term was apt.

Major Finnley Macbeth, Scottish baron and late of his majesty's Highland Brigade, shifted his weight from the leg that still ached like the devil, and scanned the room for his quarry, an undersecretary in the Home Office who he'd met at the army's winter quarters in Frenada.

From his spot near a damask covered wall, he measured each breath, trying to calm his rising unease. The heavy scent of perfume mixed with fine beeswax and hothouse florals unsettled more than his stomach. The shimmering silks and waving plumes threatened to stir the disquieting visions plaguing him lately.

Fire, explosions, rain, the screams of men and horse.

He squeezed his hands into fists. These were not the hellish memories of the recent past, dammit, but rattling visions of some battle yet to come.

Or not. Foretelling the future was for Travellers and crones, wasn't it? Not battle-hardened men like himself.

He inhaled slowly, holding the breath for a count, and then eased the air out. Best keep his purpose in mind—he was here to track down Sir Thomas Abernathy, lately arrived in London, and rumored to be attending this rout.

His gaze swept the room, seeking the distinctive bald pate. In spite of his own forty-three years, his eyesight was still keen enough to make out a sniper or spot the dust of a fleeing stag. Keen enough as well to relish the deep décolletages and clinging, delicate, almost transparent skirts on display this night, a vision far more cheering than the one the Sight was showing him.

A more modestly clad woman stood alone halfway across the ballroom, her back turned to him, surveying the room as he was doing.

A memory stabbed him, laced with an old shame. He'd once known a lass with hair like this, so abundant, so near to black. The lady tonight had crowned all the loveliness with dark feathers, like a glorious cormorant. His hand itched to pull out those feathers and rake his hands through the tumble of hair, as he'd once done...

He caught a steadying breath. It couldn't be her. He'd simply been without a woman too long.

And these visions plaguing him of he knew not what? That foolishness grew from naught but fatigue, the wages of war, and the steady company of too much death. Napoleon had been defeated. He must put the memories of battle and that more distant passion aside. The lovely lady with feathers atop her head was only a stranger wondering where her man had got to.

Yet he couldn't turn away. As he watched, she pivoted one way, and then the other, allowing a glimpse of dangling earbobs and a firm chin.

Drawn to her, he stepped out on his bad leg just as she turned.

Pain shot through his hip. The room threatened to fall away but he held onto the pain, let it shore him up whilst he swore a silent curse.

It *was* her.

Earlier that evening

As the lights of London came into view, Greer Douglas smoothed the silk skirt of her evening gown and glanced out the coach window again. "I wondered if we should be quite safe traveling so late at night." Chelsea seemed such a great distance from Mayfair, though at home in Scotland, she'd often journeyed farther back and forth on market day.

Her companion grunted. "I'd rather have stayed home and read the proposed Corn Law. Not to mention that it is Lent."

Greer would have chuckled, had she not been so nervous. Malcolm Comyn, Earl of Menteith, was a sober young man, but not a pious one. "We are in England now, Malcolm, two fish out of water and we must learn to swim. As long as we don't have to surrender my new earbobs to a highwayman."

"Aunt Fiona read the tea leaves and felt the coachman and groom shall be adequate protection." He patted her hand. "Do not ye worry, Cousin. I'm not wholly incapable of handling a dirk and a pistol. Though I had rather not."

"Ye had rather not mingle, either."

"So true. But Aunt Fiona insisted we must honor her friend by attending this affair, and so we are here."

Lady Fiona Carlin, who'd been widowed longer than Greer's thirty-eight years, had surprised them both at breakfast with this invitation to her friend's small gathering. The elderly lady did not herself feel up to attending. Nor would Lady Fiona allow Greer's daughter, Lucie, to attend until she had made her come-out.

When that would be, was anyone's guess. Poor Lucie. At the age of almost twenty, she was anxious to experience more of London, especially the social events of the *ton*.

Greer feared that her daughter's manners needed further refinement. Like her mother, Lucie was a country girl, unused to higher society. Life had smoothed out most of her own rough edges, but Lucie was often too direct, too outspoken. And her temper...

Greer pressed a hand to her chest and tried to breathe through the bad memories. Lucie's temper was an inherited gift from the father who had never met her.

"I suppose that honoring her friend is the least we can do to repay your aunt's hospitality," she said.

Two weeks after Malcolm's departure from Scotland, a letter had arrived for Greer from Lady Fiona inviting her and Lucie to join Malcolm as her guests for the London season. She'd even sent the means for hiring a chaise and post riders.

Greer had made up her mind to write back declining—Malcolm would not want his irksome relations crowding him in London. But as she read on, Lady Fiona mentioned the upcoming celebrations of the end of two decades of war, and the latest gossip.

And among the items of gossip she'd included the tidbit that Major Finnley Macbeth had arrived in London.

The time would come when they would speak— and just let her have a piece of him. But not tonight. Tonight, she wanted to see how the great world of London would welcome a woman like herself.

When their carriage jerked to its final stop in front of the brightly lit townhouse, Malcolm handed her out, and escorted her through the receiving line where their elderly hostess, Lady Estelle Walby, looked her over with a gleam in her eye that matched Lady Fiona's.

And then Malcolm abandoned her.

"I must step away to the gentleman's," he said, with his usual bluntness. "Where will I find ye?"

"Since I don't know a soul, I'll seek out Lady Estelle when she's free."

He shook his head. "Proceed to the middle of the room, and I'll find ye there shortly."

"Yes, my lord," she teased.

Wandering deeper into the room, she scanned the groupings of people. Not one familiar face. Not one. At home, in the Highlands, she'd know every soul at a local assembly.

Oh, but the gowns were far more magnificent here. The glow from the candelabra gleamed off exquisite jewels and sparkled in mirrors arranged to brighten the room. Large urns filled with roses and gladioli stood on pillars, and along one wall, chaperones kept eagle eyes on girls Lucie's age. Some of the young ladies looked as nervous as herself.

Across the room, she caught the curious gaze of three young bucks. One whispered to the others. She lifted her chin and turned fully around.

And for one desperate moment her heart stopped, and then started up again in a wild gallop.

A man stood watching her, a tall, broad chested man in a gold waistcoat and a fine dark coat, golden-eyed and handsome, with hair flaming in bright tones of red, hair pulled back into an old-fashioned queue, hair that used to fall to strong shoulders in wild tangled waves.

Finnley was here.

Available at all major booksellers.